THE SUNDAY BROTHERS NOVELLAS

MAY ARCHER

Cover Design: Beth Cranford
Editing: One Love Editing

All the good bits are theirs, and any mistakes are my own!

PICK ONE

A SUNDAY BROTHERS NOVELLA

CHAPTER ONE

TEAGAN

"The guy's not coming," I told my friend Fern in a slightly panicked tone, holding the phone to my ear with one hand while yanking at my hair with the other. "I have been waiting in the lobby of my new apartment building for forty-seven minutes, exactly as agreed. Forty-seven minutes does not suggest 'oops, I was stuck in traffic.' Forty-seven minutes suggests my brother's friend forgot he was supposed to help me. Or that Jace forgot to ask him in the first place. Forty-seven minutes means I have been *forsaken*, Fern. Forty-seven minutes means my sofa is in *peril*."

Fern sighed in my ear, like the fate of my hand-tufted green Chesterfield was of no particular importance to her. "Teagan, babe, are you sure you need to be worrying about this right now? You've had a hell of a week, and in the end, it's just a sofa. Replaceable."

She had a point. But that point was not *my* point.

"No, Fern." I tugged my hair harder. "It's not just a sofa. This sofa is a *symbol*, okay? This sofa is the perfect combination of form and function. This sofa is firm, it's supportive, and it cradles my ass lovingly, which is more than I can say about any man I've ever dated, *especially* Martin. This sofa is the proverbial line in the sand between what I am willing to forego and what I refuse to give up. It's bad enough that I came home early from my Intro to Creative Writing TA hours Tuesday to make soup for my flu-ridden boyfriend, only to find him being *ridden* by someone who was blond and twinky and decidedly *not the flu*." I sniffed. "I refuse to let the bastard have my sofa, too. Martin doesn't deserve hand-tufting."

"Martin doesn't deserve to keep your apartment," she retorted. "As I explained to you at length."

Oh, she had. She most definitely had. Through our entire shared shift at Campus Connection on Wednesday, even the part where I ended up sorting stock in the back because I'd been crying off and on—she'd simply raised her voice so I could hear her.

The "Come to Jesus" discussion was Fern's preferred love language.

"You should've made him move out," she concluded.

"I know, I heard what you said. But then I'd have had to pay to live in that building, and grad school stipends and part-time work at Coffee Connections would not make that happen," I reminded her. "I'd be another innocent ingenue forced to sell my body on the street, and anyone who's ever seen a Broadway musical could tell you how *that* would end." I paused, then remembered Fern was a biology grad student when she wasn't a barista and probably hadn't been listening to show tunes since high school. "Death, Fern. It ends in death."

"Teagan." Fern said my name like it was a complete sentence, expressing exasperation and warning and fondness all at once.

"Besides," I went on quickly, "this way I get to show Martin how utterly unaffected I am by his treachery." I stared at my reflection in the lobby's plate-glass window and assumed a calm, distant expression. "I plan to stay cool and remote and slay him with my quiet dignity. Let him writhe in guilt."

"Oh, honey. The man cheated on you in your own bed. You really think your quiet dignity will get him?"

"It might." I sighed and curled in on myself again. "I mean, yes, what Martin did was unforgivable. And to be perfectly honest, things between us hadn't been right in a while, no matter how hard I tried, so I'm not sorry things are over. But he was a kind, caring person at one point." I stared out at the distressingly empty sidewalk. "He still has those qualities, deep down."

"No," she said flatly. "He doesn't. He never did. The day you met, he ordered a latte, paid in exact change, said one witty thing about Shakespeare that I swear he didn't even intend to be funny, and said your hair was 'seriously sexy.' Then all of a sudden, your brain started churning like a broken ATM spitting twenties, filling in all the blanks that made him your personal Prince Charming."

"But... wait, really?" I frowned. "I don't remember this! And if you knew it all along, why didn't you ever say anything?"

"Oh, for— You're kidding, right? Dude, I staged an intervention in August before you moved in with the guy, but you wouldn't listen. You told me, 'Pick one, Fern: potentially losing your greatest chance at happiness or potentially losing your heart' when you *know* how I feel about your 'this or that' questions—"

"I think you mean my amusing philosophical conundrums," I teased.

"I think I mean your false dichotomies," she retorted. "Because humans almost always have more than two choices. But anyway, then you quoted some poem at me about buds of love—"

Ugh. Now *that* sounded like something I would do. "It's Shakespeare," I said grimly.

"Right. And at that point, I washed my hands of you."

"I don't blame you," I said sadly. "It's not even a particularly good poem."

"Yes. Uh-huh. *That's* the takeaway here, Teagan. Your judgment of *poetry* was skewed." Fern huffed. "Honey, have you ever considered just being less…" She broke off.

"Less?" I prompted.

"I don't know how to say this without it sounding shitty, and I don't mean it that way, but less… volatile? Less emotional? Less likely to jump in with both feet." She sounded frustrated. "Just… just *less*."

Ouch. I leaned back against the bank of mailboxes that lined one wall of the lobby.

"Not everything has to be sweeping and dramatic and overly gushy. You need stability more than you need romance. So next time you meet a guy, approach with caution. Chill. For your own well-being. Because next time, you might not find an apartment on short notice or coerce your brother into finding someone to help you move your couch. Next time, you might lose something that's not replaceable. You know what I mean?"

"Yeah," I said in a small voice.

This was not the first time I'd heard this speech from someone in my life. More like the billionth. My dad used to angrily inform me that people would "take advantage of me" if I insisted on being so "high-strung." My mom told everyone in an only half-joking way that I was her most exhausting child—which was particularly funny if you knew that I was the only one of the three Donahue brothers who'd never been arrested. My friends loved and appreciated me, because they knew I was loyal to the death… but they also never seemed very surprised when my boyfriends tossed me over because I'd gotten attached too quickly and moved too fast.

"Just contain yourself, Teagan," they'd say. "Don't laugh

so loud. Don't speak so passionately. Don't be so *extra*. Moderation is the key."

But it wasn't that easy. I felt things deeply, and it was hard to hold back. I hated approaching life that way. Plus… even knowing that Fern meant well, it hurt to be told that I was always too much or too little of something to please the people in my life.

I liked myself the way I was. I wanted other people to like me, too.

"Fern," I said softly. "When in the entire eight years, five *Star Wars* releases, and two Adele albums of our friendship have you known me to chill?"

She made a noise that was half grumble, half sigh. "Never."

"Exactly. I am a man who has been blessed with a few specific talents," I reminded her. Then I counted them off on my fingers. "I make a mean sourdough."

"The best," she admitted.

"I can analyze Prufrock like nobody's business."

She snorted. "Whatever that means."

"I can suck a man's brains out through his dick in under twelve minutes."

"Did not need to know that."

"I come up with the most amusing philosophical conundrums—"

"Once again, I argue that your 'Pick One' games are not conundrums, they're logical fallacies that contribute to your very black-and-white view of—"

"But they're the most *amusing* logical fallacies."

Fern laughed helplessly. "Okay, yes. Granted."

"And I haven't missed a Trivia Night question in three years, except for that weirdly worded one about the marmosets, which you agreed was robbery."

"It was," she confirmed loyally.

"But *chilling* is *not* a talent of mine," I informed her seriously. "Indeed, legend says that when the tiny fairies went flying through the hospital nursery, flinging out talents to the newborn babies like Mardi Gras beads, the Chill Fairy passed directly over my crib and shook her head. She said, 'Oh, no, sisters, I cannot bless this one.' And do you know why, Fern?"

"I'm going to regret asking this," she muttered, but I could hear the smile in her voice. "No, Teagan, please tell me why legend says you were not blessed by the Chill Fairy."

"Because the fairies must pick and choose the gifts they bestow to provide *balance*. So the Chill Fairy said, 'Sisters, this child has already been given a fondness for crop tops that makes a mockery of his love of sourdough. This child shall have an eidetic memory for Broadway show tunes and the vocal abilities of a cat in heat so that his friends will refuse to karaoke with him. This child—" I threw my head back, squeezed my eyes shut, and lifted both hands toward the ceiling, lost in my own vision. "—will be given an unquenchable thirst for love and be doomed to one day have his heart shredded and mangled, sacked and pillaged, burned and salted, by a man he's devoted the best six months of his life to, until nothing remains but a desiccated husk barely useful for sustaining life and utterly incapable of nurturing romantic affection ever again. There is no room in this child for chill! Indeed, it is his very *un*-chill-ness that will save him!" I lowered my hands, cleared my throat, and concluded in a normal tone. "So, like, who am I to argue with the Chill Fairy?"

"Amen," a deep voice said from way too close to me.

My eyes flew open, and I found a tall guy in a snap-back hat watching me with an awestruck look that quickly faded into embarrassment when I met his gaze.

"Holy mother of fuck!" I exclaimed, scrambling back further against the mailboxes. "Where'd you come from?"

From my daydreams, apparently. The man was tall and solid, deliciously thick in all the right places, with shoulders that stretched his Hannabury College sweatshirt and thighs that strained the seams of his otherwise baggy khaki pants. A flush climbed his cheeks beneath his thick beard, and he looked down at his boots nervously.

"Teagan?" Fern asked in concern.

"Sorry," he said in that same deep voice. He held up his hands to show me he was unarmed except for his keys. "I didn't mean to startle you, and I wasn't trying to eavesdrop. I'm just here to… " He made a vague, anxious motion toward me where I leaned against the mailboxes. "But you know what? I… I can come back. You look busy." He nodded to himself. "Yeah, okay. I'm gonna leave now—"

"Oh my God!" I squealed, putting the pieces together—the way the guy was standing there, watching me, had to mean he was there for *me*. Or, at least, for my sofa.

Jace hadn't forgotten about me after all. I was saved!

"No, wait, stop! Don't leave!" I cried. Into the phone, I said, "Fern? I've gotta go. Fate has sent me a knight in shining armor after all!"

The guy blinked in surprise, but when he saw my smile, he smiled back, tentatively at first and then *gloriously*, transforming his whole face from fairly attractive to breath-stealingly, blindingly handsome. His eyes were a deep, soft brown and crinkled at the corners like he was used to laughing *a lot*, and his whole personality just magnified peace and gladness, the way a prism turned sunlight into rainbows.

How incredible, I thought, *would it be to be the reason this man with the soft eyes smiled?*

How amazing would it feel to bask in his sunshine?

"Wow-ow-ow," I breathed, and the all-consuming feeling of rightness in my gut gave the words a little shudder. "Wow."

"No. *No!* Teagan Donahue, you stop this shit right now," Fern said impatiently in my ear. "Fate's name is Jace

Donahue, and you told me he once waterboarded your Barbie doll in the toilet."

"He's forgiven," I said breathlessly, staring at the man in front of me with hearts in my eyes.

"Jesus Christ, you're even doing that weird stutter-breathing thing. Can I call 9-1-1 for an emergency involving my friend being an utter dumbass who cannot learn lessons? Would I request an ambulance or the police?"

"Fire department," I whispered, because I legitimately felt like I was burning up. I had *never* felt this way before—not about any guy I'd ever met, let alone any guy I'd ever dated. This guy was holding my gaze, and I'd swear I could *feel* the electrons zip-zip-zipping between us, like we were two halves of the same—

"Teagan," Fern said severely. "If you never listen to a single thing I say ever again, listen to me now. You *cannot* jump into something with the man who's come to move your sofa out of the apartment you shared with the *last* guy you jumped into a relationship with. This is not love! It might be infatuation. It's probably lust. It's almost definitely rebounding with a capital *R*. It's... Jesus fuck, I don't even know what it is, but it's unhealthy, and you've been wrong before! Remember the buds of love?"

I blinked as Fern's words finally penetrated the haze around me and hit me like a blast of icy water. I stood up straighter. "What? No. This isn't... that. I'm a desiccated husk now. I told you."

But I couldn't make my eyes move away from the gorgeous man, who was shifting his weight a little nervously from foot to foot, probably because I was being a total creeper.

God.

I forced myself to look away. "Things are fine," I told Fern. "Everything is great. Don't worry."

"They're so not fine." Fern sounded resigned. "You're

gonna convince yourself you love this guy, because you won't be able to help yourself, then one of you will end up with your heart broken, because even if the Self-Preservation Fairy appeared in front of you right now, you wouldn't take his gift." She sighed gustily. "Anyway. I love you, but my break is over, and the line is out the door. See you at work tomorrow?"

"Absolutely," I agreed before hanging up. "Sorry about that," I told the guy, motioning toward my phone. "My friend Fern." I leaned toward him confidingly. "She's a bit dramatic, but I love her."

"She is, huh?" The guy's mouth twitched like he was holding back a smile. "Look, I…"

"God, I'm so glad to see you!" I blurted. I blew out a relieved breath. "Sorry. It's just that I've been waiting forever for you, and I worried you weren't coming, and— Is the traffic bad out there?"

"You are?" He blinked. "I mean, you…? I mean… no. I didn't find it too bad. It's still early yet." He frowned out at the street. "Wait, are you…"

"God, sorry. I'm Teagan," I confirmed, pressing a hand to my chest. "And I promise I'm not usually this…" I threw my hands in the air. "Discombobulated. It's been a trying week."

"Yeah." The guy nodded sympathetically. "It sure sounded like it."

Right. I winced. He'd overheard all the best parts of my phone call.

"But it's gonna be great," I assured him quickly. "I'm going to focus on the positive, starting now."

"Yeah?" He rubbed the back of his neck. "My mom says that's the secret to life."

"Your mom is wise." I grinned. "For example… I have sweet friends who love me despite my penchant for charming philosophical conundrums."

He tilted his head, the smile playing around his mouth again. "Philosophical—?"

"Pick one: guacamole without chips or chips without guac?"

"I don't…" He tilted his head in the opposite direction. "What?"

"Never mind. Irrelevant." I waved a hand dismissively and continued my list. "I also have a friend of a friend who just happened to get an amazing work opportunity in Finland, right at the moment my ex-boyfriend doubled down on being an utter jerk."

The guy blinked at the change of subject. "Yeah? That's cool." After a second, he offered, "I know a guy from Finland."

We had so much in common! I beamed at him. "Best of all, now I have you. My hero."

The man's expression blanked. "Me? Oh. I'm afraid I'm not… No."

"Don't be modest. I'm truly grateful that you're here. I was getting kind of desperate," I admitted. "Hey, what's your name, by the way? Jace didn't mention it—shocking, right?— and I figure the epic poem I write about your heroism will be more compelling if I'm not referring to you as Snap-Back-Hat-Guy." I grinned and joked, "The rhyming would be tricky."

"Oh." He touched the hat on his head, which made his sweatshirt ride up just enough for me to see the dark hair on his stomach. *Yum.* "It's John?" He cleared his throat and said more decisively, "John Curran."

"John Curran," I repeated. Possibly the most boring name ever. Way too boring for such a beautiful, sweet man. But it was simple and honest, and I liked it. "Well, at least I'll have no trouble spelling it. Alrighty, then. Shall we go collect my couch?"

"Your couch," he repeated flatly, like he'd never heard the

words before. He squinted at me slightly, but his extreme confusion did nothing to make him less attractive.

"Jesus, Jace." I rolled my eyes to the ceiling. Of course my brother hadn't given the man pertinent details. Probably hadn't told him the right time to show up, either. "You didn't even know what you were going to be moving today, did you?"

John shook his head slowly… almost warily. "I definitely didn't."

"It's a couch—the world's best couch, by the by—and we need to move it into my new apartment." I pointed upstairs. "I was able to haul the rest of my stuff over here with my little Nissan earlier this afternoon, but the sofa is over at my old apartment—my ex-boyfriend's apartment—so we need to… Oh, shit."

If Jace hadn't told this guy what he was moving…

I laid a hand on his arm. "Please tell me you at least have a truck or something?" I begged. "Because if you don't…"

"I… I do, actually." He looked down at the keys in his hand, then at my arm on his sleeve, then back at me, like he was coming to a decision. He nodded firmly. "I can help you get your couch if you want."

Sweet relief pulsed through me. "I very much want." I swept a hand toward the door. "Lead the way."

MARTIN WAS at his most Martin that afternoon, answering the door wearing a silky dressing gown I'd never seen before and carrying an honest-to-God *martini*, like some kind of alternate-universe Hugh Hefner… if Hugh were a balding, thirty-something pension administrator who didn't comprehend fine furnishings or the concept of monogamy.

"Teagan," he chided before I could get a word in. "I've been worried sick. You ran off the other day and never said when you'd be home, and you didn't answer my texts until this morning when you said you were coming by. *Tsk*. We need to talk."

I looked back at John—still wearing his hat, his sweatshirt, his unfortunate khakis, and a sweet, steady expression. Then I looked at the man in front of me—the appearance of wealth he was trying to project, the carefully styled hair that barely concealed his receding hairline, the way he started out the conversation with accusations that would make me react or likely *over*react so he could gain the upper hand—and I had a moment right there in that hall.

You know the part of Cinderella where she's running down the steps and suddenly all the magical glamour drops away and she's staring at a couple of rats and a pumpkin?

Martin was that pumpkin. Okay… maybe he was the rats. And all I could think was "Holy shit. Fern was right."

And right on the heels of that, "Holy shit. I've been such a fool."

If I'd lived with this man for months and I'd fucked up so badly, how could I trust myself anymore?

This realization was so distressing that I took a step backward, forgetting John was there. He put a hand on my back, so strong and warm that I felt it through my T-shirt. I took a shuddering breath and brushed past Martin into the apartment. "I have nothing to say to you. John, this is the couch."

"Where'd you hire this oaf?" Martin demanded.

"He didn't." John folded his arms over his chest. "I volunteered."

Martin pursed his lips like his martini was sour and set the glass down with a click.

"Well, well." He looked John up and down. "I can just imagine how Teagan plans to pay you for your services. Well, lucky you. He's talented. But I warn you… he's effort."

My jaw had dropped to the floor as I gaped at him, so hurt and… okay, yes, *mortified* that he'd said something like that in front of John… that for once in my life I was literally speechless.

John stepped in front of me, blocking Martin from my view, and folded his arms over his chest—he wasn't overtly threatening, but he was way taller than Martin, and he made that perfectly clear. "By talented, I assume you mean that Teagan makes a mean sourdough?"

I clapped a hand over my mouth to restrain a wholly inappropriate, hysterical giggle.

I heard the rustle of fake silk as Martin shifted backward.

"I have no idea what you're talking about," Martin said.

I poked John in the back. "Martin doesn't eat carbohydrates," I told him. "I've never baked for him. My talents would have been wasted."

John peered down at me over his shoulder. "Sounds like lots of your talents were wasted on him," he said gently. "But that's on *him*. Not *you*."

I blinked. I melted.

Then I heard a voice in my head that sounded like a cross between Mufasa in *The Lion King* and Fern on the phone saying, "Self-preservation, Teagan!"

So for once, I listened.

Well, mostly.

"John, I will bake for you bread every week for a year for the service you've done me this day," I told him appreciatively. "It's the least I can do."

John shook his head, his gaze steady. "You don't owe me anything, Teagan."

"I want to do it," I assured him, finding I meant it. "As much as you want."

"You might not know what you're in for," he said dubiously. "You have no idea how much I like bread, T."

It was probably pathetic, but the *T* thing twined itself around my heart. I'd never had a nickname before, unless you counted Jace calling me "runt" after I'd stopped growing at five foot six. Even my mom called me Teagan. And if you'd asked me, I would have told you that nicknames were absurd and reductive.

But it turned out that when John did it, it made me feel… important. Known.

My heart melted toward him a little more… and for the first time in my whole non-chilled life, the intensity of my emotions scared me because I wasn't sure I could trust them. I wasn't sure I could trust *me*.

So I took a step back. "M'kay. Sofa?"

John nodded.

"You know, Teagan, it's incredibly immature to throw away a half-year relationship on the basis of a single indiscretion—" Martin began.

"Seems to me like *you* did the throwing," John said mildly. Then he looked over his shoulder at me again. "Ready?"

"Unquestionably. I'll take that end." I moved around to the far side of the couch with the confidence of a person who moved his own furniture all the time.

John nodded. "Good call. That way I'll be on the lower step while you control the pivot."

"Precisely my thought," I lied. "M'kay, count of three—"

When John turned and crouched to lift the sofa, Martin saw an opportunity and darted around him to get to me. "Teagan—"

With a speed I wouldn't have expected of him, John blocked his path by settling a giant paw against Martin's silk-covered chest. "I think you should back up."

Martin took a single step back and smoothed down his robe. "And *I* think nobody's interested in your ignorant mumblings. You're here to lift things." His eyes found mine. "Are you going to let him talk to me like this?"

John looked at me also, like he was waiting for me to decide.

I folded my arms over my chest, copying John's earlier stance. "Absolutely, I am."

John chuckled briefly, his eyes dancing, then looked back at Martin, and he sobered. "For what it's worth, I did my undergrad in applied math at Hannabury up in Vermont. Graduate degrees—both of 'em—at BU. Doctorate at Covington, which is where I teach now." He shook his head in disgust. "But it doesn't take any education at all to know how to treat people decently or to see that Teagan is a really special, vibrant, caring person who was badly hurt by your… indiscretion. You had your chance. You need to own that, and you need to stand aside."

His words were soft, spoken with the quiet dignity that I'd been so incredibly unsuccessful at conjuring up, but they were effective… especially the last two, which came out in a near growl.

Martin rocked his jaw from side to side for a second before he took a step back, threw his chin in the air, and retreated to the kitchen. "Fine, then. Do what you want."

"Oh, he will," John said firmly, then looked at me and shrugged apologetically. "Sorry. That should have been your line, but I was on a roll."

"You delivered it *so* well." I couldn't hold back my grin, but tears pricked my eyes, too, from relief and gratitude and… *ugh*. Attraction. Overwhelming, all-encompassing attraction, not just to John's height and his muscles but to everything he was.

Everything I *thought* he was, I silently corrected, Fern's warnings echoing in my head.

We got the sofa out to the truck without further incident, and both of us stayed silent on the ride back to my new place, which was not usual for me, but even the silence with John felt comfortable. It wasn't until we arrived back at the lobby of my new building, with John carrying most of the weight of the sofa between us, that he finally broke the silence.

"Chips," he said firmly.

"Chips?" I frowned. "Oh! Oh my gosh, you must be hungry. I am the *worst*." I darted a glance back out the front door of the lobby, wondering where the closest convenience store was. "Let me buy you dinner. We can—"

"No." John grinned and shook his head. "I mean your philosophical… whatever you call it. I was thinking about it on the way back here, and my answer is chips."

I stared at him, shocked. He'd been pondering this all that time?

"The chips might seem like they're plain without the guac," John explained, like he thought maybe I was staring at him because I disagreed. "But really, that subtle flavor makes them versatile. A dependent variable, if you will. They don't *need* the guac the way the guac needs them, which ultimately makes them better, as a food."

He cleared his throat when I continued to stare at him and said nervously, "Or did I completely misunderstand the question?"

"No," I whispered. "No, that's… that's the perfect answer."

I could fall in love with this man, I thought. *I might be falling already.*

And six months from now, I could be moving this couch out of *his* apartment.

I forced myself to look away from him. "This is getting a little heavy, so maybe we could…"

"Oh, fuck. Right." John snapped to attention. "Okay, let's turn so you can go up first. You said you were upstairs?"

"Yeah, I— Actually, hang on. Can we set this down for a second?" I put the sofa down to shake out my hands, which were genuinely cramping. "I know it's hard to tell from my incredibly defined musculature, but I don't do heavy lifting all that often."

"Believe it or not, neither do I. Not since I left my moms'

farm, anyway. I'm just built this way." He winked, inviting me to share the joke. "To lift heavy things."

But I didn't find it funny. I grimaced. "About what Martin said—"

John waved a hand. "T, I couldn't care less what that guy said, and neither should you. He cheated on you. He's an idiot."

The words were so simple but said with a confidence that soothed me. "Yes, well. I was *deluded*, which is every bit as bad. I fooled myself into seeing him as something he wasn't. Into thinking we had a connection."

John took a seat on the stairs and regarded me steadily. "Or it means that the Optimism Fairy gave you a gift for believing the best of people and situations, because life is hard enough, and it'd be even worse if you went through life expecting it to shit on you."

My eyes flew to his. That was maybe the kindest thing anyone had ever said about me. And also…

"You, uh… you really heard that *whole* speech I gave Fern, huh?"

"Yep. Pretty sure." His grin was probably supposed to be apologetic, but his sparkling eyes gave him away.

I sniffed. "You probably think it was very *extra*—"

"Yeah, extra-*awesome*," he interrupted. His steady brown gaze held mine. "People who don't get that shouldn't get to have you in their lives, Teagan. And let me just tell you, if I ever run into Martin at a coffee shop, I am one hundred percent not letting him cut me in line, no matter how long the wait is or how much of a hurry he's in."

I sputtered out a laugh… then realized he was serious.

Holy fuck, John Curran was a Disney princess in a snapback hat.

And, even holier fuck, it was working for me in a major way.

"You're so… *nice*," I said, because it was the highest

compliment I could think of. He was smart and he was funny, and his smile was perfection, but there was this feeling of *goodness* coming off the man that made me want to curl up beside him and bask in his warmth forever.

And I really, really hoped I wasn't imagining it.

"Oh." John's smile faltered a little. "Yeah. Thanks. You, ah… you good to keep going?" He stood and dusted his hands before tilting his chin up the stairs.

I smacked my forehead. "Jeez. Yeah, otherwise I'll keep you here all night. Let's go. Two more flights."

John froze in his crouch by the sofa. "You're on the third floor?"

"I didn't say? Yes, third floor. I just got the keys a few hours ago from the guy who was moving out." The words came tumbling from my mouth with a combination of nerves and excitement. "These old buildings are full of charming details, but I can't lie, an elevator would've been nice. I carted a bunch of boxes up here earlier, and it was a *workout*, let me just tell you. Ready? One, two—"

John lifted the sofa a beat late but managed to steady it. "Wait, hang on. Which apartment did you—?"

But I kept going. "You know that expression beggars can't be choosers? Well, that was me. This place opened exactly when I needed it, for exactly the price I could afford—I told you my friend knew a guy who was leaving Boston midsemester and needed someone to take over his half of a lease, right? I mean, what are the chances? *Finland*, for goodness' sake."

"The chances are slim," John whispered. "I would have said impossibly slim. But the probability of improbability is…" He shook his head as if to clear it. "Well. That's a subject for another day. Suffice it to say, I couldn't have calculated it. Hey, lift your end high? We need to tilt it over the… yeah. Nicely done."

I successfully maneuvered my end of the sofa over the

banister on the second floor, despite my muscles burning. But his comment reminded me of something he'd told Martin. "You couldn't calculate it… despite your many graduate degrees?"

"What? Oh." John's blush from earlier came back with a vengeance. "Yeah, that was kinda braggy, huh? Sorry you heard that."

God, this man was too pure to live, and I felt a sudden pang at the idea that he was just going to walk out of my life once we dropped off the sofa.

But what if you're wrong, Teagan?

What if you're wrong?

What if you're wrong?

I was getting tired of the Fern-voice already. I hated not trusting myself. But now that it was in my head, I also didn't know how to make it stop.

"Um. I don't suppose you drink coffee ever?" I asked as we hiked up the second staircase and around the landing. "It's just, I work at Campus Connections when I'm not TAing, and I thought maybe you could stop by and we could…"

I broke off when I realized John was looking at me strangely. Like I was missing something. Like maybe I'd misread things.

I swallowed hard. "…grab a cup of coffee in a friendly way," I backtracked. "Just a pair of acquaintances who are acquainted. Very platonic friends, obvi. Not in a remotely date-like way, since I'm, you know…"

"A desiccated husk?" John volunteered.

My face flamed. "Yes. Exactly." I cleared my throat. "Well, here we are. Three-oh-eight. If you can just help me get it inside, I'm sure that when my new roommate gets home, he can help me arrange—"

"You should back up a little further," John interrupted. "Let me head in first. The living room's not that wide, and we won't have much room to turn it once we're in there."

"Oh." I frowned at the exterior wall of the apartment, reluctantly impressed. "That's some serious spatial awareness. I wish I had a math brain."

John huffed out a laugh and set down his end of the couch, and I followed suit. "No, you don't. It's a bunch of hamsters running in wheels, night and day. Yours seems exponentially more fun."

I highly doubted that. Especially when it was replaying Fern's voice at double speed, like a chipmunk on helium.

You're gonna fall for this guy, because you won't be able to help yourself, and you're gonna convince yourself it's love when it's not, and one of you will end up with your heart broken…

Damn it, Fern.

"Hang on. Let me get out my keys." I reached into the pocket of my tight jeans.

Once again, John looked at me a little strangely, but then he smiled, reached into his pocket, produced his *own* keys, and inserted *them* into the lock.

"So, um… you were mentioning slim odds?" He shrugged offhandedly. "It looks like I'm your new roommate."

"Nope," I responded immediately and, it must be said, irrationally, given the whole key-in-the-lock evidence. "That can't be. Ben said his roommate is impossible to talk to, and you're…"

John blushed and rubbed the back of his neck. "I mean. Ben's not entirely wrong. I, ah… I definitely didn't get the memo that he was going back to Finland this week, so…"

I laughed a little bit hysterically and rubbed both hands over my face. This was terrible. This was impossible. How the hell was I going to stay away from this guy—this incredibly attractive, incredibly wonderful guy—if we were living together?

"So you're not my brother Jace's friend," I said, stating the obvious.

John shook his head and braced the door open with a stopper. "But I'm sure he's a great guy. You ready?"

I sighed but bent obediently to pick up my end of the couch. "He's really not. He's kind of a dick. Which honestly should have been my first clue that you weren't his friend."

We walked the couch into the room, where Ben's missing sofa had left a vacant spot that was the perfect size for mine, and set it down one final time.

John dusted his hands in a satisfied way and stood back to look at the setup. "It looks great. The green looks awesome with the hardwood floor."

It really did. But I still had so many questions.

"John, you didn't even know I was your roommate. Why in the world did you help a perfect stranger move a sofa?" Who the heck did that?

"Well..." He darted an almost nervous glance at my face. "Because you seemed like an interesting person? Like a guy who needed a friend? And I was available." He shrugged.

"That simple?"

"Sure. It doesn't have to be complicated, T." He took a seat, then slid back with a delighted groan and ran his hand over the green tufted armrest. "Holy shit, is this hand-tooled leather?"

"It... yes. It is."

"Mmmm." He closed his eyes and smiled sleepily. "This really *is* the best couch ever."

I snorted. This whole situation was... it was beyond ridiculous. Still, I felt my mouth curl up in a smile I couldn't have stopped even if I wanted to.

"So you want us to be... friends?" I clarified, testing the word on my tongue.

John's eyes opened, and he frowned a little, like he was looking for the catch. "Uh... yes? Why not?"

All the reasons why not—six feet and several glorious inches of why not—were splayed out right there on my sofa with his feet propped up on the coffee table. His sturdy legs, his killer smile, his big hands that had made my body warm all over the one and only time he'd touched me *through my shirt.*

Could I really go a whole year without twisting friendship into something it wasn't?

But what was the alternative? Having this sweet man walk out of my life entirely?

And maybe it would be easier than I thought. Heck, maybe the man wasn't even gay.

Pick one, Teagan Donahue: friendship or nothing.

"Why not," I agreed, plunking myself down on the opposite end of the sofa and propping my feet on the coffee table, too. "Let's be super-platonic roommate friends."

John's bright smile sent ripples of warmth through my stomach, chasing away my doubts… at least for the moment.

"We know your thoughts on sourdough," I said pensively. "But how do you feel about karaoke with mediocre but enthusiastic singers?"

"Well. Back in Vermont, I once dated a guy who was an award-winning pig caller…"

Fuck. So, not straight, then.

But also… weirdly fascinating.

"I can learn to love it," John promised solemnly.

Then I would try my very best *not* to fall in love with him.

I leaned across the space between us and rested a hand on his shoulder, one bro to another. "John Curran," I vowed, "I am going to be the very best friend you've ever had."

And I kept the hell out of that promise…

Until the day I fucked it all up.

CHAPTER TWO

JOHN

Almost One Year Later

TEAGAN

This is your friendly reminder that it's Friday night, aka NETFLIX NIGHT, aka The Best Night of the Week.

If you get home early enough, we can watch the last five episodes of Knightfall before we crash, which MUST HAPPEN, because I will not be able to sleep until I know that Abe is happily in love.

Also, just to say, if I don't get proper sleep, I will never finish my degree, and I might go full-on Ophelia from the strain of it all.

I'm not saying my tragic descent into madness will be entirely your fault, John…

But I'm also not saying it's NOT your fault.

Did you leave yet?

Or are you and the other math dudes busy watching multiplication porn and jerking off?

I snorted. When the texts from Teagan came through, I'd already grabbed my jacket off the back of my chair and had my laptop bag in one hand and my travel coffee mug in the other. I shut off the light with my elbow, shut my office door with my foot, tucked the empty coffee cup under my chin, and typed.

> Your fantasies about life in the math department are always so spot-on.

> Also, you made me mess up my seventeens tables and threw off my rhythm. I'm limp now. Thanks a bunch.

I could hear the laughter in Teagan's voice when I read his reply.

TEAGAN

> True fact, Johnny: just KNOWING your seventeens tables is the leading cause of erectile dysfunction in men over twenty-eight.

> (I'd make up more fake stats on that, but then you'd get hard again and I'd never get to finish our show. Hurry up!)

I groaned.

The real true-fact was that I hadn't had a problem getting an erection since I'd meet my very-platonic best friend, Teagan. These days, my problem was trying to hide it, and that grew harder (no pun intended) all the time.

I'd been head over heels for the man for three hundred fifty-five days (yes, I was counting), and since then, I'd found myself doing all kinds of shit I never would have fathomed before. Like moving a random stranger's couch, yeah— because when the most beautiful man you've ever seen turns to you with his big eyes and needs a favor, you fucking do it

—but also participating in Karaoke Saturdays, and Philosophical Conundrum Taco Tuesdays, and all the other random days of the weeks that Teagan turned into holidays, complete with sacrosanct festivities and, almost always, special holiday foods.

Maybe the craziest of these, though, was Netflix Night every Friday, when I sat in the semi-darkness for hours in what had become "John's spot" on Teagan's beloved sofa and pretended I felt nothing but warm friendship for the sexy-as-fuck man sitting two feet away.

Weirder still, I somehow looked forward to this torture.

Teagan Donahue had made me a masochist.

"I am not going to have sex with my roommate," I whispered aloud, willing myself to believe it. Then I adjusted myself quickly, locked my office door, and texted back.

> I believe you believe that. FYI, smartass, I've already left the office.

There. I smiled a little to myself. This technically was not a lie, and I prided myself on being as honest as possible.

About most things, anyway.

"Professor Curran?" a voice called from an office on the left as I hurried down the hall. "John?"

I winced but quickly turned it into a smile as I turned around and doubled back to talk to the older blonde woman who'd been my mentor since I'd been here. "Marie. Hey," I said from the doorway. "Working late?"

"A little." She sat back in her desk chair and gazed at me impassively across her messy desk. "I got an interesting phone call that derailed my afternoon a bit."

My heart beat faster. "Oh?"

"A Professor—" She slid her reading glasses on to consult a paper on her desk before quickly sliding them off again. "—Osman Kheir from Hannabury. Apparently there's a full professorship open in their math department, and you're the leading contender for it. He wanted a reference, and of course I was happy to give it." She shook her head, and her face broke out in a smile. "John, why didn't you tell me you were applying for this?"

"Oh." I tapped my metal coffee cup nervously against the doorframe. "Well." I cleared my throat nervously. "It's hardly a done deal. I, ah, I applied for the position nearly a year ago. My brother-in-law Andy works in the math department at Hannabury, and he gave me a heads-up that the opening was coming, so I was the first guy in the door, so to speak. But at the time, they were hoping to promote from within, and I haven't heard anything *official* since then, so I'm pretty sure nothing will come of it."

She narrowed her eyes. "That's not how it sounded to me at all. Professor Kheir indicated that the spot is yours for the taking. And Hannabury is closer to your family, isn't it? Your parents are still up in Vermont, and your sister's family?"

I nodded, my palms dampening slightly. "My mothers have a hobby farm up in Keltyville. And Molly is pregnant with her second now. But really, Marie, I'm not sure what's going to happen with the Hannabury job—"

"John, we both know Covington won't be able to offer you a comparable position for…" She shrugged helplessly. "A long time, if ever. And positions at Vermont colleges like Hannabury are incredibly rare, what with so many schools going out of business. This is the career opportunity of a lifetime—"

"Yeah, I know," I agreed. "But there are, you know, a lot of factors to consider. So…" I forced a smile. "Don't tell anyone in case it doesn't work out, okay?"

She stared at me for a moment like I was an equation she couldn't solve. "What does Teagan say about this?"

"Oh, ah…" I licked my lips. "I'm not sure. We haven't really talked about it. He's… you know…"

Beautiful. Fascinating. Compelling. Genuinely kind. Fiercely intelligent. Entertaining as fuck.

Also sexy.

I am not going to have sex with my roommate.

"He's busy," I concluded, which was also true. "He's finishing up his degree next semester."

"Yes, I know." She smiled warmly, which was most people's reaction whenever Teagan's name was brought up. "The last time he brought you lunch, he complimented my new glasses, told me about an amazing hair salon his friend opened, and gabbed to me for ten minutes about his thesis. It sounded fascinating."

I returned her smile because I couldn't help it. "It really is. I know nothing about T.S. Eliot, and I didn't really *want* to know either, but when he talks about it, I get interested against my will. It's annoying."

Marie laughed. "You're proud of him."

"Of course." I shrugged. "He's amazing."

"And what's Teagan going to do after he graduates?"

"He's hoping for a high school teaching contract for next fall. Probably substitute teaching otherwise. And he does creative writing, too—like, he and my sister are working on these children's picture books that I think could really take off because he's an incredible storyteller, and I keep encouraging him to query an agent, but—" I coughed lightly. "Anyway. He's got a million things he could do. I want him to pick the one that makes him happy."

Marie nodded, then tilted her head. "Forgive me for asking such a personal question, but you and Teagan... Are you two...?"

The look in her eyes made it clear what she meant, and I felt my face go hot. "Us? Oh. Nah. No. We're not... together. We're roommates. Best friends. Platonic. That's all. That's... that's plenty."

I'd been telling myself that for eleven and a half months.

For two semesters, five visits to my family, and a summer road trip to the beach in Maine so terrible that it had already become funny.

For fifty-one weekly loaves of sourdough that Teagan had made me faithfully, exactly as he'd promised. Even during the blizzard that snowed us in over spring break. Even when I was ready to crawl under my mattress and hide during final exam season. Even during the sweltering summer months, when sweaty tendrils of Teagan's bright red hair had fallen out of his topknot to plaster against his neck as he worked the dough in our tiny kitchen.

And one of these damn days, if I kept saying it enough, it was going to sink in.

I am not going to have sex with my roommate.

"Ah. I'd imagined, with how close you are… " She shrugged, a little disappointed. "Well. Never mind. You know I'm here if you need to talk about career goals or anything. Covington and our students would be sad to lose you, but our loss would be Hannabury's gain. You know that, right?"

"Sure." I nodded woodenly. "Have a great weekend, Marie."

I checked my phone as I raced down the hall toward the stairs and saw the text string I'd missed.

TEAGAN

You're still standing in the math department as you type this, aren't you?

Tell Marie and Botan and whoever else you're talking to that I say hey.

Why are you not answering me, Mr. Reliable?

You will recall that failing to answer a text message is second only to people who use the thumbs-up on Facebook Messenger in Teagan's Hierarchy of Annoyance.

Then, time-stamped six minutes later…

TEAGAN

OMG. I have major, MAJOR news to share!!
Like, an incredible, once-in-a-lifetime, holy-
shit, unexpected but REALLY GOOD thing
just happened, and my emotions are all over
the place, and I need my CALM AND
STEADY BFF to talk me down. WHY ARE
YOU NOT HERE?

No, it's fine. It's FINE. I'm composing myself
and then jumping on a Zoom call in 10 mins,
so now you're gonna have to wait until you
get home for me to tell you all about it.

But actually, if all goes well, I think we need
to postpone Netflix Night!

Just until tomorrow night, I mean. Would you
mind?

Turns out I MIGHT be able to wait one more
night to find out if Abe is happy.)

Johnnnn. You're still not answering. I swear, if
you're still working right now, I'll…

Actually, I don't know what I'll do. But it's
gonna be TERRIBLE.

When I submit my list of Top Ten Most
Tragically Forsaken Humans in History to
Buzzfeed and put my own name at the top,
you'll know why and you'll have no one to
blame but yourself.

I grinned, feeling the slight panic that had gripped me in
Marie's office fade as I read Teagan's messages. It was highly
ironic that he called me calm and steady when I was in the
midst of a really annoying and uncharacteristic freak-out over
him, but just seeing his messages—and his egregious use of
capital letters—on the screen helped level me out.

Another true fact? There were times when I thought of the Hannabury job and all the things it would give me—smaller classes where I could really get to know my students, a slower pace of life, closeness with my family—and wondered if maybe I was foolish for not jumping at the chance I was being offered.

But then I'd have a moment like this one, reading Teagan's messages, when I'd remember with crystal clarity what I could and could not live without.

And that was why I would not be moving to Vermont.

Without thinking, I typed out a quick reply.

> Sorry! Marie needed to talk to me urgently. I'm for real leaving now though. What's the big news? Is there a puppy available at the shelter? Because I'm still not sure our place is big enough.

I hit Send. Then I realized my error.

Teagan was almost definitely going to ask what I'd been urgently talking with Marie about. If he learned there was a job offer from Hannabury on the table, he'd begin packing my bags *for* me, because he knew how much I loved the place. If I told him I wasn't going, he'd demand to know why (and probably check me for signs of a concussion), and I could hardly tell him the truth—that I'd miss him too much.

People weren't supposed to make life decisions based on how much they might miss their *very platonic best friends*, I was pretty sure.

And Jesus, if Teagan could see the way my palms sweat at the idea of him knowing how I actually felt, he'd never call me calm and steady ever again.

See, Teagan had gone on twenty-three dates in the past year, including one just the previous evening (and, yes, I'd counted those, too). He claimed all of them went "okay," but when I asked why none of the guys got a second date, he'd turned beet red.

"I wouldn't do that to them, Johnny," he'd said. "It's too hard being friends with someone who can't give you what you really want."

Needless to say, after that I'd been in no hurry to share my own unreciprocated feelings.

I wasn't lucky enough to have a guy like Teagan fall for me in return. I wasn't foolish enough to go back to living without him. I for sure wasn't willing to risk it when I couldn't calculate and mitigate the odds.

Back when I was a kid, I had a hoard of good-luck charms. A mountain of pennies I'd picked up, a sock my twin sister had worn when her kindergarten soccer team won the championship… even a piece of paper that I *swore* could make any wish I wrote on it come true. Strangely, none of them seemed to work consistently, but I'd been both stubborn and timid as fuck. I'd been convinced that if I found the right charm, it would make me brave.

Then the summer I turned nine, while attempting to find a four-leaf clover that my cousin Arlo *swore* he'd seen growing near the woodpile in his backyard, I acquired the worst case of poison ivy known to man—so bad I couldn't help scratching and ended up getting a terrible skin infection that landed me in the hospital on IV antibiotics, crying the whole damn time because Arlo was gonna get the clover before me and steal my luck.

Yes, really.

After a few days of this, my poor, exasperated Mom had thrown up her hands and told Ma Ann to "sit your son down and explain this stuff to him, Annie, before he concusses himself trying to steal a horse's shoe next, for Christ's sake." And Ma Ann had done just that. She'd sat on the side of my hospital bed and explained in her quiet voice the concept of probability—the science behind luck—so that I'd stop running amok looking for "flippin' clovers."

It had been a life-changing moment for me.

It turned out, outcomes tended to follow patterns. If I learned to account for the right variables, I could predict the likelihood of any outcome, because there was a probability to everything—winning bets, acing tests, scoring touchdowns, even making friends. And you didn't have to be brave when you could only take the risks you knew would pay off, right?

I'd decided Arlo could keep his damn clovers, and I'd spent my life focusing on the numbers instead.

But then three hundred fifty-five days ago, I'd driven home from Vermont after my promising Hannabury interview and found the world's most beautiful man standing in front of my mailbox, pouting his perfect, *perfect* lips, flipping his long red hair, and talking about fairies. And I—rational, shy John Curran—had for the first time in my life wanted to grab a man, run possessive hands all over his body, and never let him go.

There was no metric in the universe that could have accounted for the absurd coincidence of that meeting. No collection of data I could have evaluated that would have predicted the instant, overwhelming *click* I'd felt when his eyes met mine. No method of analysis that could have forecasted how much this one person had come to mean to me.

In short, when it came to Teagan, the numbers didn't apply.

I am not going to have sex with my roommate.

I debated taking the train home, but I knew the Green Line would be packed with commuters, so I opted for a half-hour walk home instead, figuring it would be a good chance to get my head on straight—or at least *very platonically*—before spending the evening with my best friend on the couch.

The weather was the kind of autumn-crisp that people

thought of when they imagined fall in New England—cool enough that I didn't turn the concerning shade of red that would make bystanders worry my burly ass was gonna stroke out any second, but with a warm breeze blowing in off the water that swirled the yellow and orange leaves on the ground like one of the seventeenth-century Iranian carpets in the textile exhibit Teagan had dragged me to last spring. Canada geese flew south in a tidy V-formation that soothed my soul, honking their asses off.

> Almost home. Do I get to hear the news now?

"Evening, John!" Mrs. Graziella, the elderly woman who lived downstairs, called with a wave as I hoofed it up Grand View toward home. She and her husband were taking their Pekingese, Tito, for his evening stroll, and as usual, they were linked arm in arm with their white heads bent so close together, it was impossible to tell who was supporting who.

"Hi, guys. Hey, Tito," I said, smiling as I passed them. "Sorry, I'm running late."

"What's the rush?" Mr. Graziella called. "Got a hot date with your young man? Tell him he left his muffin plate at our place this morning, and he can bring me more muffins when he comes to collect it!"

"Dante." Mrs. Graziella smacked her husband lightly and spoke in an urgent whisper that people on the next block could probably hear. "What did I tell you? I asked Teagan, and he said they aren't dating."

"Ah, baloney. I seen the way this kid looks at him." I could feel Mr. Graziella's gaze on my back as I jogged up the steps from the sidewalk to my building. "Wait, no kidding? Then who's Teagan dating? You might think I'm going deaf, but I swear I heard you and Teagan this morning talking about him going on dates and finding *the one*."

"Jesus, Mary, and Joseph, Dante," Mrs. Graziella hissed. "I thought you were watching your car auctions on the television!"

My face went hot as I opened the building door, and when I hit the lobby, I could feel sweat soaking my temples as my heart pounded. It took me a second to recognize the feeling for what it was—panic—because I couldn't remember the last time I'd felt that way.

Shit. If both Marie and Mr. Graziella had noticed my feelings for Teagan, I was doing a shit job of hiding it. How long before Teagan noticed?

Calm and Steady John had officially left the building.

My phone buzzed in my hand, and I looked down, expecting a reply from Teagan, but instead the words EVIL TWIN appeared above a picture of my sister sticking her tongue out.

Jesus. Why had the whole world decided to descend on me at once?

I knew exactly why Molly was calling… and I didn't have an answer for her any more than I had for Professor Kheir or Marie.

I darted a guilty glance around the lobby and declined the call, hoping that Molly would drop it, but I should have known better. A moment later, the text messages began.

EVIL TWIN

> John. Bernard. Curran. Stop ducking my calls.

> You think I'm calling to ask WHAT THE FUCK YOU'RE THINKING, not jumping at this job at Hannabury, don't you?

> Well, you're only half right. And I'm also reminding you that you're coming home for Ma Annie's birthday next weekend. Good luck ignoring me when we're in the same house, jerkface.

My groan echoed around the empty lobby. I suddenly felt a tickle of Ebola in my throat that I was confident would flare into a full-blown disease just in time for next weekend.

> EVIL TWIN
>
> And don't think you're gonna play sick, because I texted Teagan, too, and he said he'd be HAPPY TO COME. Mwahahahaha. #playingdirty
>
> By the way, let me know what you think when Teagan tells you the news!!! The excitement is so real. Love you.

Fuck. *Triple* fuck. I couldn't even feel annoyed that Molly knew Teagan's news before I did, because I was too busy imagining what would happen when I brought Teagan home with me. He'd find out *everything*.

I had a week to avert this crisis.

Sure. No problem.

"Oh, John, thank goodness you're home." My across-the-hall neighbor pulled her door wide as I clomped up the steps to my own apartment like she'd been lying in wait for me. "What is going on with Teagan?" she demanded.

I'd lived across from the woman for nearly two years, and we'd never exchanged names. But then last winter Teagan had heard her playing "Turn It Off" from the Book of Mormon soundtrack at full volume. He'd gasped like a Broadway refugee who'd found someone to speak his native tongue and pounded on her door, and now Monica—who was thirty-three, an Aquarius, had three cats of varying temperaments, worked as a labor and delivery nurse, and was seriously considering dying her black hair platinum blonde but wasn't able to commit—came over a few times a month for what T called "Charcuterie and Show Tunes."

"Teagan?" I repeated, frowning down at my phone. He

still hadn't answered me. "He seemed fine a little while ago. I think he's on a Zoom call now. Why?"

"Because." Monica looked left, then right, then grabbed my arm and drew me into her living room, which was the mirror image of mine. "Because," she whispered, "we walked in together when he came home from work, but he seemed… off."

"Okayyyy. *Off* like when they ran out of oat milk at Campus Connections? Or *off*, like when Shawn Mendes and Camilla Cabello broke up and he thought he had a chance with Shawn?"

"Neither." Monica wrinkled her nose. "Worse. Like… like I asked him how his date went last night, and he bit his lip and looked down at his phone and got all gooey-eyed and dreamy. And I was like, 'Hey, yo, talk to me here!' And he blinked a bunch, like he was coming out of his own little world, then he said something about how 'big things' might be happening, but 'I've gotta talk to John first before I tell anyone else.'"

I shrugged. "He mentioned big news to me, but I have no idea what it could be. He seemed happy about it, though. I don't think it's anything bad."

"Well, there's bad, and then there's *bad*, isn't there?" Monica mused, which was the kind of statement Teagan would have totally understood on a level I did *not*. She lowered her voice and said significantly, "He went on a date last night."

"Yeah, I know. He goes on lots of dates." Twenty-three. Exactly. "So?"

"Soooo, it was with the guy from the seminar on technology in education last week."

"Was it?" I said nonchalantly. "I didn't get details."

No details other than the fact that the guy's name was John, just like mine, that Teagan had been gone precisely two hours and fifty-three minutes, that he'd driven his own car, that he'd brought me home some leftover chicken scampi that reeked of garlic, and that he'd looked tired but not *disheveled-tired* when he'd plunked down beside me on our sofa to watch the news, which had allowed me to finally draw a deep breath.

Any more details would've made me a full-blown stalker.

"Well, I'm worried that maybe..." She lowered her voice to a whisper. "It went well."

I blinked at her uncomprehendingly.

She nodded. "Right? You see what I'm saying here? So I called Fern immediately, of course—Teagan gave me her number for emergencies, and this fits the bill—and she agreed that we're at Threat Level Scarlet. She'll be here any minute for something I'm calling Margaritas and Mischief Night. It's kind of a Teagan-inspired name, which I thought was fitting. Mrs. Graziella is bringing up some lasagne in half an hour, too, and don't you worry, because we're not leaving until we've made a plan to handle your situation. *Oooh!* Maybe we can lock Teagan in a room until you have a chance to correct things. Something like that."

"Lock him in a—? What the heck are you talking about?" I demanded. "Monica, what do I need to correct?"

Monica heaved a frustrated sigh, like *I* was the one being dense. "This situation that you've allowed to occur, obviously! I mean, it's bad enough that we've all been watching you guys do this weird hide-your-feelings dance for *yearrrrrs*—"

"Less than a year," I corrected. Then belatedly added, "Not that I have... feelings."

"Oh, please." She rolled her eyes. "Sorry to crush your illusions, but you are the worst feelings-hider in the world, second only to your roommate. The tension has been driving all of us crazy for months, waiting for you to sort your shit."

Wait, what? "Who's 'all of us'?"

"Um. Let's see. Me. Fern. The Graziellas. Mr. Sincero from

2B. Kasim from the market. Pauline and Jen from the bakery. Um, Stephen and Carl, the ones with the mini schnauzers Teagan liked to pet whenever you guys went for coffee on summer weekends." She tapped her lips. "I'm probably forgetting some. Teagan knows a lot of people."

He really did. He had a magnetic personality that drew people in. But not a lot of people knew *Teagan*. I loved knowing that I did. I actually felt kind of… almost… possessive about it. About him. Which was wrong on all sorts of levels.

"Anyway. Mrs. Graziella said to let you two work things out in your own time, but I'm afraid that's no longer an option here, John. It seems like he really likes this guy." She cast a worried look in the direction of my apartment. "So what are you gonna do about it?"

I clutched my coffee cup more tightly in my hand. "What *can* I do? I mean, it's… good. It's… great. That he… that he likes someone," I managed to choke out.

"Other-John," Monica reminded me sadly.

"Right. Yes. Other-John," I agreed grimly, like the bottom wasn't falling out of my world. "Teagan deserves to be happy."

"Sure he does." Monica grabbed my arm. "But he deserves to be happy with *you*. No one else can love him like you can! And this whole clusterfuck is *your* fault, because *you* haven't told him how you feel. He might like Other-John, but the original is always the best." She laid her hand on my arm. "Go be the original-John, John. Just talk to him."

For a long moment, I stared at her, my muscles too frozen to move. Downstairs, I heard the main door to the building open and close with a click and Tito barking excitedly.

My first thought was *I don't even have a week to sort this. I have to do it now.*

Just talk to him… God, she made it sound so easy. Like it

was just a matter of being determined enough. Like there weren't very real stakes.

I had no numbers to run, no formulas to input, no lucky charms to stuff in my pockets. I wasn't sure how to even begin.

"I've gotta go," I blurted, taking out my keys. "I promised T I'd be home. I'll... I'll let you get back to your... mischief."

I strode across the hall, let myself inside, set down my belongings, and leaned back against the door to catch my breath. The apartment smelled like a fall candle Teagan must have had burning somewhere, and the dust motes twirled lazily through the late-afternoon light filtering through the wide-open curtains at the window. From Teagan's room came the sound of his sweet voice chatting animatedly, and a plate of muffins sat under a glass dome on the kitchen counter. But it wasn't until I walked down the short hall toward Teagan's bedroom and found him sitting at his desk, his long hair tied up in a knot and his legs pretzeled beneath him, that I could really draw a deep breath.

Teagan's gaze shot to mine as I hovered in the doorway, careful to stay off-camera, and the polite smile he'd been giving the person on the screen warmed a fraction. Became something special. Something that was *mine*.

Or maybe I only had it temporarily. Until he moved on to this Other-John.

I gulped nervously and choked on my own saliva. Teagan looked concerned.

"Patsy, can you hang on while I mute you for two seconds?" he asked the person on the screen. He clicked a button, then looked at me. "You okay, Johnny?"

I nodded, not trusting myself to speak. Dear God, he was so beautiful.

"Okay. Well..." He bit his lip—that full lower lip I fucking dreamed of feeling on my dick—almost nervously. "I'm gonna need like ten… maybe fifteen more minutes here, and then I'm gonna jump in the shower and get ready."

"Ready?" I was way too distracted to hold a conversation.

"Yeah. To go out." He grinned. "Things are looking really good. But I…"

"Teagan?" The woman on the Zoom call prompted at the same moment that a phone began *quacking* somewhere in the living room.

"Shit," Teagan muttered. "That's my alarm to start getting ready. I have like fifty-seven things to tell you, and I *will*, I promise. Wait for me?"

"I… I'll go shut off your alarm." I hooked a thumb toward the living room, and he gave me a wide, grateful smile.

"Ten minutes," he reiterated. "Maybe fifteen."

Right. Yeah. Great.

Fifteen minutes to figure out a solution I hadn't been able to come up with in a year. Fifteen minutes to find a way to convince Teagan that, yes, I had romantic feelings for him, but I could handle them. That things between us didn't have to change. That he wasn't the sole reason I was staying in Boston. That I hardly ever jerked off at night thinking about the curve of his ass when he leaned over to take bread out of the oven and that I hadn't had to add ten minutes to my shower time every morning because the green-grass scent of his bodywash had a very consistent effect on certain parts of my anatomy.

What could go wrong?

I found Teagan's phone sitting on the charger by the sofa, and I wiped my damp palms on my pants before I picked it up and hit Stop to silence the alarm. On the lock screen were the unread texts I'd sent Teagan on the way home.

JOHNNY

Sorry! Marie needed to talk to me urgently.
I'm for real leaving now though. What's the
big news? Is there a puppy available at the
shelter? Because I'm still not sure our place
is big enough.

For half a second, I wished I could unlock the phone and quickly delete all reference to Marie, but I told myself it was too late for that anyway. I needed to move forward and come clean. I needed to…

The name on the message underneath mine snagged my attention, and I read it before I'd consciously decided to.

JOHN D

It's only been one day, but I already miss you.

What the fuck?

I scrolled further, to the bottom of an extraordinarily long text string, and started reading.

JOHN D

Last night was so magical, Teagan.

The connection between us was unlike
anything I've ever felt before.

The way you listened to me like you really
cared what I was saying…

The way you immediately understood me
and encouraged me to follow my dreams…

The way you finished my sentences.

The way you looked when you blinked your
bright blue eyes at me.

I scowled. Teagan's eyes were gray-blue. Changeable as storm clouds. Idiot.

JOHN D

> You dazzle me.

> You inspire me.

> The way I feel about you is so huge and overwhelming.

> It feels like… it feels like LOVE, Teagan. And I know that's crazy, and it's probably too soon…

> But you deserve to know, and I couldn't wait another minute before telling you.

> I need to see you tonight.

> Please, baby.

I clutched Teagan's phone so hard the glass squeaked under my hand, and I forced myself to put it down gently.

Baby. He'd called my Teagan *baby*.

Every word that Other-John had written was one I could have said.

But it turned out I didn't have even fifteen minutes to sort my shit and come clean. I was already too late. I'd missed my chance to tell Teagan how I felt, and he'd already found someone else. Someone who'd made him… what had Monica said? Gooey and dreamy? Someone he'd told Mrs. Graziella might be *the one*.

So many other things started slotting into place, too. Postponing our Netflix Night? Needing to talk to me about his once-in-a-lifetime, unexpected good news?

In the other room, Teagan laughed lightly, happily, and my stomach flipped with genuine nausea. In just a few minutes, Teagan would come out here and talk to me about his magical date and his true love, and because I was his platonic best friend John, he'd expect me to listen and smile supportively. I would have to show him how happy I was that he was happy, even while my heart was breaking.

And I… couldn't. I just couldn't.

Later, after the shock had worn off, after the buzzing in my brain slowed down, after the panic had subsided, maybe after I'd accepted the job at Hannabury, I'd be able to be the best friend he deserved, but I knew that right then I would only ruin his excitement with my own disappointment.

I typed out a quick text on my own phone, and by the time Teagan's phone quacked to signal that he'd received it, I already had my keys in my hand.

I let the door slam shut behind me.

CHAPTER THREE

TEAGAN

"Sounds great, Patsy! Talk soon."

I slammed my laptop shut, stared at the wall, and grinned dopily. I liked to think I'd always been a fairly optimistic person, but if someone had told me a year ago just how much my life would change for the better in such a short time, I would've told them to fuck off with their manifestation bullshit because I didn't believe in that stuff. Then this guy—the world's sweetest, strongest, most gorgeous man—had offered to move a random stranger's sofa… and here I was.

I sat there for ten whole seconds, letting my giddy excitement wash over me.

Then I did what I always did when I got good news.

"John! Johnny, come here! You are not going to *belieeeeve* —" I broke off as the apartment door slammed shut.

What the heck? I'd asked him to wait.

"John?" I demanded. I walked down the hall to the empty living room, where my phone was quacking forlornly. I swiped it off the couch before heading to the apartment door.

"John?" I called into the echoing hallway. "If you forgot the mail, just leave it. I need to—"

Belatedly, I looked down at my phone.

JOHNNY

Hey. Congrats on your big news. I'm not
feeling like great company tonight, so we'll
celebrate soon, okay? Have a great evening
with John.

What in the fucking fucksticks?

A great evening with *John*?

Also, since when did either of us care about whether we were great company or not? John had gotten me Boston Cream Pie ice cream and deleted the Grindr app in solidarity with me back in June after a particularly horrible date. I'd made him chicken soup and brought him cold compresses when he was sick back in April, because he'd been so miserably feverish that nothing in the apartment had felt like the right temperature.

We were not "company" friends.

Also-also, he was acting like he knew what my big news was when he couldn't possibly, because *I* hadn't officially known about it until five minutes ago, and I hadn't told anyone the details ahead of time, because I'd wanted John to be the first to know.

"John?" I yelled, louder now, leaning over the railing so I could see down to the lobby. "What the heck is—"

But I heard the distant sound of the outside door clicking as John left the building.

"Teagan? What's going on, boo?"

Our across-the-hall neighbor, Monica, stood in her doorway wearing pajamas and carrying something that looked suspiciously like a margarita in her hand.

"It's John. He's acting bizarre all of a sudden. I wanted to talk to him—"

"About your big news, right." Monica nodded. She winced sympathetically. "He didn't take it well when you told him? Did he... did he cry?"

"What? Why would he cry?" I shook my head. "I didn't

even get to talk to him. I was on a Zoom, and when I finished, he was gone. Then he sends me this." I gestured with my cell phone, and Monica stepped into the hall to read it over my shoulder.

"Is that Teagan?" a voice called from inside Monica's apartment. My friend Fern appeared a second later, also in pajamas and holding a drink.

"Fern?" I blinked. "What are you doing here?"

"A little something I'm calling Margaritas and Mischief—" Monica began.

Fern interrupted her. "*Bupbupbup.* Hey. We'll ask the questions." The teal-dipped ends of her dark hair bounced as she pointed an accusing finger at me. "You'd best get in here and explain yourself, young man."

"What?" I asked, bewildered.

Monica took my phone and handed it to Fern, who scanned it quickly.

"What does John mean, 'enjoy your night with John'?" she asked.

"John means, you know, *John*." Monica widened her eyes significantly. "Not *John*-John, but *Other*-John. The one Teagan went out with last night."

"And you're seeing *Other*-John two nights in a row? Teagan, really." Fern shook her head disappointedly. "What about *John*-John? Have you considered his feelings at all?"

Wait, what the hell was going on?

And how was this somehow my fault?

The word "John" had been repeated so much it was starting to lose all meaning.

"I'm not seeing John tonight! I was supposed to have plans with *my* John." My cheeks went hot. "I mean, my *roommate* John. We were going to watch *Knightfall,* but then I told him I had news and said I wanted to postpone Netflix Night so we could go out and celebrate my news instead, and…" I shook my head again. "I have no idea what's going on."

Fern and Monica exchanged a look. "Come in, honey," Monica said, gesturing me toward her apartment. "Let's get you a drink."

"Give me back my phone," I told Fern once we'd gotten inside. "I'm going to text my… *roommate*… and ask him what the fuck."

But Fern didn't give the phone back. Instead, Monica handed me a giant water glass full of slushy strawberry margarita and pushed me down onto the overstuffed sofa.

"So, what *is* your news?" Fern asked, sitting on the coffee table right in front of me.

I squirmed, reluctant. "Do you remember me mentioning how John's sister and I wrote a children's book? Well, it's about that. And I wanted to tell John before I told everyone, because he's the one who inspired everything, and… yeah."

I *still* wanted to tell John first. This felt like his news as much as mine, in a way.

I gulped down my margarita.

"You wrote a book," Monica said flatly. "*That's* your news?"

"Could you sound a *little* more excited?" I demanded. "Yes, that's the news. Jeez. When was the last time *you* wrote a book?"

Monica and Fern exchanged another look.

"We thought the news was about John," Fern said. "*Other*-John."

I stared at her blankly. "Why the heck would you think that? We went on one date. It was… fine, I guess? Not newsworthy."

"But." Monica frowned and sat on the sofa beside me. "You got all dreamy over him. When we were walking in earlier, I asked how your date was last night, and you were all moony and distracted."

"Not because of my date," I assured her. "Because I'd just gotten an email about the book."

"Ohhh." Monica winced. "Uh. I may have jumped to a teeny, tiny conclusion…"

"Question." Fern lifted a finger in the air but kept her eyes on my phone screen. "Does this Other-John person realize that your date with him was only meh? Because these texts… 'Last night was so magical, Teagan'? 'I need to see you tonight'? That doesn't sound meh."

"What texts? Give me that." I snatched the phone away from her and quickly scrolled. "Oh, *ew*. Noooo. Nope." I flashed Fern a guilty grimace. "He was nice enough, but I was actually sitting across from the poor guy the whole night thinking how much I'd rather have been home. He caught me daydreaming like *twice* while he was talking about his five-year goals, and I felt so bad I hadn't been listening that I did that overly enthusiastic encouragement thing, you know? Like 'Oh my gosh, wow! That, um, thing you said was, like, so inspiring that I needed to, like, sit with it for a minute and take it all in! Live, laugh, love, you know?'" I shrugged. "I guess I was more convincing than I'd hoped."

Monica snickered.

I frowned and looked up at Fern. "When the heck did these messages come in, anyway? I didn't see them."

Fern shrugged. "Check the time stamps, silly. They were on your lock screen under John's last text, so… sometime before that? Ohhhh, wait! Is it possible that *your* John saw them? Because if so…"

I shook my head. "He'd never look at my phone unless… *Ugh*." I rubbed a hand over my eyes. "Unless I asked him to shut off my alarm while I was on my Zoom call, which I did. But fuck, just because this dude wants to see me doesn't mean I want to be seen!" I whined. "It was supposed to be Netflix Night!"

"Which you postponed," Fern reminded me.

"So *my* John and I could go out!"

"Did you tell your John you wanted to go out with *him*?" Monica asked. "Or just that you wanted to go out?"

"I—" I deflated slightly. "I can't remember. But what in the world would make him think I'd cancel our plans for *this* random guy?" I brandished my phone.

Fern gave Monica a stern look. "Yeah, Monica, why would he think that?"

"Um. *Well*." Monica quickly exchanged her full margarita glass for mine... which had somehow become empty in the short time I'd been sitting on the sofa. "That teeny, tiny conclusion I jumped to? It's, ah... possible that I told your John about our conversation regarding *Other*-John. And I may have, um... saidyouhaddreamyeyes," she finished in a rush.

"You what?"

"And it's possible that *your* John looked a bit dejected and depressed when I suggested things seemed serious with you and Other-John. And, um... I'm kind of wondering if these texts might have confirmed that for him?" She bit her lip. "I think he was jealous."

I leaned back in my seat and groaned. "Well, that's ridiculous. Because even if I had been romantically interested in Other-John, *my* John is... he's my John. No one will ever be as important to me as he is."

Fern and Monica did their eyeball-talking schtick again.

"What?" I demanded. "Stop with the looky-looks! What am I missing?"

"Your John's the most important person to you," Fern reiterated. "Have you ever told him this?"

"Well, no. But I've also never told him the sky was blue. Some things are just... obvious." I shrugged. "Besides, guys don't talk to their friends that way. 'Hey, John, could you bring me a soda while you're up? And bee-tee-dubs, you're my favorite person in the universe! K, thanks, bro.'"

"If anyone could get away with that, you could," Fern muttered.

"Yeah, but I couldn't." My cheeks got hotter, and I sucked down more liquid. "If I did, it'd seem like I wanted more than friendship."

"And you don't?" Monica exchanged my empty margarita glass for Fern's, which was still mostly full.

It was funny how Monica's glasses held less liquid than average glasses, and I was totally gonna ask her about that at some point.

"No, I do. Of course I do." I plucked my shirt away from my body. "Is it warm in here?"

"Wait, you *admit* you have romantic feelings?" Fern demanded. "For fuck's sake, Teagan. Monica called me over here to stage an intervention—"

"Mischief and Margaritas," Monica corrected.

"Well, we got the mischief part down," Fern said pointedly. "But meanwhile you're all 'Oh, yeah, sure, of course I love him. Like it's no big deal.'"

I shrugged. "It's not new. I've loved him from the first minute. Or, okay, maybe the second," I allowed. "You were there, Fern. On the phone, remember? You were the one who told me not to jump into things. That I had been wrong before. That I would ruin everything if I started putting all kinds of expectations on John..."

"Because you didn't know him then!" Fern lifted a hand and let it fall. "Because you had literally met seconds before. Because you claimed you'd fallen for him and you hadn't even asked his *name*."

I opened my mouth, then clacked it shut. That was true.

"I wanted you to wait a couple of *weeks*." Fern shook her head. "But nooo, you had to go to extremes and wait a whole year *and* decide to keep a secret for the first time in your life?"

"I wasn't keeping a secret. It's just... he became my best friend," I said quietly. "I'm not just *in* love with him in a romantic way, like I want to kiss the hell out of him and rub my face against his chest—"

"Seriously, Teagan, I do not need to know this shit," Fern sighed.

"I do." Monica clasped her chin under her hands.

"—I love him. Like, I just want to be in the same room with him. And to know that he's well and happy. But I suck at romance," I said softly. "I've been on twenty-three dates this year, and all of them were crappy. I didn't want to fuck up my friendship with John trying for more."

"But now John's hurt, thinking you threw him over for Other-John," Fern said softly.

"Because I think your John has feelings for you, too," Monica said just as softly.

"Oh. Wow. That's…" Despite all the fantasies I'd had about John, that was one dream I'd never dreamed. It would have been too soul-crushing to wake up from it.

I swallowed hard and set down my empty glass on the floor beside the couch. I stood up and, strangely, felt a little wobbly. "John still should have talked to me and not assumed."

Fern nodded. Both of her. I blinked to clear my vision.

"So I'm gonna kish… I mean, *kick*, his ass."

"You should," Monica agreed happily. "Go find him and do that."

I frowned. "But I don't know where he is."

Fern rolled his eyes. "Your John is a creature of habit. You know exactly where he'll be."

There was a commotion at the door, and then Mrs. Graziella from downstairs bustled in, carrying a delicious-smelling lasagna and looking put out. "Good Lord. Sorry I'm late, girls. Dante wouldn't let me leave until he'd shown me a car video on the YouTubes." She sighed as she put her casserole dish on the kitchen counter. "But I'm here! So let's figure out a plan to help… Teagan!" she exclaimed, noticing me for the first time.

"You're late, Mrs. G.," Monica said. "We've already gotten

through the mischief, and Teagan's drunk most of the margaritas, and now we're at the point where Teagan is ready to confess his undying love to John. Tonight."

"Wait." I paused, and the room swayed, so I steadied myself with a hand on Fern's head. "I am?"

"You are," Fern confirmed, slapping my hand away. "You're heading to BarZ."

"Because your John is *your John*," Monica said firmly. "And he needs to know that you don't want any others."

"Oh." When she put it like that, it suddenly made so much sense. "Yes, he hecking does! It is right and just! I should write him a poem. Or, like, an original song!"

"Maybe not a song, sweetie." Monica wrinkled her nose.

Fern grimaced. "Definitely not a song."

"Oooh, my granddaughter Nicki works at BarZ!" Mrs. Graziella exclaimed. "Hang on half a sec."

Mrs. Graziella removed an enormous phone from her bra and tapped on it with bejeweled fingernails. "Nicki *is* working tonight, and she confirms John *is* at the bar."

"Ha! It's a sign," Monica crowed.

Mrs. Graziella pursed her lips. "She also says John's flirting with a cute guy who's been buying him gin and tonics." She looked up at me. "She thinks he's from out of town."

"The fuck you say!" I exclaimed, a little too loudly. I pulled at my hair band, releasing it from its topknot.

"Easy, killer," Fern began. "We don't know for sure—"

"How dare he be flirting with some imported interloper on the night when I am to sing the song of my undying love to him!" I yelled. "This is outrageous. I am marching down there—"

I took a wobbly step away from the couch, and Mrs. Graziella grabbed my elbow to steady me. "Or maybe you'll catch a taxi," she suggested.

"—and I am taking what is mine. *John is mine.*"

"Sweet Jesus." Fern sighed and rolled her eyes. "Maybe don't lead with that line, m'kay?"

Monica grabbed my shoulders and drew me into an impulsive hug. "Don't listen to a word she says," she whispered. "You should *definitely* lead with that."

———

IT TOOK me a little longer than I would have liked to get to the bar, since Fern had pointed out that I was wearing boxer shorts and fuzzy socks, and this attire might be frowned upon, even at a casual spot like our local hangout. By the time they'd sent me on my way in a pair of tight jeans and my favorite blue crop top, I was already sober again.

Well, okay, more like sober-ish.

Way too sober for original love songs, that was for damn sure. Which meant I was gonna have to wing it.

I scanned the bar area when I first got inside and found the place was *packed*. But John's height and bulk made it pretty hard for him to hide, and he definitely wasn't there.

"Nicki," I called, lifting a hand in greeting to the small, dark-haired woman behind the bar.

She gave me a small return smile, then tilted her chin toward the dance floor with an unhappy look.

I turned my head and sure enough, John—*my* John—was part of the throng of people packing the small space. Under the flashing strobe lights, his dark hair shone, and he moved with a kind of unself-conscious grace he usually only had when he'd been drinking.

The guy he was with... *ugh*. He *was* cute. He was tall—well, taller than me—and younger than either of us, with a smile I could tell from a distance was playful and sweet. His hair was golden brown and incredibly messy, like he—or maybe *my John*—had been running his fingers through it. They looked... really good together.

My throat went dry, and as I stood on the edge of the dance floor and watched them moving together in perfect rhythm, I had a moment of overwhelming self-doubt.

Maybe this guy was good for John. Maybe Mr. Cute-and-Playful was less of a drama queen than me, less inclined to turn to John when he was just trying to enjoy his Tuesday tacos and present him with annoying conundrums like, "Okay, pick one, Johnny, world peace *or* a cure for cancer..." Less likely to cry while watching Netflix or attach sentimental value to his sofa.

And, heck, John had never shown any romantic interest in me. Maybe Monica had been wrong. Maybe he wasn't here because he'd misunderstood my intentions with Other-John. Maybe he'd come out to meet this guy and had stood me up on purpose.

He certainly didn't seem to be thinking of me at the moment.

As I hesitated, a man came up and stood beside me. Like me, he didn't seem eager to join the throng.

He gazed down at me and said abruptly, "That bearded guy. You know him?"

I nodded miserably. "That's my best friend, John."

He grunted in acknowledgement, and I noticed that he was watching, too. Specifically, he was watching the man in John's arms.

"You know *that* guy? The one with the..." I made a tornado-like motion at the front of my head.

The man nodded slowly.

"Is he *your* best friend?" I asked hopefully.

He snorted in surprise. "Goodman? Fuck no. He's my..." He paused for a second and gave the Goodman person a look that was a little impatient and a whole lot *longing*. "Something."

I nodded. "They seem happy," I volunteered a moment later. It came out sounding like an accusation.

"Goodman seems drunk off his ass," the man replied. He glanced down at me again. "I'm Knox, by the way."

"Teagan." I pushed my hair back indecisively. "Well…"

"Teagan, I have an idea," the man said suddenly. "Would you like to dance?"

Anything seemed better than standing there overthinking, so I let him lead me out on the floor. But when we got close to where John and… Goodman, or whatever his name was… were dancing, and I saw just exactly how fucking *close* they were dancing, I kind of lost my mind. I stalked right up to them.

"You must be John's roommate, Teagan!" the Goodman person said, all gross cheerfulness and smiles.

Overly enthusiastic people were *so* annoying.

"Yeah," I said witheringly, trying to peer over his shoulder at my best friend, who'd plastered himself to this stranger's back. "John, are you—?"

"Teagan! Hey! Didn't see you there!" John straightened up and leaned against the guy's side affectionately. "This is Gay."

Gay?

"Gage," the Goodman person corrected.

"Are you sure?" John asked.

"Entirely," the guy corrected, beaming up at him.

"Gage," John agreed, giving him a fond look. He dragged the man up against his side. "He's my new boyfriend."

My stomach cramped like a giant had clenched it in his enormous fist and squeezed tightly. To the best of my knowledge, John hadn't dated anyone since last December, and they'd never gotten serious enough for him to invite the guy over to our place. The man had been history by Christmas, and John had spent New Year's Eve with *me*. So to hear him call this other guy his boyfriend was… horrifying.

"He's what?" I repeated softly.

"Oh, John," the Goodman person simpered in this cloying,

utterly fake sort of way as my sweet pure John smiled down at him, steady and calm and unshakable as ever.

What. the. fuck? Could John not see that this guy wasn't really into him? My protective instincts—yes, it turned out I had some—kicked in, and I set my jaw.

"Did you get him drunk on purpose?" I demanded of Goodman, probably way too loudly. "Are you trying to take advantage of him?"

Goodman acted all shocked and innocent, but I knew better.

"Goodman," Knox said impatiently, coming up on the man's other side. "What the hell are you doing?"

Precisely what I wanted to know.

"Knox!" The little asshole sounded way too happy. "Hey! Meet John. He's my… we're… boyfriends, so…"

He droned on and on about whatever the fuck, but I wasn't listening. I was too busy staring at John, who looked miserable, and defiant, and… and *miserable*.

"—Grindr hookup?" Knox said, looking from John to Goodman.

I gasped. "John! You were on Grindr?" The betrayal of it all! "You said you weren't doing that anymore. You pinky promised."

"I…" John looked at Goodman guiltily. "It's…"

"We didn't meet on Grindr," Goodman said. "We met at the bar earlier. The specifics are all a blur, but we're very committed. Aren't we, honey bear?"

I pressed a hand to my stomach. *Honey bear?*

"Committed," John agreed, looking at me sadly. Then he let Goodman spin him back into the crush of dancing bodies.

Oh, God, how mortifying. John clearly hadn't been that upset about the idea of me being with Other-John if he'd moved on this quickly, and yet here I was, practically stalking him at the bar. I needed to leave, immediately, before I did something that really would ruin my friendship with John far more than a declaration of affection would have.

I turned to leave… and Knox blocked my path.

"Let's dance," he said again. "Trust me."

I didn't really want to, but I was obviously a glutton for punishment, because I let him take my hand and spin me through the crowd until we were standing next to John and Goodman again.

We got there just in time to see John spin the man around and hold him so that John's broad chest was plastered to Goodman's back and John's big hand was on the man's hip as they swayed.

Knox was a decent dancer, and he kept our bodies moving in time, which I was distantly grateful for. Meanwhile, the entire focus of my consciousness was centered on John's hand where it held Goodman in place. It was so wrong, so fucking *wrong*, to see him holding someone else while feeling in my bones that it should have been me in his arms instead.

The flashing lights caught on John's soulful eyes, high-lighted the fine filaments of his beard, caught a drop of sweat that rolled from his temple to his cheek. Goodman reached behind him, wrapping his arm around the back of my John's neck, pulling John down to whisper something in his ear that made John's eyelids flutter momentarily.

It felt unbearably intimate, watching him like this, and I knew that if John looked at me, there'd be no way to hide my hurt, let alone my overwhelming jealousy.

I lifted up on my tiptoes and pulled Knox's head down. "Sorry, but I think I need to go. I—"

Goodman stumbled into me, knocking me sideways. "Oops! My bad!" He smirked at me, but his gaze kept straying to the place where I was touching Knox.

Oh, really.

I narrowed my eyes and very deliberately ran a hand through Knox's hair.

The asshole looked like he was trying to murder me with his laser eyeballs, and I felt a faint glimmer of satisfaction… before I remembered that the asshole was dancing with *my John*, and what the fuck was he doing being jealous of anyone else?

He swallowed hard and turned his attention back to John. Then suddenly they were plastered together with Goodman nearly bent in half, doing a bump and grind that was hotter than anything in my porn folder.

Mother. Fucker. My hands clenched into fists, and I briefly contemplated throwing *down*, right there in the club, despite never having been involved in a physical confrontation in my entire life.

I would *enjoy* it.

"Hey." Knox put a hand on my waist comfortingly. "It's okay. Chill," he whispered in my ear, not understanding my chronic, congenital un-chill-ness. He obviously didn't know about the fairy. I bit my lip so hard it stung.

"I don't know how," I moaned. If John and Goodman were acting like this at the fucking club, it was only a matter of time before they slipped away to the back. Or, Jesus fuck, went back to Goodman's place. Or *ours*.

I was seriously going to be ill.

Suddenly, I felt a familiar hand on my wrist, pulling me away from Knox's almost-embrace. "T," John said, low and urgent. "Can I speak to you, please? Right now? Outside?"

For a second, I almost refused. I didn't know if I could speak to him without bursting into tears. This was the part where he would tell me that he and Goodman wanted to go back to our apartment, wasn't it? How could I refuse?

Then I would have to stay the night at Monica's apartment so I didn't murder Gage Goodman in cold blood. Or, no. Maybe I needed to get a hotel room someplace further away. Like downtown Boston. Or Vermont. Or Sri Lanka. That way, I wouldn't be tempted to go across the hall and refuse to leave until Goodman had answered a comprehensive list of questions to prove his worthiness as John's potential suitor, including an essay question that I did *not* intend to grade on a curve.

I sighed, then nodded woodenly and let John lead me away.

"Can I be arrested for refusing to leave our apartment, even if you ask me to?" I demanded as he towed me through the crowd. I didn't pull my wrist away—I wanted his hands on me, and I told myself this might be the last time I got to enjoy it.

Because John was incredibly quick-witted—and, yes, used to dealing with my random thoughts after a year of friendship—even while slightly inebriated, he didn't hesitate. "No, you couldn't. But then, I'd never ask you to, so the point is moot."

I hustled faster to stay by his side and used my free hand to grasp his bicep. "Pick one, John!" I insisted passionately. "Showing consideration for your best friend and roommate, even if it means no sex... Or having loud, passionate sex with a guy just to get your rocks off, even if it leads your roommate to abject misery later."

John stopped and blinked down at me sadly. "Those the only choices?" he asked, his voice so low I had to read his lips. "Friendship or sex?"

I nodded solemnly, making my hair fall over my eye. "I just don't know how else it can work. I'm sorry. I know you're disappointed."

His whole face collapsed, but he nodded slowly. "Yeah, that's... that's safe to say. Well, that answers that, I guess. Thanks for letting me know. I'm heading out. Enjoy your night with..." He glanced back at the dance floor. "Whoever."

I blinked at him, definitely feeling a few margaritas shy of comprehending what was going on here.

"John!" I yelled, my voice getting lost in the buzz of

chatter as I darted around patrons in an attempt to catch up. "Excuse me. John, wait, I— Oh, oops. Pardon me. *John!*"

Miraculously, he heard me and turned toward me.

"John, why are you—"

I slipped on a wet patch of floor, and suddenly I was falling. I grabbed for the closest thing to break my fall and ended up yanking Nicki to the ground along with me...

Or, more accurately, yanking Nicki *and the full tray of drinks she carried* to the ground along with me.

I screamed in shock as a torrent of icy liquid ran down my back and arm, plastering my shirt to my body. Nicki's tray thumped down on my head.

"Oh, shit! Teagan!" Nicki cried, grabbing the tray. "Are you okay?"

Was I? I landed hard on one knee and one palm, and I knew both would bruise. But far, far worse was the sting to my pride. "Yeah," I sniffled. "I'm okay." A small sob bubbled out of my chest before I could help it.

"T? Oh, fuck. Oh, Jesus. Teagan?" John's voice held none of its usual calm steadiness. As soon as he reached me, he knelt and scooped me bodily off the floor like I weighed nothing, then held me in his strong arms. "Are you okay? Baby, your head. Are you...?"

For one second, I let myself revel in the feeling of him holding me. It was everything I wanted.

"I need to go home," I told him. And not just because I smelled like several breweries, a distillery, and an orange grove had all vomited on me simultaneously.

"I'll take you," John said firmly. He set me on my feet but held me against his side, much the way he'd held Goodman earlier. I was too weak-willed to push him away.

After spending ten minutes assuring Nicki and her manager that I was okay, and apologizing profusely for the chaos, I let John lead me out.

Outside, the night had gotten much cooler. A cold breeze blew against my soaked shirt, and I set my teeth.

A group of women chatted noisily while smoking cigarettes, and a pair of men were huddled on the curb, one holding his head in his hands while the second hovered protectively. The second man stood up as we approached.

"Teagan?" Knox asked, his deep voice concerned. "You alright?"

"Yeah. Hey. I… had a little incident with a tray of drinks." I massaged my sore palm. "I'm fine. Just soaked."

Knox looked at John with narrowed eyes, like maybe he was responsible for this debacle, then back at me. "I'm taking Goodman to our hotel. Our ride's on the way. But we can take you to—"

"John!" Goodman called drunkenly without looking up from the sidewalk. "John! D'you remember what I said earlier?"

John looked at me a little guiltily and licked his lips. "Uh. The one where you compared men and… murder cows?"

"Jesus," Knox muttered.

"No!" Goodman said defensively. "Although, dude, I stand by that. I mean the part I told you when we were dancing." He lowered his voice to a very loud whisper. "The part about… *eyeballs*?"

"Oh. Yeah, I remember."

Eyeballs? Oh, fucking lovely. They had inside jokes now? Had they exchanged numbers, too? Were they going to see each other again? I was miserable and jealous and soaked to the skin, and now I felt tiny and inconsequential, too.

I tried to step away, but John's arm tightened around me.

"Are you okay, Gage?" he asked.

"Me? Fuck yeah. Doing *great*," Goodman confirmed. "In fact, we should go dance some more. Because I got mooooves and—" He started to push himself to his feet, but Knox held him in place with a hand on his shoulder.

"How about you settle down, Magic Mike," Knox said dryly. "Before the world starts spinning again." He turned to me. "Our ride's arriving. Come with us, T, and we'll drop you off on the way."

I started to shake my head, but John spoke up before I could. "His name is *Teagan*, and we're all set. I already got us a ride. Thanks anyway."

Knox grunted. "You good with that... T?"

I found his concern really, really sweet, and in my emotional state, I got a little teary. "Yeah, we'll be fine."

He opened the rear door of their Lyft for Goodman but turned to look back at me. "I'd feel better if you take my number and send me a quick text when you're home."

I nodded and plugged his number into my phone, ignoring John's growing impatience. "Got it."

Knox still didn't seem convinced. "If you'd like, I could—"

"*Thanks anyway*," John repeated, all but growling this time. "But Teagan's with me. I've got him."

I buried my face in his chest and shivered, suddenly exhausted.

"I wish you really had me," I murmured.

CHAPTER FOUR

JOHN

THE WIND PICKED up as Teagan and I stood on the curb outside BarZ waiting for our ride, and Teagan shivered despite being tucked against my side. I let him go just long enough to pull off my jacket and wrap it around him.

"I'm f-fine," he said, pushing half-heartedly at my hands as I zipped it up. "It's going to get all sticky and ruined."

"Shush." As if I cared about that. As if I cared about anything but Teagan.

I zipped it all the way to his chin, and he finally, reluctantly, pushed his arms through the sleeves. It was too big on him—the hem fell to the top of his thighs, and the cuffs covered his hands—but the sight soothed some caveman impulse inside me. An impulse I only ever felt around this one particular person.

I wrapped him back up in *both* my arms this time and savored the feeling while I could, the image of him dancing cheek-to-cheek with another man still throbbing in my brain.

Get used to it, I told myself. *That's gonna be your life.*

After I'd dragged Teagan off the dance floor, I'd been mere seconds away from spilling my guts and telling him every one of my secrets—how much I loved him, how much I wished he'd be mine, how I wanted to build a life with him in Vermont as so much more than his very platonic best friend—but then he'd stopped me in my tracks, literally and figuratively, with his pick-one question.

Would I rather have friendship or sex?

I wasn't sure where that question had come from, but there was zero question which one I would pick, even if it meant my right hand was going to continue to get a workout until the end of time. Even if it meant I was gonna have to learn to watch him dancing with other guys without wanting to break things.

Teagan—having him whole and happy and *in my life*—was the most important thing.

It always would be.

"Four minutes until our driver arrives," I told him after a glance at my phone. "When we get home, I'll order us some dinner while you warm up in the shower, and we can…" I hesitated. I wanted to ask what had happened to his plans with Other-John, but I wasn't sure whether that would upset him more. "We can watch *Knightfall* if you want."

Teagan shrugged. "Don't worry about me if you have other stuff to do," he said dully. "I'll be okay on my own."

My arms tightened around him in concern.

Teagan didn't do *dull*.

He was sometimes sad, and occasionally outraged, especially over injustices. He spoke with conviction about everything. His energy was inspiring and soothing at the same time. But right then, it was like the light inside him had gone out.

Had he been into that bossy, overbearing Knox guy? Had things not worked out with Other-John and their date for tonight? Was he pissed that I'd left the apartment earlier without hearing his news? Once again, I wanted to ask, but for the first time since we'd met, I couldn't sense his mood, and Teagan wasn't sharing.

I hated it.

He stayed quiet the whole ride home, and my worry increased with every minute. Was he more badly injured than he'd let on? Was he depressed? Had Other-John hurt him? Had Knox?

"I wish you really had me," Teagan had whispered outside the bar, so softly the wind had chased the words away. The idea that Teagan felt like I wasn't there for him, that there was *anything* I wouldn't do for him, made my chest go tight.

"Sounds like Monica and Fern are playing *Hamilton*," I said as I unlocked our apartment door while someone across the hall sang a very off-key rendition of "Satisfied." Seemed at least someone was enjoying Mischief and Margarita Night. "Did you want to go over there and be the third Schuyler sister?"

Teagan rubbed a hand over his forehead. "Not tonight."

This was more serious than I'd thought.

I wanted to cuddle him against me and kiss the life back into his eyes. I wanted to protect him and fight back anything that might dare to steal his spark. But I wasn't sure exactly what was wrong with him at that moment, so I didn't know how to make it better.

But I kept trying.

"Okay, here we go." I opened our door and steered him inside. "Get in the bath. I'll be back in twenty minutes with medicinal dessert, okay? Please don't leave or… or… make any other plans in the meantime. Yeah?"

The real Teagan would have gone on a short-lived but very outraged rant about how "*he* had not been the one who'd made a habit of walking out on people this night, *John*," but this imposter-Teagan nodded meekly, walked into the bathroom, and shut the door behind him with a *click*.

Fuck.

It took me only fifteen minutes to jog to the expensive

little bakery cafe two blocks over, beg them for their last cheesecake even though they'd just closed up for the night ("Please, Pauline? It's for Teagan."), make a quick stop at the liquor store on the corner for a bottle of Teagan's favorite sweet wine, and jog back.

When I got home, Teagan was still in his bathroom. The apartment was dark, chilly, and silent, with no scent of bread or fall candles in the air. A blanket my mom had crocheted lay in a haphazard puddle on the floor by the sofa. Everything was dull and empty, just like my life before Teagan had been.

I put the food and wine in the refrigerator and knocked cautiously on the bathroom door. "T?"

He didn't reply, so I knocked louder.

"Teagan? I got cheesecake from PJ's."

He sighed softly.

"You coming out of there at any point?" I asked gently. "I got wine, too. We can still have our Netflix Night."

"No." Teagan's small, quiet sniffle made me want to beat down the door to get at him, but I refrained, and after a moment, he added, "I'm not coming out. I'm going to stay in the tub until I die of exposure. They shall find my corpse here in the water, like Tennyson's Lady of Shalott."

As usual, I had no fucking clue what he was talking about. And also as usual, Teagan knew it. But the very fact that he was saying anything at all was a relief. I forced myself to sound casual.

"Was the Lady of Shalott kinda pruny and wrinkled, like grapes that have been sitting in the fridge for a week? Because that's kind of how I'm imagining you."

An outraged noise was followed by a loud splash and then the sound of water gurgling down the drain. The door opened so quickly I nearly fell forward into the bathroom, and my roommate, my best friend, my... my *Teagan*... emerged in a billowing cloud of steam, with one enormous towel wrapped around his hair and another, much smaller towel wrapped around his waist.

"You make a compelling point," he said in a dignified way.

I nodded.

To be perfectly honest, I'd forgotten the point I'd been making the second I'd laid eyes on him. The smooth, creamy perfection of his skin where it flared over his hip bones, his high, sharp cheeks and pouty lips, the long, lean muscles of his body that I'd been salivating over while he was dancing with another man, were way too distracting. I wanted my hands on him. I wanted to know what the precise texture of his nipples was if I sucked on them. I wanted…

I am not going to have sex with my roommate.

I swallowed hard, praying for my cock to deflate, and the two of us stood in the hallway staring at each other in our first-ever awkward silence.

"Well." Teagan cleared his throat and folded his arms over his chest. "I really could have gotten home on my own, but thanks for the assist. I think I'll go to bed early. But if you leave now, Goodman might still be up."

"Huh?" I lifted my gaze from my focused non-contemplation of Teagan's nipples. "Who?"

Teagan rolled his eyes impatiently. "*Gage*, then. The guy you were dancing with."

"Oh." I shook my head and managed to say, "No, I… I'm staying in. With you."

"Suit yourself." He uncrossed his arms and went to slide past me, toward his room. "G'night."

"No, wait!" I blurted. "Are you… is your hand okay? Did you hurt it when you fell?" I reached for his wrist, but he snatched his arm behind him.

"It's fine. It hardly stings anymore."

"Good. That's… good. Did you, um… did you want to talk about anything? Anyone?" I gritted my teeth, determined to be supportive if it killed me. "Like the guy you went out with last night? I caught his texts to you when I was shutting off your alarm earlier. He seems very... passionate."

"Yeah, right." Teagan huffed out a half laugh. "No, I don't want to talk about him."

"T, please. Are you mad at me for leaving earlier? I was being selfish, and I'm sorry—"

"I'm not angry," he said bleakly.

"Then *talk* to me!" I demanded. "Yell at me. Sing Sondheim at me. Recite haikus. Make today a holiday so you can refuse to celebrate it. Pour all your emotions into baking a pavlova, like you did that one time, and then drop it out the window. Give me one of your Teaganisms, like you usually do when you're feeling sad. 'I may never feel joy again, John!' Or 'Why are mortals born only to suffer?' That one's a classic. Anything, Teagan. Do *anything*—"

"Jesus Christ, John!" He clapped a hand to his head to hold his hair towel in place, blushing furiously. "You make me sound deranged. I'm trying to deal with this situation rationally and not be as fucking *extra* as I usually am. I'm trying to be normal for once."

"Why the hell would you do that?" I yelled back. "You're not normal, you're *Teagan*."

"Thank you! Delightful. It's good to know what you really think of me." He sniffled. "Jerk."

What?

"T, that's not what I—"

"You want to know what's wrong with me?" He threw back his slim shoulders and his lovely eyes filled with tears. "I'm broken," he said, as serious and sorrowful as I'd ever heard him. He swiped at his nose. "And I don't know how to fix me."

He looked so small and sad that my stomach plummeted and I reached for him with both hands, heedless of all the reasons why that was a terrible idea. I drew his damp form against my chest and held him there, where he belonged.

"Teagan, babe. What happened tonight?" I ran my hands up and down his back and tried not to enjoy the feel of him in my arms, his lithe body pressed against my larger frame... but I couldn't help the way my stomach swooped and settled into a feeling of rightness.

Teagan shook his head against my chest, which loosened the towel around his head. Fragrant, damp strands of his hair fell down to his shoulders, and I sucked in a greedy lungful of clean, warm Teagan before I thought twice.

Enough. Jesus. Some best friend you're being. Control yourself.

I was not going to have sex with my...

"I had a decent date last night, John," Teagan murmured against my shirt. "He was a little boring, but really okay. The last guy I dated, in September? Same thing. Guy at the coffee shop who keeps giving me his phone number? Same."

"Oh-kay? Did... did they say or do something, T?" I whispered. "Did they disappoint you somehow?"

"No." I felt the huff of Teagan's laugh, but then he sniffled once again. "That's the problem. I'm not disappointed."

I blinked. "I... I don't follow."

"It used to be that I could catch feelings for a guy at the drop of a hat. I could look at someone and say, 'Yes, I see the potential here.' Fern used to despair of me because I sometimes saw potential that wasn't even there, like with Martin. But now?" He waved a hand up and down himself. "Look at me. The Potential Fairy doesn't visit this desolate landscape anymore. I am a ruined shell, unable to sense romantic possibilities with any man who happens to show interest in me. John is a decent guy. All of them were. But I don't want any of them. I'm *broken*."

I grabbed his shoulders hard—too hard—and had to force myself to loosen my grip. "That's not true. Look, I don't entirely get what's going on here, but—"

"I'm telling you, I'm—"

"Stop it, Teagan. Don't you dare say you're fucking *broken*." I shook him gently. "Whatever happened tonight, or with those other guys, it wasn't your fault. It couldn't possibly be. So don't take that on—"

Teagan's voice was uncharacteristically bitter. "You said that the first day we met, remember? About Martin."

"I remember. It was true then, and it's true now," I growled in a voice that didn't sound anything like my usual voice. I held his bare waist against me with one hand, bending him back slightly, while my other hand cupped his chin and tilted his head to look at me. "It's *not* your fault. You know how I know? Because you're perfect, Teagan Donahue. You're gorgeous. You're brilliant. You're witty. The way you genuinely care about people is a superpower. You make people's lives better. You've made *my* life better. You are infinitely better than *normal*—"

"Then Jesus, why can't I feel a spark with anyone but y—" He broke off with a shake of his head and pushed away from me. "Forget it."

I snatched his hands and tugged him into my arms again. "I won't forget it. Anyone who doesn't want you is a fucking fool, Teagan, and that's the truth."

"Oh, really? Really? Do *you* want me, John Curran?" he asked defiantly.

My throat went entirely dry in an instant, and my hands went numb.

"M-me?" I searched his eyes, feeling like I'd missed a crucial piece of data somewhere in my calculations. "But, Teagan, I…"

I am not going to have sex with my roommate.

Teagan closed his eyes, and his posture deflated as he slipped out of my grasp. "Yeah. That's what I figured. Don't worry about it. I'm going to bed. Maybe tomorrow we can wake up and pretend tonight never—"

Ah, fuck it.

Without giving either of us a chance to think or overthink anymore, I grabbed Teagan's hand and spun him against the wall by the door to my room.

"Yes I fucking *do*," I snarled, and for the first and only time in three hundred and—Jesus, at that moment I couldn't remember how many—days, I pressed my lips to his.

Teagan gasped in surprise, but his arms immediately rose to twine around my neck, and his tongue licked into my mouth eagerly, leaving me zero room to doubt that he somehow, miraculously, wanted this, too. Arousal clenched my gut as I closed my eyes and sank into the mint-and-margarita taste of his mouth, the tantalizing heat of his body, pouring months of longing into this one simple, perfect act.

I pulled back to bite his full lower lip—the lip that had been tormenting me on a daily basis for as long as I'd known him—just because I finally could, and my already hard cock throbbed against my zipper, begging for release.

"John," he moaned breathlessly, his fingers grasping the short strands of my hair as he tilted his neck to one side so I could slide my lips down his throat. "Oh, my actual God. Is this happening? Is this real? Did I hit my head in the tub and fall into some kind of—*oh, fuck, yeah*—some kind of coma, where I'm living an incredibly realistic alternate u-u-universe that I'll have to fight to make a reality once I finally regain consciousness, like in that—*God, yeah. Right there!*—that Hallmark movie I made us watch that one time?"

There he was. *This* was my Teagan. My hands tightened on him with bruising force.

"I dunno, babe. This feels pretty real to me." I slid my knee between his and found that he was every bit as hard as I was. He rubbed his towel-clad erection against my thigh shamelessly, whining at the friction.

My hands dipped down to cup his ass and pull him more firmly against me so his hard length pressed against mine, and I groaned at the pleasure of it. My head swam with a mixture of relief and desire that was way more potent than any of the drinks I'd consumed earlier.

"Yeah, that… that seems pretty fucking real," he gasped. "But prove it. Say something only you would say."

I ran my teeth over his collarbone the way I'd imagined doing a million times, just to watch him shiver, and I inhaled his green-grass scent like a drug. "Want you, Teagan Donahue," I whispered. "I've wanted you and *only* you, for so damn long."

"Oh, God. Oh, wait, really? That doesn't help me decide at *all*," he groaned. He cradled my jaw in both of his hands and pulled my head back so he could look up at me. "But say it again anyway," he commanded.

I couldn't help but smile down at him goofily, and then all the words I'd been holding back for eleven goddamn months started spilling out of me in a torrent. "I want you. I have wanted you from the moment you first ranted in the lobby. You were the most beautiful human being I'd ever seen." I ran a possessive hand up the center of his chest to clench around the base of his throat. "And I think I knew even then that you were *it* for me. But you'd just gotten out of a relationship. And you wanted to stay very platonic friends—"

"I did not! I thought *you* did!"

I shook my head. "I went out to the bar tonight because I thought you were going out with Other-John, and the jealousy was eating me. I thought I'd missed my chance—" Just remembering how close I'd thought I was to losing him made my voice rough, and Teagan must have heard it because he yanked me down into another drugging, consuming kiss.

He ran his hands up and down my back, tugging fretfully at my shirt. "Want to touch you. Want your skin."

I reached behind me and yanked my T-shirt up and off. Teagan had seen me shirtless a billion times before, but never like *this*, and for a half second, I wondered if he found my uncut bulk and furry chest attracti—

"Oh, God," Teagan groaned breathlessly, staring at my stomach. His hands trembled just a little before his palms touched me, and then he skated them up to tangle in my chest hair. "I've decided the coma can have me. I'm not waking up." He bit his lip and looked up at me with heat in his eyes. "You're gorgeous, John."

I wrapped his long, silky hair around my fist as amusement and *belonging* sang through my blood in a potent combination. "You're ridiculous." I tugged gently.

"You're *sexy*." He nuzzled his face into my chest hair.

"You're so fucking sweet." I tugged harder.

"I'm in love with you," he blurted.

I froze.

"I... I mean." He swallowed convulsively, looking suddenly afraid, but then he straightened his spine. "Actually, I mean exactly what I said. I'm in love with you. And I'm tired of pretending I'm not. I'm tired of pretending I only want you as a friend when you're so much more."

So was I.

His neck and jaw were smooth under my lips as I kissed my way back up his neck to take his mouth once again.

But before I did, I leaned in and whispered. "Good. Because I love you, too. I always have."

Teagan surged up on his toes, pushing me against the opposite wall, and fused our mouths together. God, I loved the way he kissed. Then he dropped to his knees right there on the floor, kissing his way down my happy trail and fumbling with the button on my pants. *Fuck*, I really loved that, too. So much that my breath stuttered and my hips surged forward, wanting the hard press of his hands.

Together we managed to wrestle my pants down and off. My cock bounced against my stomach, and Teagan stared at it while slowly licking those perfect lips.

"Please, T," I begged softly.

He smiled up at me brilliantly. Then, he gripped the base of my cock with one smooth hand, and his tongue darted out to lick the tip. He closed his eyes like he was enjoying the flavor.

"Oh, yeah," I approved.

Then the scalding heat of his mouth engulfed me as he took me to the back of his throat in one smooth movement.

"H-holy fuck!" I yelled. My hand tightened in Teagan's hair while the other scrabbled against the wall, trying to find something to hold on to since gravity had ceased to exist.

Teagan moaned lewdly in response, like he was enjoying this as much as I was, which simply couldn't be possible.

He braced his forearm against my thigh as he sucked me, using his tongue to swirl around my sensitive cock head, and his fingertips dug in to my muscles, leaving five distinct Teagan-shaped impressions.

I fucking approved.

"God, Teagan. So fucking good, baby. Don't stop."

I wanted to close my eyes and savor every sensation, but the view was too compelling to close my eyes. Teagan, on his knees, his mouth stretched wide around me, his eyes sex-hazed and watering just a little, and then below that, Teagan's own straining cock, freed from his towel, which he was jerking with his free hand in time to the pull of his lips. Utter fucking perfection.

Way, way too fast, I felt my orgasm building, but I didn't want this to end. I tried to stave it off by doing math problems, but even my fucking seventeens' tables reminded me of Teagan and sex. He'd invaded every part of my brain… and I liked it.

"I'm close. I— *Baby, please.*"

He abandoned his own cock and dipped his hand between my legs, cupping my balls and rolling them gently. I widened my legs, silently begging him for more. He could do anything he wanted to me. My body was his.

He popped off and took a giant, trembling gulp of air.

"Come for me, John," he whispered fiercely, his voice deeper than I'd ever heard it, positively wrecked from my cock. "Want to taste you."

"Fuck yes. *Fuck. Yes.*" I pounded each syllable into the wall with my fist. I wanted that. I wanted to own that mouth. Ruin it for anyone but me—

And holy shit, since when had my shy, nerdy self gone full-on Cro-Magnon chest-beater?

Oh, right. Since Teagan.

"I'm coming. Baby. I'm… Yeah, *fuck*, Teagan." I held him in place by his hair as my hips stuttered once, twice, and then I came in wave after fucking wave, filling up that beautiful throat.

Teagan swallowed me down feverishly, greedily, like he didn't want to miss a drop, and it was the single hottest thing I'd ever seen. Even hotter than all that had come before.

He slid off me finally with a low groan and gripped himself again while staring up at me.

"Oh, God, I love the way you watched me," he moaned. "That was so sexy. I wanted to know what you were thinking. Next time… *hnfhhh*… next time you have to tell me every dirty thought, and—"

"Get up here," I growled, pulling him to his feet. I spun him around so his back was to the wall, and I thumbed that swollen bottom lip. "You wanna know what I was thinking, Teagan? I'll tell you. I was thinking that I have watched this lip for three hundred fifty-five days. I have watched you bite it. I have watched you lick it. I have imagined what it would feel like under my tongue. Between my *teeth*. Wrapped around my dick. You said you could suck a man's brain out through his dick in under twelve minutes," I reminded him. "I had a *lot* of fantasies about this lip."

"Oh, fuck." His head *thunked* back against the wall, and his fever-bright eyes lost focus. "John." His tongue darted out nervously to wet that lip and ended up licking my thumb, too, and my very, incredibly satisfied cock nevertheless perked up. "I'm a little bit out of practice."

"It was so much better than I'd imagined," I whispered.

I licked into his mouth, tasting myself there, and it was so good, so *right*, I didn't know how I'd gone without this for as long as I had. It seemed impossible.

I thumbed his nipples as I kissed him, then made my way down his gorgeous body, paying attention to all the beautiful places I'd longed to touch. I ran my tongue down the tendon of his shoulder, sucked the salt from his nipple, and nuzzled my face into his armpit. Green grass and Teagan was my new forever-favorite scent.

His fingers tangled in my hair. "Fuck me, John. Do you… will you…?"

I pulled back. For all that Teagan and I knew about one another, I had no idea what he liked in bed—whether he liked to bottom, whether he liked anal at all. Looking back, maybe the fact that we'd shared so much but both of us had very carefully avoided talking about *this* was a giant red flag we'd both ignored.

"Hell yes. Anything you want, baby." I ran a hand over the jut of his hip. "Your room or mine?"

He led me down the hall to his bedroom and frantically rummaged through his nightstand while I pressed ardent kisses to his neck and the tops of his shoulders, everywhere I could reach, distracting him and making the job take twice as long.

When he finally found what he needed, I laid him out on his cool sheets like a buffet all the things I loved best. I teased his hole with lube-slicked fingers, teasing him all the while by nipping and sucking and licking over every inch of his body. By the time I'd finished preparing him, his creamy skin was sweaty and flushed with arousal, and he babbled my name over and over incoherently.

"John. *Fuck.* This is torture! There are… there are *statutes* about this. There are… *Oh my fuck…* there are *UN Resolutions* about this. If you don't get inside me right this second, I will… I will… I will *protest.*" He writhed on the bed, his hair tangling as he shifted side to side. "There will be posters. There will be songs." He broke off for a particularly loud groan as I sucked on his nipple. "I'll begin a letter-writing campaign the likes of which you've *never seen!*"

Good God, I loved this man.

I grasped his leaking cock in my fist and tugged him, twisting my thumb over his crown. His eyes rolled back as he groaned. I was already rock hard again, myself, so I wasted no time putting on a condom and slicking myself up.

I climbed over him on my hands and knees and peered down at him. "Just so I understand… you're going to start a letter-writing campaign?"

"What?" His eyes blinked blearily up at me.

"You're threatening me with a letter-writing campaign if I don't fuck you."

"I… Yes." He grabbed my ass, forcing our cocks into alignment. I pushed against him, and he whined. "And that's only the beginning. There will be a bread strike, John."

And that was how I came to be laughing as I pushed inside my best friend—the love of my life—for the first time. I figured, all things considered, that was pretty fucking fitting.

"Oh, gahhh…" he moaned, his hands grasping at me. "Baby."

The snug heat of him clenched around me so tightly I had to squeeze my eyes shut so I wouldn't lose it on the spot. Yes, it had been a whole year since the last time I'd topped anyone —hell, a year since I'd last *touched* anyone—but I didn't remember it ever being like this. His throaty groans, his distinctive scent, and the scrape of his fingers as he tugged on my ass and shoulders all reminded me that this was Teagan under me, letting me inside him.

I opened my eyes and found him staring up at me like he couldn't quite believe this was happening either.

"John," he whispered. "Move, baby."

I began thrusting in and out of him, and he lifted his hips in time with mine. The sound of our lubed skin slapping together was obscenely loud, and that combined with the little moans Teagan gave every time I hit his prostate sent shock waves of pleasure rolling down my back and thighs.

"Oh, God. John, I need…"

He reached for his cock, but I batted his hand away and wrapped my own fingers around him instead, jerking him in time to my thrusts. He erupted with a glad little cry all over both of our stomachs.

"So. Fucking. *Beautiful*," I gritted out, watching his face contort with pleasure and jacking him through his orgasm. The tight clench of his muscles had me on the edge again in no time.

My hips moved faster, snapping against him, wanting to imprint myself inside him. My orgasm was like an ecstasy avalanche, rocking me to my core and sending me over the edge so hard I nearly blacked out.

After I pulled out and removed the condom, I collapsed onto the bed beside him and buried my face in his pillow.

"Holy shit," Teagan breathed. "That was…"

"Not bad for a guy you once called '*nice*'?" I snorted.

"Shut up. You *are* nice," he insisted. "You're the best man I've ever known. That's the first thing that drew me to you."

"Really?" I turned my head to the side so I could grin at him.

"Yeah. That… and your big hands."

"My hands." I trailed my fingers through the cooling release on his stomach. "Tell me more."

"I wanted them all over my body."

"How convenient, since that's exactly where I've wanted them, too."

"Since the first day?" Teagan asked, his eyes shining.

"Since the first minute," I confirmed.

He grabbed my wrist in both his hands and trapped my hand against his chest, sighing happily.

"I don't suppose this had anything to do with your big news, did it?"

"Oh, my God!" Teagan inhaled sharply. "I still haven't told you. You remember the book series Molly and I were working on?"

I frowned. "Of course."

"Well… Molly actually finished up the final illustrations a few weeks ago. And she has a friend or a friend from college who works at a literary agency, and… they really like the book and want to represent us."

I lifted my head off the pillow. "Baby, that's incredible."

"I know. I *know*. And it's still not the biggest news of the day." He lifted our joined hands to his lips and pressed a kiss to my palm.

"I love you so much." I couldn't believe I got to say that to him finally.

"Yeah, well, wait until you read the books." He grinned. "The first one is about a boy on a quest for good-luck charms who falls into a patch of poison ivy."

I groaned. "You did not immortalize that."

"We so did! If I hadn't loved you already, I would have fallen for you the day I heard that story," he said staunchly. "And in the end, the boy realizes he's smart and brave on his own."

I shook my head. "Well, it's definitely not drawn from my life, then. If I'd had the courage to tell you how I felt a year ago…"

Teagan's mouth twisted up in a lopsided smile. "Yeah, I dunno about that. I might have pushed too hard, too fast. I definitely wouldn't have trusted that it was real. I might have been waiting for the other shoe to drop once you got to know the real me." He rolled into me and pressed a kiss to my lips before flopping back down. "I definitely wouldn't have thought we could be friends *and* be in love, since I'd never experienced it before."

"We definitely don't have to pick one," I teased.

"As it happens, we don't." He grinned. "So I'm not going to regret the year we spent as friends. But we will have a *lot* of sex to make up for. Just to kinda warn you about that."

"I appreciate the warning," I said solemnly. "I will start addressing that this very weekend. In fact, we can address it again in about... hmm." I gauged my own exhaustion level, my refractory period, my age, my lack of sustenance, and Teagan's need for another shower and calculated eight hours. Then I looked over at the naked perfection beside me, his hair spilling like red flames across his pillow, and realized that things with Teagan would never go according to the numbers. "Thirty minutes," I said hoarsely. "Maybe sooner if you let me tell you my dirty fantasies about your couch."

His laughter shook the bed, and I mentally revised thirty minutes to twenty.

Then he grinned. "Speaking of weekends... we're gonna have to spend ours in Vermont, least for the next little while, since Molly won't be able to travel with a newborn, and we're gonna have lots of work to do. You up for that?"

"Oh. Ha." I cleared my throat. I couldn't believe I'd forgotten. "Now that you mention it..." How could I tell him about the job opportunity without upsetting him? I didn't want him to think I had any regrets about choosing him.

I didn't. Not one, not ever.

"Now that I mention it..." He looked at me expectantly.

"Well, I mean... I got this maybe job offer. Or, I'm expecting one anyway." I filled him in on the details of the position. "But it's in Vermont, at Hannabury, so I already decided it wasn't important."

Teagan stared at me. "Not important? How so? You love Vermont. You love Hannabury."

I shrugged. "Yeah, but… I love you more, and you're here, so…"

Teagan's eyes got suspiciously wet.

Damn it.

This was exactly what I had been hoping to avoid. "Babe," I began. "It's fine, really."

He sat up on the bed and clasped the top of still-damp head with both hands. "Oh my God, John. This… it's the good luck you've been waiting for! You finally got your dream job. It's perfect for you. Of course you're going to take it." He squirmed and made a shimmying move that I recognized as his good-news wiggle, the one he did when our favorite pizza was on sale or when he'd found out my sister was having a baby. "We're moving to Vermont!"

"We are?" I asked stupidly. "But what about your career plans?"

"My plans were to find a teaching job and to keep writing with Molly, both of which I can do from our new home in Vermont."

"Our new home," I breathed, hardly daring to believe it.

Teagan squeezed my bicep with both hands. "Our new home with room for a *dog*," he clarified. "I can picture it so clearly. Can't you?" He proceeded to describe in great detail what our life was going to be like in Vermont, how we'd have to plan for Guncle Groundhog Day and Teagan Is My Favorite Uncle Tuesdays, and just like that I suddenly *could* picture it. Me and Teagan, together forever. "There will, of course, be sparkling apple juice and those fruit roll-up things that… ah… kids like."

I thought about the hidden box of fruit roll-ups that were

currently behind the fiber cereal in our kitchen cabinet. "Yes. The kids. You're so thoughtful, baby."

His eyes shone with excitement and joy—the things that made him the most Teagan of Teagans—the things that made him bright like a shining sun I wanted to revolve around all of my days. "John," he said, meeting my gaze. "It's going to be amazing."

My entire body felt like a zipping parade of tiny sparklers. It *was* going to be amazing. But the *job* was not the luckiest thing that had ever happened to me.

I swallowed my fears and reached for his hand.

"T. Pick one: are we going as boyfriends or husbands?"

EPILOGUE
TEAGAN

"You're not coming, are you?" I accused the second Fern's voicemail beeped. "Fern, you are fifty-two minutes late. Fifty-two minutes is not 'Surprise! John and I stopped to get you maple donuts, Teagan!' Fifty-two minutes is not 'Oops, we turned left instead of right coming off the highway and ended up at the Little Pippin Hollow Tree Museum.' Fifty-two minutes is 'Sorry, Teagan, I have decided to forsake nine years of friendship and abscond with the U-Haul containing your sofa, every single one of your loaf pans, and *oh yeah, the love of your life* to build a life in Canada amongst the moose and Mounties, leaving you all alone in your brand-new house in the wilds of Vermont!'" I closed my eyes and sniffled delicately, feeling incredibly put-upon by this turn of events. "Let me remind you that you don't even like Celine Dion."

And I was pretty sure that was a requirement for Canadian immigration.

"But I do."

"Holy shit!" The deep voice startled me so badly that I took a giant step backward, directly into the shiny metal surface of the vintage refrigerator that had come with the cottage John and I had purchased just two weeks before. "Where did you come from?"

The hot guy in my kitchen doorway looked me up and down, and his lips twitched beneath his thick beard. He wore a bright green T-shirt that did amazing things for his eyes—which was why his husband had picked it out for him—and an old snap-back hat that had seen better days.

He was *not* wearing his Hannabury hoodie, because his husband had stolen it from him. And, I thought as I disconnected my call and shoved my phone in the large pocket, I was not gonna give it back.

"I didn't mean to startle you," John said, his eyes gleaming as he recited the words he'd first said to me more than a year and a half ago. "I'm just here to..." He tilted his head in my direction.

"Check your mail?" I said dryly, folding my arms over my chest.

He grinned. "Nope. I'm the perfect stranger who's here to help move your sofa." He wiggled his eyebrows, and I fought hard not to laugh.

"Really? You're sure you're here for the sofa?" I narrowed my eyes. "Because you wouldn't *believe* how many cases of mistaken identity involving sofa moving occur each year."

"Oh, I'd believe it. Feel free to tell me more about it, though. You might not know this about me, since we only just met..." He lowered his voice and stepped closer, getting allllll up in my personal space... which was exactly where I always wanted him. "But gorgeous redheads who quote random statistics at me are my biggest turn-on."

"How oddly specific," I exclaimed, not having to fake my excitement as he rucked up my—I mean, technically *his*, but whatever—sweatshirt and spread his big hands on my bare waist.

"One thing you'll get to know about me, baby—you don't mind if I call you baby, do you? —is that I am all about oddly specific kinks. For example, karaoke with charming-if-not-particularly-tuneful singers. Also, baked goods."

"You're attracted to baked goods?"

"Mmmm. Mostly the men who bake them."

"*Men?*"

"Man," he corrected, nipping at my lower lip. "Just one man." He kissed me more deeply, sliding his tongue against mine and reminding me just how much I'd missed him for the two days we'd been apart. "Just one incredible man."

"You're very forward," I said breathlessly. "For a perfect stranger who's just volunteered to move my sofa."

"But it's a really nice sofa." He moved his hands under the waistband of my shorts to cup my ass.

I collapsed into laughter as I pulled his lips back to mine. "I missed you, baby."

"Me, too," he said. "A really pathetic amount for having only spent thirty-two-point-five hours away from you. Not that I was counting."

"Of course not. Did you get Fern moved into our old place?"

John nodded. "Moved our stuff out, moved her stuff in, then we jumped in the truck. Monica and the Graziellas are unpacking Fern's stuff for her, God help everyone involved, and then they're driving up here tomorrow. I left Fern outside having a Come to Jesus with Monica about allowing Monica's cats to sleep on a pile of Fern's unmentionables. How about you? Were you bored while I was gone?"

"Bored?" I rolled my eyes. "Not quite. Thursday night, I hung out at Molly's with the new baby, and we concepted a whole new book series. Friday morning, I had a meeting with the principal at Averill Union and got the keys to my new classroom so I can start preparing for the fall. A bunch of the other teachers took me out for a welcome lunch at this little diner-type place in Little Pippin Hollow—"

"Panini Jack's?" John demanded, and when I nodded, he

groaned enviously. "Oh, damn. I forgot that was only the next town over from us. I feel like we're going to be eating in the Hollow a *lot* from now on."

"Uh-huh. But it turns out Knox's little brother works there, and he wanted to hear the whole story about how we'd met Knox and Gage down in Boston—"

"The probability of us meeting guys from Vermont at our local bar in Boston was…" He shook his head.

"Only slightly lower than the probability of what ended up with happening with Knox and Gage after that?" I finished. "Yes, agreed. But I kind of like how it all worked out. It's nice to already have friends here, in addition to Molly and your moms. And Gage isn't a *terrible* person," I allowed, "despite our tragic first meeting."

John grinned and nipped at my earlobe. "I love when you get jealous."

I sniffed but didn't argue. I *was* just a trifle jealous when it came to him, which worked out nicely since I was really into how caveman-possessive my guy could be.

"*As I was saying,*" I continued as he chuckled knowingly and squeezed my ass more firmly. "I met Knox's little brother, Hawkins, who works at the restaurant. And then Knox's *other* brothers came in—the lumberjacky one we met last winter—"

"Webb Sunday," John supplied. "The guy with that whole *bugle* drama."

"Yes, right! And oh, God, you're not gonna *believe* how that story turned out. But he was also with their other brother Porter, who's going to be a senior at Hannabury—"

"Small world."

"Seriously. And their *other-other* brother Reed, who's home for a quick vacation from DC—"

"Jesus Christ. How many Sunday brothers are there?"

"So many," I said gleefully, because each one was cuter and lumberjackier than the last, and while there would never be anyone for me but John, a man could *look*. "Then Gage came in with *his* brothers—"

"No shit! The Goodmans came up from Florida?"

"From Whispering Key," I confirmed. "Gage's two brothers, their partners, his cousin and *his* partner, his dad and stepmom, and some guy who kept offering to score me some pheromone supplements—whatever those are—are all up here for a visit." I bit my lip apologetically. "I was so caught up in the excitement that I mayyyy have accepted an invitation for all of us to attend a cookout tonight with all of them over at the orchard after we get moved in. And, um, I may also have indicated a willingness to consider a puppy from his dog's latest litter?"

"Did you now?" He laughed out loud. "So, *definitely* not bored while I was gone, then."

I shook my head. "Not even remotely bored."

John sighed and withdrew his hands from my shorts. "So, we won't be christening the couch in our new home just yet, is what you're telling me."

Considering Fern was just outside, we wouldn't be doing that for a couple more nights, but I didn't remind him of this.

"I'm afraid so, yes. But, hey, we waited a whole *year* to have sex, right? We're delayed-gratification experts, aren't we?"

John's lips pursed. "You know, we already skipped Netflix Night this week."

"I know." I grimaced. And it had been awful, because cuddling John was maybe the one sport I could gold medal in. "I really missed that."

"Same. And now we're missing Karaoke Saturday." He took my hand and led me down the hall toward the front door.

"Yeah," I sighed, running a hand through my hair. "That's true. I—*oof*. John, this is our coat closet!"

"So perceptive," he agreed. "I'm feeling a distinct lack of

Teagan in my life, husband. So may I introduce you to the concept of Coat Closet Blowjob Afternoons?"

"I… what?"

"My husband taught me that anything can be a holiday if you give it a fancy name." He grinned as he shut the door, enclosing us in the darkness. "Should I explain how we celebrate this holiday? It's like delayed gratification, but with way more orgasms. And we still have a year's worth to make up for."

I sputtered out a laugh. "Oh my God, I've created a monster. Fern is…"

"Very used to walking away and complaining loudly when she hears you moaning?" John suggested, mouthing his way down my neck. "Yes, she is."

"She… she really is," I sighed, giving in as his hands found their way to my ass once again.

"You know, I once had a very quiet life," John groaned as I reached for his belt buckle.

"Uh-huh. And then you met me, and it became exponentially louder?" I teased.

"Then I met you," he agreed. "And it became exponentially more fun. Love you, baby."

Fuck, I loved him, too.

"So pick one, Teagan Donahue. You wanna get on your knees for me, or want me on mine for you?"

"Both," I said without hesitation. Because the best part of being in love with my best friend was that I didn't have to pick at all.

Thanks so much for reading! Want to know what happened to Knox Sunday and Gage Goodman after they left the bar? Read Pick Me, book one in the Sunday Brothers series, available here → http:// readerlinks.com/l/2235263 or turn the page for a sneak peek!

BONE TO PICK

A SUNDAY BROTHERS NOVELLA

CHAPTER ONE

PORTER

I was three tequila shots past my limit, otherwise I would have never considered confronting Dr. Hancock at his own home.

Or, okay, knowing me, maybe I *would* have, but I definitely wouldn't have done it quite so... aggressively.

In my defense, though, my friends at the bar had made it sound like such a good idea.

"Doctor Hot-Cock needs to understand how he screwed you over, Porter," Nolan said, nodding at his empty beer glass as if having a conversation with it rather than with the group of us who'd come straight from the Advanced Creative Non-Fiction critique group meeting we had every Thursday.

The after-session bar meet-up had become something of a tradition over the past couple of months, and since I was only taking *one* class this semester, I appreciated the social hour with my fellow students. Otherwise, I'd be back in my apartment feeling sorry for myself for being a twenty-six-year-old sixth-year senior, and I sure as hell didn't need more of that.

Toru waved their slender fingers in the air and sniffed. "If that asshole had failed *me* the way he did *you*—having it out for you practically from the jump, forcing you to put your whole life on hold just so you could repeat this stupid class —*mmmpfh.* Honey. Best believe I would sit him down for a *serious* conversation about it."

Now I was the one nodding. Remembering the injustices that had been dished out to me all last spring kindled a fire in my gut… or possibly that was the tequila, too. "I had a 3.8 GPA until that class," I confessed. "And now it's fucked. I was supposed to have embarked on my big career by now. I should be in Boston or New York or… I dunno, London? Doesn't matter, really. The epic journey of my life has been…" I burped delicately. "…derailed."

Sean nudged me. "There *is* one silver lining. At least you get to work at the Hub for another semester."

"Well… true." I sighed. I loved my job at the Hannabury Youth Hub, and leaving to pursue a real job after graduation would be painful. The one and only upside of fucking Dr. Hancock fucking ruining my fucking life was the fact I hadn't had to say goodbye to the kids yet. But… "The Hub doesn't have enough money to give me more paid hours, so I'm mostly volunteering at this point," I admitted. "Volunteering," I repeated, the word feeling so strange on my tongue that I couldn't help giggling. "*Volunteeeeeering.*"

It occurred to me at this point that I might be getting just a tiny bit inebriated, so I forced myself to take a sip from the glass of ice water in front of me, which I'd ordered specifically so I wouldn't get hammered that night. Sadly, the water didn't taste nearly as good as the salty tang of the tequila, so after that single sip—*look at me, being responsible!*—I waved to our server for another round of shots.

Sean grabbed a potato skin off the nearly decimated platter on the table and took a big bite. "Another bright spot," he mumbled around a mouth of melty cheese, "is that old Professor Burton is the faculty member teaching Advanced Creative Non-Fiction this semester, and he seems to like you just fine. Because if you'd gotten stuck having you-know-who as a professor again…" He wrinkled his nose in drunken concentration. "What's a word that means more-screwed-than-screwed?"

Beck nearly snorted her tequila. "In Porter Sunday's case, the word is *Hancocked*," she laughed.

I gave her a sour look.

"Eh. Disagree. Professor Burton's ancient and bald, and he talks like a human white-noise machine," Toru complained. "Gotta say, even though Doctor Hot-Cock is a terrible human and we *hates* him, I'm a little jealous you got to take this class with him your first time around, Porter. He's young and passionate and scrumptious, *and* he was the faculty advisor for the Hannabury LGBT alliance. Might've been worth getting screwed over if it meant getting to stare at him during lectures for a whole semester. Those eyes…"

I pictured my nemesis, the ruiner of all things good in my life, and… I couldn't disagree. Dr. Theodore Hancock, aka Doctor Hot-Cock, professor of English at Hannabury College, was God's gift to humanity. Or his body was anyway. His attitude could go to one of Dante's infernal rings of damnation as far as I was concerned.

"Which circle of hell is violence?" I asked abruptly, but no one was listening.

"…and that *ass*," Toru continued, nearly drooling.

"God, and that *dimple*." Beck flipped her long, blonde ponytail back and waved at her flushed face. "Jesus save me from staring at the dimple in my Shakespeare's Sonnets class. Pretty sure Hot-Cock caught me doing it the other day. Can't even say I'm sorry."

"Wait, you're taking his Shakespeare's Sonnets class?" I demanded, blinking at her. "How did I not know this?"

"Um…" Beck shrugged a bit guiltily. "It never came up, I guess? But it's been fine. Great, actually. He's really nice… and not just to look at. He's really engaging and charismatic, and he makes the subject matter accessible, so it's super fun

—*ow!*" She jumped slightly in her chair and scowled at Nolan, who tilted his head pointedly in my direction. Beck winced and gave me an apologetic look. "Oh. Uh. I mean… I mean it's super fun-*ny* that such a horrible person could seem so nice," she concluded lamely.

I sighed down at my water glass. I couldn't blame Becks for enjoying the class. If anything, I was a little jealous. I'd never told anybody this because it was *way* too woo-woo and embarrassing to admit, but Dr. Hancock's Shakespeare's Sonnets class had actually changed my life… even though I'd never taken it.

I'd been hanging around in the corridor of the English building one afternoon sophomore year, impatiently scanning the flyers on the message board in the hallway while I waited for a friend, when a voice began to read Sonnet 116 aloud.

Now, I'd recognized the poem right away because I'd had to do an essay on it back in high school, and I'd hated every minute of it. I'd thought it was overwrought and a little silly —I mean, love admits no flaws, when all humans are flawed and imperfect? Pfft. Ridiculous, right?—which is not the sort of thing you're allowed to say about Shakespeare, at least not if you don't want Mrs. Titelbaum to give you a C- and a note to see her after school.

But as that deep, self-assured voice rumbled through the pin-drop silence of the lecture hall, I realized that no matter how many times I'd read it, I'd never truly *understood* the poem before. Something about that voice made the words twine around my chest, urgent and right and unignorable. I'd stood stock-still in the hallway outside the open door, heard the line "…*That looks on tempests and is never shaken,*" and I'd… well…

I'd been *Hancocked*, without ever laying eyes on the man.

I'd been toying with the idea of an English major (to go along with my Nonprofit Management minor) before that day, but as a person from a tiny town who'd only made it to college thanks to a combo of scholarships, a hardworking (generous) brother, and my own steady employment since age sixteen, I'd sort of figured I should pick something more practical for career purposes. Business marketing, maybe. Or supply-chain management.

But, *shit*, after hearing that recitation, I'd felt sucker punched. Words were *power*. You could use them to make up worlds and suspend people in an alternate reality. To hold an entire audience in the palm of your hand. To teach them facts and hard truths. To change their minds. To make them *feel things*.

I'd gone to the student office that very day to declare an English major, and I'd never regretted it…

At least, not until last semester. And that was thanks to Dr. Hancock, too.

I shook my head to clear it of those stupid memories, but all that did was make my brain slosh precariously like the goldfish in a bag my nephew Aiden had once brought home from a fair.

"Dr. Hancock's good at sonnets," I admitted in a defeated voice, slumping further into my seat. "And he's a good professor." Except, inexplicably, with *me*.

Nolan scowled at me, almost managing to focus on my face. "He's also good at ruining lives, my man. Stop getting distracted with the sonnet thing. That's what they want you to do. English professors lure us into this major with the rhyming couplets and the… the… *iambic pentameter.* Next thing you know, they have us doing a biographical analysis of David Foster Wallace's *Consider the Lobster* and writing personal essays on 'memory and place.' It's all the sonnets' fault." He brandished a fist at the ceiling. "Fucking *sonnets.*"

"Fucking sonnets," we all agreed before throwing back another shot.

Beck paused for a beat as the tequila burned on its way

down. "Okay, so, like, what if you… what if you *took back the sonnet*, Porter?"

I squinted at her. "Took back… which sonnet?"

"The one you're going to write!"

"Huh?" Either she was very drunk, or I was.

"*Listen*," she insisted, leaning toward me with tequila-infused earnestness. "What if you wrote out your anger in an angry sonnet for Professor Hancock?"

"An angry sonnet," Toru said, testing the idea on their tongue. "Hmmmm."

"You mean like Sonnet 147? '*Black as hell and dark as night*'? That kind of thing?" I tilted my head, considering. "I *have* always enjoyed an angry sonnet."

"Same," Nolan said, nodding at the same empty beer glass in front of him. "Same! I mean, who doesn't?"

Beck tapped a fingernail on a beer mat. "And what if you delivered that sonnet *spoken word style* to his face."

I blinked. "To his face? But…"

Toru closed their eyes. "A performance piece," they breathed. "*Yes*. Brilliant."

Beck elbowed me harder than she'd intended. "Sonnet 147: Porter's Version!"

Nolan, with the fucking nodding that was making me semi-pukey, managed to recite, "'*Now reason is past care, And frantic-mad with evermore unrest.*' I dig it. Porter's frantic-mad! Right, Porter?"

Despite being shit-faced, Nolan was right.

It was too late to change anything, of course, but every time I thought about Dr. Jerkface Hancock, my chest went hot and my stomach dropped. I'd done my *best* in that class. Poured my heart into it. Spent every waking moment when I wasn't at the Hub crafting my papers, desperate to impress him.

But he'd failed me anyway.

He'd taken a thing I loved and tarnished it. He'd made me doubt myself. And it somehow felt *personal*.

Yes. Yes, I was very much frantic-mad.

Which was my only excuse for what happened an hour later.

"Get the fuck out here, you asshole!" I shouted into the dark night.

Shivering in the cold, my Vans planted in the dead grass outside my professor's house—a miniature log cabin set so far back in the woods that moonlight barely penetrated the dense trees around it—might have felt really unwise on another night.

Fortunately, I had my friends with me and more than enough tequila on board to overcome such a trifling concern.

From the back seat of the rideshare SUV, my friends flashed thumbs-up gestures and cheered me on through the open window. The only one who wasn't cheering was Steve, our rideshare driver, who seemed as annoyed as I was that Dr. Hancock wasn't coming out to meet his fate.

"You guys," Beck called. "Are we sure that this is actually where Doctor Hot-Cock lives? 'Cause, I-D-K, his vibe is more tasteful-artwork and industrial-penthouse, and this place is giving… animal trophies and *woodland hut*."

Toru answered, "Villains have lairs, Beck. Make peace with it."

Nolan bobbed his head. "Probs a serial killer, too. Nobody has sculpted cheekbones like that without using them to lure unsuspecting undergrads to their death."

"I guess." Beck stuck her phone out the window and snapped pictures of the darkened cabin. "This is gonna get me street cred with all those fuckers in my Sonnets class who have crushes on him."

Toru snickered. "That's everyone on campus, babe."

My friends collapsed into drunken laughter behind me. But from the house itself, there was no response whatsoever.

No light, no noise, no angry professor storming out in his smoking jacket, ascot, and pipe like I would have expected from the haughty know-it-all who was gonna take over as head of the English department when Professor Burton retired next semester.

"This gonna take much longer?" Steve demanded. "I've got another pickup back on campus."

"Uh…" A hint of sobriety nudged my subconscious, and my resolve weakened. "You know, Steve's right. Maybe we should go."

Toru scoffed. "Nuh-uh. You're not going anywhere, Porter. *Performance. Piece.*"

"Exactly," Beck agreed. "Frantic-mad, remember?"

"Failed you into a whole 'nother semester of college, bro," Nolan chimed in. "Under *no circumstances* are you leaving until the seething, roiling vortex of your fury has been unleashed upon his head! Don't let the hot ass fool you. The man is hellfire incarnate."

Someone in the car murmured, "But it's *such* a hot ass," with a plaintive whimper. I couldn't disagree.

"Seriously, guys," Steve insisted. "I gotta get back, or I…"

"Right," I muttered, ignoring whatever was happening in the car. "Okay." I refocused, calling up Sonnet 147 like a good little drunken English major, in case that might summon my quarry. *"Thou art as black as hell, as dark as night!"* I called into the… well… dark night.

"Awesome, bro," Nolan approved. "You're killing it! Listen, Steve says we have to pay a hundred extra if we delay him anymore, so we've gotta jet. But you keep doing what you're doing. Vent that vortex, baby! Good luck and godspeed!"

"Wha—?" Before my mouth could catch up with my shocked and still-sloshy brain, the SUV's headlights backed down the long-ass driveway to the windy mountain road and disappeared into the night.

"Shakespeare didn't use the word *thou*. He said *who*," a deep, vibratey, and oh-so-calm voice said from the front porch of the cabin. "If you must quote Shakespeare at me, Sunday, do it properly."

I whipped around, nearly losing my balance in the process, and found none other than my *nemesis*, Dr. Theodore Hancock himself, braced against one edge of his doorframe in the dark. Instead of his usual button-down and trousers, he wore thin gray sweatpants—*nghh*—and a Hannabury T-shirt. His short, brown hair—always ruthlessly tidy in real life— was a sleep-rumpled mess, and his dark-framed glasses were a little crooked. He almost, *almost* looked like a normal person, rather than what he actually was: the human embodi- ment of sex and poetry and evil all rolled into one drool- worthy package.

"Did I… wake you?" I asked stupidly.

Did evil villains need sleep?

Dr. Hancock tilted his head. "Mr. Sunday, it's two in the morning on a weeknight. Yes, you woke me. The question is, *why*?"

"Why?" I stared at him blankly. That was a really good question, damn him. It was bad enough that he was good at poetry. Why did he have to be so good at questions, too?

He huffed out a breath. "Yes, *why*. What are you doing in my front yard?"

"I…" I began. *Strong start, Porter.* "Well, I…"

Dr. Hancock ran a hand through his hair, and his biceps bulged out at me like one of those magic-eye 3D images. *Boing.* The whole world spun.

"I came here…" I started again. "Because I needed to tell you…"

Dr. Hancock leaned further against the open doorframe like he had all the time in the world and crossed his feet at the ankles. His very *bare* feet. There was something oddly vulnerable about seeing him like that, with no armor on at all. He looked almost... touchable.

I tried to stand a little taller, but it seemed that all of my muscles had frozen solid in the cold because I forgot how to move. I parted my lips to deliver my frantic-mad hate sonnet, but saliva pooled in my mouth, making speech impossible. I tried to breathe deeply and remember my purpose, but my throat constricted in a funny way that made breathing tricky, too.

As I lurched helplessly toward Dr. Hancock, the words that flashed through the Tilt-a-Whirl in my brain weren't from a Shakespearean sonnet but a line from another poet entirely.

I have a bone to pick with Fate...

Then I bent over and hurled tequila-soaked potato skins into the darkness.

CHAPTER TWO

THEO

I STOOD on my front porch in the unseasonable late-autumn cold and stared down at my new lawn ornament.

Some people decorated their grass with gnomes, or flamingos, or those garish inflatable Santas that belted out Christmas carols. My mother, bless her Southern-transplant heart, was partial to twee blown-glass birds that her gardener arranged to peek out of her manicured flower beds. But nothing so mundane would do for me! Oh, no, I'd just *had* to pursue a career in academia despite my father's objections. And now I had six-plus feet of partially frozen undergrad beefcake spread out like a welcome mat at the foot of my steps as a result.

At least he wasn't singing "Jingle Bells."

I sighed and picked my way down the steps to where Porter Sunday lay face-up and groaning on the crunchy grass. He'd managed to avoid landing in his own sick by mere inches. A few snowflakes were beginning to fall, landing and melting on his sweatshirt, his jeans, his thick, wavy hair.

I nudged him in the side with my bare toe. "Honestly, Sunday. Why are you here?"

He dropped the forearm he'd thrown over his head and

blinked up at me, but his eyes—eyes I happened to know were a shade of green so deep and intense that the first time I'd seen them, last January, I'd assumed they were contacts—seemed to have trouble focusing on my face. He frowned, and his full lips pursed in such a comically befuddled expression that I felt my own mouth twitch up in a smile before I ruthlessly suppressed it.

Porter Sunday was not adorable. He wasn't.

He wrinkled his nose and garbled out something that sounded like, "Wanneda talktaya."

I folded my arms over my chest and ignored the cold seeping into the soles of my feet. "Indeed? Then by all means, talk."

"Well…" He watched a few white flakes tumble through the air as if perplexed by the concept of snow, then scowled at me. "I forgot what I wanneda say now. S'your fault, lookin' at me like that. But it was fucking *poetic*," he assured me. "*Frantic-mad* poetic. An' you were gonna feel *bad*. Like… *super* bad."

I whistled through my teeth. "Judging by your current level of eloquence, I can only imagine. The mind boggles." I shifted from foot to foot so as not to lose both extremities to frostbite. "I am cold, and damp, and viciously annoyed, Mr. Sunday. I assure you, I have rarely felt worse. So, well done, you. You can leave anytime now."

He sighed. "S'not fair, you know. Why you gotta be so…" He lifted one meaty arm, gestured at my body, and let it flop back to the dead grass. "…*you*?"

"I could ask the same." It was utterly ridiculous that this creature—this thoughtless, entitled, frat-bro man-child who'd invaded my peace to yell at me and hurled toxic sludge in my grass—should still manage to look so damn sweet and bewildered and make *me* feel like the villain of the piece. "You should call your friends, Sunday. Get them to come back and get you."

"Can't," he mumbled. "Steve's got a mother pig up."

Only years spent listening to people butcher *Beowulf* enabled me to understand him. "If Steve has another pickup, order yourself a new Lyft."

He gave an approximation of a nod. "Mkay. Will do. Jus needa minnit because… tequila. *I have a bone to pick with fate.*" He grinned wildly at the sky. "Bone," he chortled like a twelve-year-old. Then he closed his eyes.

I snorted. "Was this the poetry you wanted to quote at me? Ogden Nash is rolling in his grave. Get up, Sunday."

When the man didn't respond, I nudged him with my toe once more. This time, he grunted and then emitted a soft, sleepy sound.

"Jesus Christ. Sunday?" I demanded, bending down to shake him and tap his cheek. He barely roused. "Sunday!"

My entire body was icing over from my feet up. I wanted desperately to be back inside my little cabin, in my nice, warm bed, curled up with my down duvet and the premium memory foam pillows I'd splurged on as an early birthday present, *alone*.

But I couldn't very well leave the man lying out here in the cold. I'd earned a bit of a reputation for being a hard-ass because I didn't hand out easy A's or tolerate students who tried to slack off in my classes, but I hadn't achieved "leaving a student to suffer hypothermia so they'd learn natural conse-quences"-level heartlessness. At least not yet.

I growled impatiently and knelt by his head to grab him under the armpits and drag-carry him inside. If I'd ever contemplated what it would be like to have Porter Sunday's enormous, incredibly muscled body under my hands—and I definitely hadn't, certainly not more than once, in the shower, with my dick in my grasp—it would not have involved me trying to haul his corporeal sack around while breathing through my mouth to keep the stench of vomit from causing a sympathy-puking event that would be difficult to recover from.

Fortunately, by the time I'd dragged him the few feet to the stairs, he'd woken up enough to turn over and crawl the rest of the way.

"Sorry," he mumbled. "So sorry. I didn't mean…"

I push-pulled him to his feet and led him over to the kitchen area of the one-room cabin, where I propped him against the sink and grabbed some paper towels.

"Sunday, what in the world caused you to show up at my house at two in the morning?" I scrubbed at his nose, lips, and chin with the wet paper, and he lurched away as violently as if I'd been waterboarding him. "How did you even know where to find me?"

"Internet?" He groaned the word like a question, reaching for the tap so he could rinse out his mouth. "Dr. Hancock. Hannabury. *Boom.*"

Boom was right, I thought sourly. Porter had dropped into my quiet evening like a shrapnel bomb.

"If I let go, can you stand without me?" I demanded. "No puking on my floor, Sunday, and I mean it, or I *will* kick you out, and I won't care if the fucking 'autumn snowpocalypse' the meteorologists have been salivating over will bury you until spring."

With that dire warning, I left him just long enough to retrieve a spare toothbrush and toothpaste from the bathroom cabinet. When I returned, he was bent over on the counter by the sink with his eyes closed, resting his face on his bent arms. I tried not to notice the muscular ass on display in his wash-worn jeans.

Eyes up here, Professor.

I blinked into the bright kitchen light to punish my eyeballs for straying. Only the creepiest of teachers got visible hard-ons for their students. Especially students they weren't even sure they liked much on a personal level.

I cleared my throat and nudged his cheek with the tooth-brush package. "Here. Clean your teeth, and then I'll drive you home myself." I retreated to the living area, trying to put as much physical distance between myself and that ass—I mean, that *man*—as I possibly could in a twenty-by-twenty-foot space.

After taking three scream-inducing minutes to get the brush unwrapped, another four to puzzle out how to apply toothpaste to it, and ten full minutes brushing every surface of his teeth at least twice, Porter finally turned to me.

"I'm done," he said dully. "My head hurts. Can I have a glass of water? Please?"

Impatient as I was, I couldn't say no when he tacked that polite little *please* on the end.

"Yeah. Of course. There's a glass on that shelf," I said, pointing. But then I recalled all the very good reasons I had to be annoyed and scowled as I added, "You have precisely one minute to hydrate while I get my parka out of the closet, then you can wait by the door."

Unsurprisingly, Sunday ignored my firm command. He was not waiting by the door when I'd unearthed my heavy winter coat a few minutes later. Instead, he'd collapsed into my reading chair by the roaring fireplace and propped his big feet on my footstool, looking entirely too comfortable in my space.

I folded my arms over my chest. "Is now a convenient time for me to drive you home, Mr. Sunday?" I asked. "I'd *hate* to rush you."

"You shouldn't be nice," my uninvited guest informed me. "It's confusing."

"I *wasn't* being nice. I was being sarcastic—"

He rolled his eyes tiredly. "I'm not talking about what you said. I meant, like… bringing me inside. And lending me a toothbrush. And giving me a ride home." He squirmed, unable to meet my eyes. "You were a grumpy, life-destroying jerk all last semester for no reason. Now, when you actually have a reason to be mean, you're *not*. It's weird. And wrong."

I opened my mouth to inform him of all the ways *he* was wrong in that little diatribe—not to mention insulting and impertinent—but then I remembered that despite having the body of a fully grown person, Porter Sunday was still a Hannabury student. A *drunk* student. Whereas I was not only a sober thirty-four-year-old, but I was a Hannabury professor. One of us needed to show a little sense tonight, and it was clearly not going to be him.

Professional distance, I told myself. *Do not engage.*

As if in agreement with my thoughts, the wind picked up, pushing icy snowflakes against the window. It was an audible reminder that I had a limited window to get my interloper safely away from here before the situation got worse.

Which was why I was mystified to find myself propping my hands on my hips and smartly retorting, "Excuse me if I refuse to take criticism from a man who drives around *hurling* poetry at people in the middle of the night, without so much as a *winter coat* on him, when a fucking *snowstorm* is coming."

So much for not engaging. I shut my eyes and blew out a breath.

"I did not destroy your life, Sunday," I went on in a much calmer voice. "Nor do I believe I was ever a jerk. By the end of the semester, I may have been... less patient with you than I would have liked," I admitted, "but that was not without reason. And unlike certain people who appear to have been carrying a grudge for half a year, I'm capable of reacting in different ways to different situations. It's called being a mature and fully articulate human being. Try it sometime."

Yeah, I was totally failing at *professional distance*, too.

I winced, expecting an angry retort, but Porter merely blinked at me some more. While he didn't seem as drunk as he had been—probably because most of the tequila he'd ingested was now fertilizing my lawn—he clearly wasn't capable of processing all the words I'd spoken. Instead, he latched onto one fragment of my first statement and ignored the rest.

"Pffft. No storm tonight, silly. Storm's *Friday*." He shifted his huge frame lower in the chair cushions, and his eyes drifted closed.

Oh, no. Nope.

"Yes. *Friday*. Which is *today*, as of…" I consulted my watch. "Two and a half hours ago."

Porter's eyes opened, and that deep, perfect green assessed me for a beat. "Are you sure?"

"Porter Sunday, you would try the patience of a saint." And needless to say, I had never been a candidate for sainthood.

I turned to the collection of fall jackets and hoodies on the hook behind my front door and tossed the largest, warmest one into Porter's lap.

"Put that on. The no-puking rule still applies, both for the jacket *and* my car." After jamming a wool hat on my head, I grabbed my keys from the hook on the wall, pulled open the front door, and made a sweeping motion with my hand. "Come on now. We're leaving. And we will *never* speak of this incident after this day. Understand?"

In just the short time Porter and I had been inside, the snow had started falling in earnest. Not much had accumulated by local standards—maybe an inch—but what there was refused to lie still. Wind stronger than any we'd gotten since a brief round of summer storms back in July positively whistled through the trees, stirring up the flakes around my feet on the doorstep like I'd been caught in a snow globe.

Contrary to popular belief—at least, popular amongst people like my mother, who refused to leave Palm Beach after Halloween—it was relatively rare to get much snowfall in Vermont in autumn unless you lived up on a mountain. It was rarer still to get full-on blizzard-force winds this time of year. And the likelihood of getting this kind of wind, *plus* this much snow, *plus* the student I'd spent way too much time trying *not* to think about last semester landing on my doorstep all at once? Infinitesimal. Microscopic. So statistically improbable that it didn't bear consideration.

And yet here we were. *I have a bone to pick with fate*, indeed.

"I was supposed to be sleeping my way through this storm tonight," I muttered to Porter, who was grinning goofily at the fire. He didn't appear to be listening to me, let alone moving from his comfy spot... by which I meant *my* comfy spot. "When I came home this afternoon, I promised myself I wasn't leaving the house again all weekend except to shovel. I brought in firewood. I downloaded a new novel. I got all the grocery foods you're supposed to get for snow-storms—enough milk and bread and eggs to feed the whole town french toast, and I don't even *like* french toast! It was going to be *delightful*."

Now my lovely three-day weekend was being delayed by a child's revenge fantasy gone wrong.

"Sunday? Sunday!" I nudged his knee with my own none too gently. "*Christ.*"

Porter's eyes had slid shut, and he startled guiltily. "I... yes? Sorry. I was just..." He yawned, his jaw opening so wide it cracked.

"Yes, I'm sure sonnet-bombing really takes it out of a man," I said waspishly, but fucking Porter had already zoned out again.

Hauling his semiconscious self to my truck wasn't going to be easy. Driving in these conditions wouldn't be ideal either, but the storm was only going to get worse. It was now or never.

I yanked Porter up and slid an arm around him to help him to the door. The warmth of his body permeated my clothing layers, and thankfully, the scent of warm woodsmoke and mint wafted off him rather than the stench of vomit. Even though he hadn't been in the cabin long, he still smelled like home…

I quickly cut *that* thought off, then leaned away from him and took a deep breath of frigid mountain air to clear my head.

"Where do you live?" I asked, carefully navigating the shallow porch steps with him at my side.

"That's easy." Porter took a deep breath, like the cold air was clearing his head, too. "Little Pippin Hollow," he said confidently.

Jesus Christ. Clearly, the cold wasn't clearing his head *much*. He'd named a town over an hour away.

"I wasn't asking where you're from," I said through my teeth. "I mean where do you live at Hannabury? An apartment? Dorm? Frat house?"

He snorted. "I'm twenty-six. Not really dorm or frat material anymore, Professor."

This surprised me, perhaps more than it should have. Tonight's debacle aside, Porter Sunday *had* always seemed more mature than my average undergraduate student—he never missed a class or turned in a paper late—but I hadn't guessed he was a full four years older than most of the seniors.

Not that it mattered. Or made it any more acceptable to be unreasonably turned on by the feel of his heavy frame against me.

"Address. Please," I repeated, picking my way carefully over the slippery ground to the passenger-side door of the truck.

He looked around us at the snow-covered branches of the encroaching forest. "Your address?" An adorable little divot formed between his eyebrows. "Don't you know? Or are you like that guy in that movie from the film class where it's all backwards and tattoos and… oh my God, does that make you the killer?"

He laughed so hard I lost my grip on his waist, but rather than tumbling to the ground, he managed to get his feet under him. Then he began stumbling down the driveway as if he planned to walk back to town in the cold, dark night.

"Mr. Sunday," I snapped. "I haven't killed anyone *yet*. Stop where you are before you nosedive into the bushes."

"I figured I'd check the mail in your box and figure out where we are," he called back with a careless wave of his arm that nearly sent him sprawling again. "That's what we call smart thinkin'."

Jesus fuck. It was *something* alright.

But it was a good thing Porter wasn't facing me because I couldn't help letting out a soft laugh, despite clapping a hand to my mouth to restrain it.

I hadn't been charmed by a drunk college guy since I *was* a drunk college guy nearly a decade ago. I wasn't sure why Porter Sunday was the exception… but then, he was the exception to a lot of people's rules.

People at Hannabury College were drawn to Porter Sunday like he was the damned Pied Piper. Faculty members in every department found him charming and magnetic. Students regarded him as friendly and kind. And everyone knew the man was gorgeous, judging by how many of the men on campus got hearts in their eyes when he flirted with them.

But I'd still been surprised when Jean Chenault, my English department colleague and Sunday's academic advisor, had come to me at the start of last semester and positively gushed about what a "brilliant young man" Porter was, with a "keen eye for social justice" and a "poet's soul." She'd begged me to find a spot for him in my Creative Non-Fiction class, and I had. Gladly.

Later in the semester, Jean had come to me again, asking for clemency on Porter's behalf—the first and only time I'd known her to interfere on behalf of a student that way, which just went to show that Sunday could talk anyone into anything—and I'd told her sadly that if he had bothered to display his supposed "brilliance" in his classwork, I wouldn't have had to fail him.

Another gust of wind blew in, and a sharp crack like a gunshot filled the snowy air, drawing my thoughts back to my current ridiculous predicament.

I whipped my head back and forth for the sound of the noise as Porter continued to meander slowly toward the street, shuffling along to a beat only he could hear.

Crack! The sound came again, this time followed by a strange creaking sound. My body identified the noise long before my brain did, and I began rushing down the driveway.

"Porter!" I grabbed his hood and hauled him back toward the safety of the house. "Porter, come on. *Move!*"

I'd only managed to pull him a few stumbling feet before he lost his balance and fell on his ass, knocking me backward. Both of us hit the snow-covered driveway with jarring force. Before I was able to process more than stunned surprise, a shower of snow fell from a nearby tree, and another *crack* rent the air, this one followed by a horrific series of *pops* as a giant tree halfway down my driveway fell toward us in slow motion.

We sat there frozen, watching in horror as the thick branches of the falling tree landed against the smaller tree beside it. For a second, it felt like the whole world went motionless, as if someone had pressed pause on a video. Porter and I each held our breath, waiting. Then the branches of the second tree gave way with a shower of white snow pellets. The tree landed with a dramatic crash lengthwise up the driveway, its heavy branches scattered atop and beside it so that it almost looked like the forest had reclaimed the land. The tips of the closest branches landed maybe six feet away… exactly where Porter had been before I grabbed him.

Porter's breath came in soft pants, and he turned his head

so his wide eyes met mine. "This… was not on my disaster bingo card."

"No," I agreed, probably looking just as wide-eyed and panicky as he did. "Mine either." And fuck had that been close. Even just a few feet nearer and someone would have been injured. "Come on," I growled. "Back inside, immediately. The cabin was built with a reinforced roof." And now I understood why my grandfather had insisted on that.

But it occurred to me as soon as Porter pushed open the door to the house and we stood shivering on the braided rug in my tiny living area that while we had possibly avoided death-by-tree, we had not fully avoided disaster.

Not by any means.

My grandfather and I had designed this cabin to be his retirement escape. The place he'd called his "hermitage." I hadn't changed much when I inherited the place because as far as I was concerned, the small, square, single-story cabin had everything a person required in a dwelling—a kitchen area in the front right corner with a small table, an area in front of the fireplace just big enough for a comfortable reading chair and hassock, an updated bathroom supplied by an enormous hot water tank, and a sleeping area with a queen-sized bed and armoire. Best of all, the entire wall around the fireplace and all the way back to the sleeping area was lined with bookshelves—enough to hold my grandfather's entire collection of scientific tomes and some of my precious first editions.

But, I was realizing way too late, what the cabin did *not* have was a convenient guest bed.

Or a sofa.

Or any fucking privacy whatsoever.

"S-sorry," Porter offered. "I'm r-really, *really* sorry."

"Me too," I gritted out.

"It wasn't supposed to happen like this." He looked at me

with those big, green eyes, now shiny with shock instead of tequila, and his huge frame shook.

I was freezing myself, and I wasn't the one who'd drunk enough alcohol to float a barge. Didn't alcohol make it harder to regulate body temperature? I sighed. "Look, go take a hot shower, and I'll make some tea to warm us up while we figure out a way to get you home. Unless… do you even drink tea?"

Of course he doesn't drink tea, Theo. He's built like the offspring of Paul Bunyan and the Rock. He probably drinks raw eggs and hot sauce—

"Fuck, yeah, I love tea!" he said earnestly. "My uncle Drew makes a blend with star anise and organic dried apples that…" He cleared his throat and hunched his shoulders. "You, ah… you probably don't care about that right now, I'm guessing?"

I snorted. "Look who's sobering up."

I grabbed my largest pair of sweatpants and an oversized sweatshirt from the armoire and turned to hand them to him, only to find that he'd followed me to the back of the house and was standing way too close, right between me and the rumpled bed I'd been sleeping in just a little while before.

I stared at him. There was no doubt Porter Sunday was a beautiful man. Even when he'd been arguing with me in class last semester, that big, capable body, shiny brown hair, cherry-red lips, and ridiculously green eyes sparking with challenge had been temptation incarnate. And now, all damp and uncertain, he was…

Ugh.

"Shower, Sunday," I croaked. "And throw your clothes out of the bathroom so I can put them in the dryer. Show me you can follow simple directions."

Before I lose control entirely.

Porter's eyes met mine. "I follow directions really well, Dr.

Hancock," the man said softly. "You just have to tell me what you want."

I was sure he didn't mean to throw around that fucking sexy voice, to have his words come out in a breathy rumble that vibrated directly through my bones and down to my cock…

But like so many things with Porter Sunday, what he intended didn't matter when the result was so unavoidably, cataclysmically terrible.

I clenched my hands behind my back and tilted my head expectantly. He gave me a sweet, almost sheepish smile, then turned and went into the bathroom. A second later, his clothes —including my jacket—hit the bedroom floor with a damp *plop*, and then the bathroom door closed again.

As soon as I heard the water running, I sank onto the edge of the bed and let out a shaky breath. *Right. Okay.* I had dealt with lots of unexpected and difficult situations before—my grandfather's death, the slow implosion of my last relationship, my parents' perpetual disappointment over my career choice—and I'd managed to handle all of them deftly and responsibly, without losing control.

I would handle this, too.

First things first, I stripped out of my own wet pants and, darting a look at the bathroom door to make sure it stayed closed, quickly changed. I collected the wet clothes and brought them to the small laundry machine in the kitchen area, then set the kettle on to heat and grabbed my phone to quickly google my options.

Unfortunately, there were none.

The impassible driveway might quickly become an emergency, but according to the town website, it wasn't yet. Not when all the emergency crews in the area would be busy dealing with actual life-threatening situations, like cars sliding off roads that hadn't been treated this early in the season and downed trees snapping power lines. Non-emergency vehicles were asked to stay off the streets, meaning no Lyft or Uber driver in Vermont would be coming back out this way voluntarily. And it would be unsafe for Porter to attempt to walk several miles back to town under these conditions, even if he wasn't still mostly inebriated.

Like it or not, he was stuck here for now.

He could sleep in the chair by the fire, I decided, just as the water shut off in the bathroom. He'd certainly seemed comfortable enough there before.

I heard the bathroom door open and immediately got very busy with tea preparations.

"Your clothes are in the wash, and the tea will be ready in a minute," I said without turning around.

"Mkay," he said tiredly.

"The only solution I can figure out right now is that you'll have to sleep *here* for the night." I waved over my shoulder at the chair and footstool. "It's not ideal, but your safety is paramount. The good news is, you'll be warm and dry. And while sleeping upright might have killed *my* back on multiple occasions, you're younger than I am, Sunday, and probably bendier—" *Jesus Christ, Theo, do not think about Porter being bendy.* "—uh, I mean, much sturdier—" *Ditto on thinking about how sturdy he is.* "—you shouldn't have any trouble."

Porter exhaled deeply, almost a sigh, and I smiled to myself as I added honey to our mugs.

"Yes, well, if you're unhappy, you only have yourself to blame, Sunday," I said a trifle smugly. "It's only for one night, after all. The storm should break for several hours tomorrow, and you can figure out a way home then. Tonight, you can deal with the consequences of your actions like an adult. As the old adage says, beggars who came to hurl angry sonnets at their professors can't be choosers."

Porter didn't reply, clearly unable to find a flaw with my logic.

"Don't you agree, Sunday?" I persisted.

When Porter didn't reply that time, I finally turned my head…

And found the man had pulled back my down duvet, curled up on my bed—wearing nothing but a towel, for fuck's sake, so that acres and acres of damp, tanned skin were on display against the white cotton—and buried his face in my brand-fucking-new memory foam pillow.

"Porter Sunday!" I exclaimed, bouncing the end of the mattress to wake him because I didn't quite trust myself to touch him in that moment. "Why is your ass in my bed?"

Definitely, definitely do not think about Porter and asses, Theo, you colossal idiot.

Porter stretched out on his back with a lusty groan and spread his legs like a starfish, leaving nothing but the scrap of white terry cloth—Christ, had my bath towels always been so tiny?—standing between me and… insanity.

I swallowed hard.

"I got *Hancocked* again," he whispered.

I sprung away guiltily. "You… *what*?" I demanded. "Sunday? Wake up right now, you lummox!"

But Porter's only response was another sigh, followed by a blissful snore.

Apparently, the only adult who'd be dealing with the consequences of their actions this night would be *me*.

CHAPTER THREE

PORTER

I HAD ALWAYS BEEN an early riser—a habit that came from growing up on an orchard where there were chores to be done before school. Getting up early had served me well when I'd started working my way through college as a barista. But the fact that I was waking up to warmth and silence this morning, rather than drafty windows and my roommate's *Sabaton* playlist blaring at full volume, was the first clue I wasn't in my own bed.

Eyes closed, my mind raced through the events of the previous evening, but my memories got a little hazy after the fourth shot of tequila. I remembered *frantic-mad*. I remembered lots of drunken giggling. I remembered Steve, the rideshare driver. I definitely didn't remember deciding to hook up with anyone or even crash at their place. Besides, no one I knew had pillows quite this comfy.

I cracked one eye open, and the rustic log walls immediately reminded me of where I was.

Professor Theodore Hancock's cabin.

Shit, *right*. I'd come to call out my sworn enemy with an angry sonnet. There'd been vomit, which was humiliating, and a tree had fallen right near me, which had been scary, and then... nothing. My mind hit a big, black roadblock of self-protection, like the bits I couldn't remember were too disgraceful for me to process at the moment.

I stifled a groan. One thing was certain: Dr. Hancock would waste no time filling me in on whatever events had led me to be his uninvited overnight guest. He'd use that very precise, cultured, ironic tone he always took on when he was dressing someone down—the tone that made me want to laugh appreciatively even while I squirmed—and he'd do it while wearing his customary disapproving frown.

I closed my eyes again and flopped onto my back.

Really, I thought, as I scratched idly at my bare chest, *no one should look so good while frowning. It's a weird kind of superpower—*

I felt warm breath against my face and gasped. "Holy motherfucking shit!" I whisper-yelled.

I slid my gaze to the right and found the breath belonged to a man curled up in bed beside me. A sleeping man whose face was mere inches from my face. A messy-haired man who looked a whole lot like my normally very-put-together former professor.

Oh. My. God.

Thankfully, I was one of the lucky few in my family who didn't experience terrible hangovers on the rare occasions when I overindulged, because if I was the type who woke up queasy and half-dead, I'd have passed out right then and there.

I'm in bed with Doctor Hot-Cock.

It was like something out of one of my more fantastical fantasies. The kind that, even while I was dreaming about them and jerking off to them, I knew were too far-fetched to ever actually happen. Except this time it *had*... and I'd apparently been too drunk to remember a damn thing.

Wasn't *that* some next-level, Dante-esque, divine justice bullshit?

If Theo Hancock's hands had been on my naked body... if I'd heard him moaning and panting... if I'd worshipped his dick... if I'd witnessed his cum-face... and I'd *forgotten*? Oh, God. Was there anything worse?

Pretty quickly, I realized that yes, there was, because... *Jesus*, what if he hadn't come at all? What if tequila-dick had struck right in the middle, and I'd had to "it's not you, it's me" him? What if he'd had to pity-cuddle me and tell me that this happened to a lot of guys?

Suddenly, I *did* feel queasy and extremely close to passing out.

My first instinct was to bolt out of bed, but I worried that the moment I moved an inch, it would wake him and begin the most awkward morning-after of my life. Of course, remaining in the bed and pretending to be asleep until he woke up on his own was guaranteed to be equally awkward. Frozen, I could only stare at the man beside me helplessly.

Theo Hancock was the most gorgeous professor on campus, hands down. Everyone talked about him like he was Henry Cavill and Shawn Mendes rolled into one, and... yeah, okay, I was part of "everyone." Even though he was my mortal enemy, the man who'd failed me in what should have been the final, *final* semester of the longest college slog in history, he was so fucking sexy that if he started an OnlyFans where he sat around reading poetry as foreplay, I'd be his first subscriber. I was so far gone over him that even his grumpy scowls turned me on...

Which was kind of a problem when the man was your professor.

Last semester, I'd found myself getting tongue-tied in his presence from the very first day, not just because of how he looked but because of who he was to me—the guy who'd made me fall in love with words. In my other classes, I'd write the kind of off-the-cuff essays that came naturally to me, but in Professor Hancock's class, I'd been so desperate to impress that I'd researched every single word before I wrote it, called in favors from friends and my new almost-brother-in-law, Gage, to edit and proofread for me, worked twice as hard as I ever had before in my entire academic career.

But with every paper I submitted, Professor Hancock would scowl a little deeper, grade a little harder, and make more pointed comments about coming to his office hours for assistance—as if I could sit that close to him without having an expulsion-worthy reaction. Every time, I'd double down to prove that I was worthy and didn't need extra help. The harder I worked, the worse I failed, until I was mad—*frantic-mad*—with self-doubt and anger, and a disapproving scowl became his default expression when he looked at me.

It had *sucked*.

Now, though, with his scowl all smoothed out in sleep, he looked... younger. More carefree. The serious mien that wrapped around him like a black shroud most days was gone.

Seeing him up close like this was a bit of a revelation—one that made it hard to hold on to my frantic-mad anger... or any anger at all. He had two tiny scars at the edge of his jaw that looked like a miniature pair of skis. Faint laugh lines bracketed his eyes, proving the man must have a whole other existence where he was something besides the strictest, sexiest professor in the entire English department.

Was it strange that I'd never wondered about what his private life was like?

I mean, yeah, maybe I'd been curious about how he was poised to become the head of the English department when most other department heads were fifty, at least. And there'd been rumors about a boyfriend years ago that made me wonder how many sonnets a guy would have to memorize before he was good enough to pass muster with someone like Theo Hancock. But I'd never tried to picture where he lived or who he lived with. I'd never wondered what music he listened to or what made him laugh.

Now… I found myself insatiably curious, not just about the *whats* but the *whys.*

Looking around the space, it was clear he lived by himself. The cabin was off the beaten path, significantly isolated away from the tiny but buzzing college town of Hannabury, Vermont. And it only had one room. One bed. Two kitchen chairs, yes, but only one easy chair and a footstool.

But why was the handsomest man in the entire county single? Why would he live in a place so isolated? Why pick a house so small you couldn't have friends over, or a desk to work at, or a *sofa*? Why read sonnets about love and friend-ship with such passion and fire and then live in a way that made it almost impossible to experience it?

Dr. Hancock—*Theo*—made a noise in his sleep, and his eyebrows puckered together in a frown, almost like he could sense my curiosity and it made him uncomfortable. He kicked a leg in my direction, and I steeled myself not to jump at the feel of his skin against mine… but all I felt was vague warmth.

Curious, I looked him up and down and realized belatedly that he'd fallen asleep on *top* of the coverlet, with only a throw blanket covering him, almost like he was trying hard to preserve his modesty… or mine. A hint of flannel peeked out where his knee was cocked to one side; he was definitely wearing pajamas.

So, okay. Had there been no sex? Or really quick sex followed by a fastidious cleanup?

The blanket situation suggested no sex, which was a relief —mostly—because it meant no impromptu tequila-dick apology soliloquies would be required this day. But it was also curiously disappointing.

Deep down, I'd hoped that the tequila I'd ingested had helped me say something meaningful to Professor Hancock that I couldn't articulate while sober. Something like, "Thanks for being an inspiration, and I'm angry at you for failing me, but mostly I'm angry at myself because I wanted you to be impressed by my writing so you'd know the work you do is meaningful."

But, like, better and smoother than that, obviously. Possibly something in haiku form. Something eloquent enough to get him to push me into his bed and ravish me.

Instead, it seemed likely that I'd passed out and he'd been stuck dragging me into his bed since the snow had prevented him from sending me off in a cab.

Chalk up another failure for Porter Sunday.

But even as awkward and ashamed of that as I was, my fingers still itched to touch the guy. I wanted to smooth over the place where his brows had puckered. To brush back a strand of golden-brown hair that had gotten tangled in his eyelashes. To drink in this precious, fragile moment, this *privilege* of seeing him up-close and vulnerable, since clearly I would not get this opportunity again.

My eyes devoured him inch by inch, memorizing each detail. The stubble on his chin and neck leading into the soft collar of the hoodie he still wore. The everyday nicks and scratches on his hands. All those little things that made my sexy, aloof professor so wildly, fascinatingly, complexly human.

He made another little sleep noise—almost a moan this time—and I felt my dick rise in response.

Oh, *no*. Oh, *fuck*. Down, boy.

What was worse than being a sixth-year senior, stuck repeating a class so you could graduate, and finding yourself passed out in your former professor's bed? Finding yourself in that situation with your *morning wood* mere inches from him.

As quietly as I could, I pressed a hand to my rapidly

inflating dick through the coverlet and clamped my lips shut against the urge to groan. *Not helping!*

Erections were normal and not always controllable, even at twenty-six. But if he woke up and saw it… if he multiplied all of last semester by the sum total of my antics last night and then raised it to the exponent of *raging boner*… Well, I was no mathematician, but I had to imagine the end product looked a lot like Professor Hancock reporting me to the administration and me not graduating at all.

I sucked in a panicked breath, nearly trembling as I tried to get the blood to exit my dick by force of will. Was this how all my years of hard work, all my hopes of the future, ended? The gaping maw of my undefined future opened up like a quicksand trap waiting to suck me down into its depths forever—

"Christ alive, Sunday. You're as intense outside of class as you were in it," he grumbled without opening his eyes. "Stop thinking so loudly."

"Oh fucking fuck!" I yelped, jumping headfirst off the bed with all the grace of a newborn calf—which was to say no grace whatsoever. My legs were still all tangled in the duvet, so while my face and arms landed on the frigid wood floor near the bathroom door, the lower half of my body remained in the warm bed.

If panic-attack-yoga wasn't already a thing, I'd just invented it.

"Fuck," I breathed again.

If biting back a giant guffaw had a sound, Dr. Hancock had perfected it. "I have to admit I've never had a man so horrified to wake up in bed with me that he tried to jump to his own doom… *from the bed*. But then, you always had to be just that little bit extra, didn't you, Sunday?"

I groaned but didn't dare move. I could feel my pulse in my eyeballs and knew I had to be flushed to a cardiac-event-level red. All the blood in my body that hadn't already rushed to my dick was now rushing to my head, which did not bode well for the other parts of me.

"What… what happened?" I managed to croak. I tried to push my torso back up onto the bed, but that only succeeded in pushing the duvet lower—as in, dick-visibly lower. Then I tried to crawl fully onto the floor, but the duvet was too firmly tucked around my feet, and there was no room to maneuver.

"Well, I don't know exactly. I assume you woke up with morning wood, freaked out spectacularly, landed face-first, and possibly concussed yourself."

"Yes, thank you," I snapped… as much as a man who found himself marooned ass up in a strange bed, tangled head to toe in bedsheets, *could* snap. "I meant, how did I end up in your bed? Why didn't you make me sleep in the chair, or push me onto the floor, or… hell, leave me laying out in your driveway covered in snow? I remember coming back inside after you saved me from the, uh, the tree incident. But then… nothing."

"So you don't remember taking a shower?"

The moment he said it, I did remember. The water had been incredibly hot and soothing, and the man's bodywash had smelled musky and intense, just like its owner.

This memory did nothing to help my dick situation.

"I… I think I discovered I was light-headed and decided to lay down to warm up afterward," I explained.

"Uh-huh." He leaned over and began yanking the covers to untangle my legs and hips. "Very Goldilocks of you. But as it happens, *I* discovered that I am not a person who leaves people to suffer hypothermia, even when they richly deserve it. You would have frozen on the floor with just this one extra throw blanket."

With a final yank of the duvet, I finally fell the rest of the way to the floor. It only took a split second to feel the cold air on my balls before I realized the situation had somehow, impossibly, gotten even more awkward.

"Arrghhh!" I yelped and scrambled for the sheet again, yanking it clear off the bed and wrapping it around my crumpled body. "Fucking fuck!"

"*Tsk.* Hasn't anyone told you cursing is a sign of a weak vocabulary? Find a more appropriate word."

I peeked up over the edge of the mattress to see my ex-professor sitting up in bed with his arms resting over his bent knees. One eyebrow lifted at me, but otherwise, his face was impossible to read.

"I promise, I'm using the *only* appropriate word. I'm *naked*." My voice had gone high, and the last word came out as a squeak. I knew my face was on fire.

I expected to see my own shock mirrored on his face, but his expression didn't change.

"Yes, you are. Not much gets by you, does it, Sunday?" he asked mildly.

I blinked. "But... *why* am I naked?"

The other eyebrow lifted to join the first. "You tell me, Sunday."

"Stop calling me that," I shot back. "Last-naming me only works if we're buddies, which we aren't, or if it's a cute nickname, like my brother calling his boyfriend Goodman, which doesn't apply here either, or if you're trying to put distance between us, which is really fucking uncool when I'm naked and tumbling out of your bed." I lifted my chin. "The *appropriate word* is Porter. Por. Ter."

Professor Hancock regarded me for a long moment—long enough to make me regret my impetuous words and wonder why I'd chosen that particular hill to die on—before finally nodding.

"You have a point," he agreed. He cleared his throat and inspected the fabric of his pajama pants as he offered awkwardly, "You may call me Theo."

A startled puff of sound escaped me, almost like a laugh but not quite. "Uh. No. I may not."

He turned to me with… ah, yes, there it was. The scowl of disapproval. "Why not?" he demanded. "If you expect me to call you Porter, then you'll call me Theo. End of subject."

I shook my head. I would swear before any court of law that Professor—*Theo*—hadn't particularly wanted me to call him Theo… until I'd refused. Why did I find that so adorable?

"For the record," he went on, "I found you passed out on my bed wearing nothing but a towel after your shower last night, despite me giving you spare clothes to wear. I couldn't tell you *why* you made that choice any more than I could explain *any* of the choices you made last night. But after cursing you heartily, using *all* the words in my very impressive vocabulary—"

"Naturally," I said, rolling my eyes.

"—I opted to let you sleep it off. I debated taking the chair, but I'm still recovering from the last time I fell asleep there, grading papers last semester. Since the floor wasn't an option for me either, I came up with the only other viable *temporary* solution." He spread his hands to indicate the rumpled bedcovers.

Despite his calm words, his cheeks were definitely rosy, and it settled something in me to know I wasn't the only one feeling the awkwardness of the situation.

"Right. Well. Good." I stood up, clutching the sheet around me like a Victorian gentlewoman. "I… appreciate that. I'm just going to…"

I bolted into the bathroom. Once behind the closed door, I let out a long, slow breath. I deliberately avoided looking in the mirror because I didn't need to see my bloodshot eyes and bloodshottier face.

"Fuck," I breathed for the millionth time. Dr. Hancock was right. I had a piss-poor vocabulary for an English Lit student.

I cleared my throat and tried again, this time using the

Bard's own words. *"O, that my tongue were in the thunder's mouth! Then with a passion would I shake the world."*

"Sun—*Porter*?" Dr. Hancock called through the door. "What the fuck are you doing in there?"

I jumped and banged my hip on the corner of the sink. "Fuck!" I cried again.

"If you're trying to convert me by showing me the many, many applications of the word, I assure you I have already discovered them all," he muttered before adding with a definite hint of amusement, "Mostly in the last twelve hours." His voice trailed off as he wandered away from the door.

I couldn't help but grin. Theo Hancock had a sense of humor. Who knew?

After splashing my face with frigid water, I looked around for the clothes he'd mentioned and found that someone, possibly me, had hung them on a row of hooks behind the bathroom door. Navy blue sweatpants, worn to softness, and a hoodie from last year's Hannabury Faculty Fun Run, which had benefitted the Hub.

I'd been at that event. I ran my fingers over the faded logo while my memory tried to place him there. I'd been a volunteer, as usual, checking people in and handing out race numbers. But I hadn't been the only volunteer at the table, and with the crowd that day, it was possible he'd escaped my notice.

Imagining him among the happy crowd wasn't easy. Even after seeing him in pajamas, it was hard to picture him without his usual dressy jeans, Oxford button-up, and textured blazer. Would he still have worn his dark-framed glasses, or would he have worn contacts for something like that?

Because I was still curious—and, okay, came from a long and proud line of nosy, small-town gossips—I nudged open the medicine cabinet door over the sink and took a peek.

No contact lenses, but among the usual items found in a

medicine cabinet, there was also a half-empty bottle of silicone lube, an unopened box of condoms, and a small black enema bulb.

Oh. Oh, shit. Okay.

My heart skittered faster. Professor Hot-Cock liked to bottom.

This knowledge did absolutely nothing to calm my flaming cheeks, so I had to rinse my face off with cold water again. And again. After the third icy-cold douse, my cheeks had faded from "call the paramedics" to "mild sunburn." That was as good as it was going to get.

I yanked on the clothes, freeballing it since there'd been no sharing of underwear, and opened the door.

Dr. Hancock stood in front of a coffee maker in the small kitchen space. The jeans he'd pulled on did loving things to his ass, which distracted me from… well, nothing, because I'd been fantasizing about his ass before, and now I still was.

"Coffee?" he asked without turning around.

"Please. Yeah." I felt painfully sober and also incredibly awkward now that I was in his small space, wearing his clothes. "And, uh… could you maybe give me a ride home after that?"

Asking him for the favor made my face heat up to "third-degree burn" again. Apparently, my embarrassment was an endless well where this man was concerned.

And rightly so, Porter. Look at what you've done.

Before Theo could answer, I cleared my throat. The man deserved an apology from me—a sober one—at the very least.

"Listen, I'm sorry. Really sorry. I mean, not for reciting an angry sonnet at you, necessarily, because while I can't actually remember that part of the night, I'm confident it was epic and justified…" Theo lifted an eyebrow, and I hurried on. "But coming here drunk? Invading your privacy when it's clear you've gone to great lengths to get some distance from campus? That was unfair and very much not cool. And I… I know I don't have any right to expect, well… *anything* from you after that display. In fact, you've already been kinder to me than I probably deserve. But… but I really hope that you'll accept my apology. Then you can drive me home, and we can forget all about this."

I ran my hand through my hair and tried to ignore how much it was shaking.

This man had my fate in his hands in so many ways. He could report me to the school or maybe even arrest me for trespassing. The last time I'd been at this man's mercy, it hadn't gone well for me at all.

Theo turned and faced me. His dark-framed glasses, tidy hair, and stern face were back in full force.

"No," he said. Then he turned back to finish pouring the coffee.

"No?" I repeated. No, as in he wouldn't drive me anywhere? No, as in he wouldn't forgive me? Both? Neither?

As usual with this man, I would have given him whatever he wanted, but I had no clue what that was.

"Not at this time, anyway," Theo elaborated, which made things zero percent clearer.

I fucking hated being on the back foot with him all the time. I hated feeling like I was constantly misunderstanding the assignment, never smart enough or mature enough to clue in. It made me feel defensive and wary—two emotions I rarely felt with anyone else.

"Right. Okay," I said lamely to the back of his head. "So… I guess I'll get out of your hair on my own, then." A quick glance at the vast whiteness out the window suggested the walk back to the road—or maybe even to town—was gonna be unpleasant.

"Sit, Porter. You're not going anywhere until I say so."

My butt was in the chair before he finished speaking, and it was only a few moments later, when he handed me a mug of steaming coffee, that the mortification of my instinctive obedience registered.

Really, at a certain point, I needed to stop registering embarrassment. Wasn't there some kind of rock-bottom-humiliation level a person could reach when they stopped falling?

I had no interest in finding out. I kept my face down and concentrated on willing my coffee to cool so I could drink it down and make my escape.

Clearly, nothing good would ever come of my fascination with Theo Hancock. At this point, the only option was to walk the heck away.

CHAPTER FOUR

THEO

I HADN'T KNOWN Porter Sunday could be skittish.

I'd seen him being a sexy, overconfident, know-it-all student too many times to count last semester. I'd seen him being a gregarious, good-natured goof with his friends around campus. As of last night, I'd even seen him being an amusingly obnoxious sonnet-screamer. More than once in the months I'd known him, I'd wished that the man would sit still and just fucking *listen to me*.

But now that Porter was sitting silent and subdued at my tiny wooden kitchen table, nearly curled in on himself, I wasn't sure this was what I'd wanted after all.

In fact, I knew it wasn't.

I set a plate of scrambled eggs and toast in front of him before taking my own seat on the opposite side of the table. "Eat," I instructed.

He picked up his fork and began shoveling hot eggs into his mouth pell-mell, like he was on the clock. I frowned at him, trying to figure out what had changed with him in the last five minutes... and whether I should try to address it or not.

Porter had had a hard night. Maybe he was hungover.

Maybe, considering the apology he'd just made, he was feeling embarrassed about his behavior. Maybe he was tired, or coming down with a cold, or sad that I didn't have oat milk creamer for his coffee, or… Christ, the possibilities were endless, really.

If Porter had been a white paper on intersectional diversity training or a few stanzas of fragmentalist poetry, I'd have been able to read, analyze, and comprehend him without a problem. Flesh and blood humans, though, were so much trickier.

There was a reason why my friends—classmates, former colleagues, or even people I'd grown close to at Hannabury, like my colleague John Curran and his husband—only called me when they needed willing bodies for their Fun Runs, or the name of a good accountant, or someone to take their extra ticket for *Les Mis* at the last minute because I probably didn't have any plans. I wasn't a heart-to-heart sort of person.

And Porter wasn't my friend. Wasn't my houseguest. Wasn't even my student anymore. He officially should not have been my problem… but it turned out, I missed the spark of mischief in those green eyes of his. I missed his humor. And his fire.

"Is something wrong?" I finally asked.

He shook his head and didn't glance up. "Nope. Good eggs. Thanks for that."

I blew out a breath and tried again. "You seem troubled. If you wanted to talk, I would listen."

He did glance up at this, at least long enough to ask incredulously, "*Now* you want to talk? I apologized. I asked you to drive me home and we could forget this ever happened. And you said—"

"No."

"Exactly!" He threw up his hands. "No, you don't forgive me? No, we can't forget it? What does that even *mean*, Professor?"

I blinked. He was upset because he thought I might be upset with *him*? That wasn't what I would have expected of Porter Sunday. But I was beginning to realize that I'd been wrong about a lot of things with him.

"Obviously, I accept your apology, Porter. I'd hardly be making you coffee and eggs if I were angry, would I? *Context clues*, yes? The *no* was in reference to me driving you home. If you recall, there's an enormous tree across the driveway, the road to town won't be plowed for ages, and there's more snow predicted later." I sipped my coffee. "Campus is closed until Monday, and even that feels optimistic."

I didn't say it out loud, but while I might forgive Porter, I wasn't sure I could forget last night had ever happened. Too many parts of the last eight hours had been written on my brain in indelible ink, and I'd be replaying them in my mind for a long while.

"Monday?" Porter repeated. "As in... as in, *three days from now*?" His eyes went comically wide, the flecks of honey in his green eyes catching the light coming in through the nearby window. "That's impossible! I have to be at the Hub tomorrow. I promised the kids we'd do a theater thing. I'll... I'll hike home."

I glanced down at his feet, which were currently snug in a pair of my wool socks but which we both knew would only be minimally protected by the thin Vans he'd left by the door.

"Sure you will," I said, turning my attention to my breakfast. "You know, the Hub will be closed because campus is closed, so you won't have to worry about that."

"But..." His eyes flicked to the bed in the middle of the room. "You and I... we... I can't stay!" The mild edge of panic was back in his voice again, lifting the pitch of his words high enough to make me bite back a smirk.

Stop finding him attractive, dammit.

"If you found my company that abhorrent, you probably should have considered that before you and your friends got

Steve to drive you out here to deliver a poetry rant," I said mildly. I took a bite of toast. "Speaking of which, have you called to let them know you're okay?"

"Yeah. I texted our group chat while you were..." Porter waved a hand at the stove. "Cooking stuff. And look, it's not that I mind your company. Jeez." He ran a hand through his dark hair. "It's just... I'm embarrassed, okay? And there's still only one bed here. And... and... you don't even like company!"

He wasn't wrong. I valued my privacy. But he wasn't correct either. "You seem to feel like you know me pretty well for a person who never had a conversation with me outside of class until last night."

"Am I wrong?" He waved a hand around the space. "If you wanted company, you'd have more than one bed and one reading chair..."

"I have two chairs at this table," I retorted. "*Four* plates in the cabinet, four glasses on the shelf."

The green eyes I was trying so hard not to notice blinked at me. "Because they came with the set!"

Once again, not entirely wrong but not entirely right either. I couldn't hold back my smile anymore. "My grandfather made these chairs by hand. One for me and one for him."

Porter looked back down at the chair he sat in. "Your grandfather did?"

I nodded before taking another sip of coffee. "Yep. This cabin was his retirement project. He made everything in here, including the cabin itself. He left me his entire estate when he passed away, but this was by far the best part."

"Oh, wow. I... I'm sorry for your loss. Sounds like you were... close?"

I nodded again.

"Rough," Porter said. "I lost my dad right before I turned seventeen. If losing your grandfather was anything like that... well. It must have sucked." He pushed his plate away and pulled his mug closer, grasping it with both hands. "Was he really handy? Or in construction or something?"

It was clear Porter was trying to make an effort, to make a *connection*, and I appreciated that. Which was why I found myself sharing more information with him than I usually shared with anyone.

"Nope. Gramps was a physics professor at Hannabury, actually, and an amateur inventor. For decades, he and my grandma lived in faculty housing, back when the college offered that as a benefit. They raised my mom there. And since they didn't have a mortgage, they bought a large parcel of land as an investment." I swept a hand out, indicating the seventy-acre plot around us. "For years, they parked an RV out here. They'd spend their summers fishing and exploring, and there's a tool shed out back where Gramps used to tinker with things. They had lots of big dreams of building a house out here as soon as he retired, but..." I took another sip of coffee. "Then Grandma died. And Gramps wasn't excited to retire anymore. Too much alone time and nothing to do, you know?"

"Yeah." Porter's bright green eyes shone with sympathy. "How did he finally decide to build the cabin?"

I smiled down at my coffee, remembering my mom's frantic phone call. *They're forcing him out, Theo. Get up there and distract him.*

"Well... I told him *I* needed a break from working on my dissertation—which wasn't a lie. I said I wanted to come stay with him for the summer and distract myself with physical labor. Chopping wood or building something. He was so excited to have company up here he immediately got to work planning our summer project. And he didn't seem to mind too much when the school suggested making him a professor emeritus and taking him off the roster for the following autumn."

"You worked on it together?" He looked around the small space as if appreciating it through a new lens. "So cool."

"Knowing how the place was put together has come in handy from time to time," I agreed. "And I've never laughed as much as I did that summer. Never worked as hard or slept as little either. When Gramps fell asleep each night, I stayed up working on my dissertation for a few more hours. I hadn't told him I had a job lead in Virginia that would require me to finish my degree as soon as possible."

"Did you make it? Did you get that job?"

I shook my head. "No, but it turned out to be a good thing. If I'd gone to Virginia, I wouldn't have gotten the job at Brown, which is how I ended up getting hired here."

Porter looked surprised. "You had a job at Brown, and you left it to come to Hannabury? Why?"

I rolled my eyes. It was a question I'd been asked many, many times. "You sound like my father," I said with a laugh. "I grew up in New York, where his side of the family is from. My mother was thrilled to get out of Hannabury and never wanted to come back, but I lived for the summers I'd spend with my grandparents up here. I enjoyed Providence, and I loved the students at Brown, but when Gramps left me this place, I just…"

"Felt the need to come back here permanently?" Porter guessed. "Like it was a thing you were supposed to do?"

After all the Porter revelations of the past few hours, maybe it shouldn't have felt so strange that this man would understand immediately what my parents and former colleagues still struggled to comprehend, but it did.

"That." I nodded. "Yeah. And it wasn't just the house. When I talked to the dean about openings in the department, it turned out Hannabury was so eager to hire me they gave me tenure *and* told me I'd be the top candidate for the department head position once Jim Burton retired. It would have taken decades to get that at Brown, if it ever happened at all. It was all—"

"Serendipity?" Porter supplied. I nodded. "Yeah," he sighed. "I keep waiting for that to happen for me, but... I mean, I guess you have to put yourself in the right place first, right? The stars didn't just align for you—you made them align."

He sounded doubtful and hopeful all at once.

"I suppose that's true," I agreed.

"And did you regret it?" he asked. "Leaving your family behind, knowing they didn't understand?"

"Nope. Because I knew it was the right thing for me, and that made everything worthwhile. Even dealing with know-it-all students who refuse to listen." I gave him a pointed look.

"I know you're not talking about *me*." He lifted an eyebrow. "All I do is listen and study. Check out the GPA I had before your class last semester—people who don't listen don't get 3.8's, *Theo*. And I'll have you know, I busted my ass in your class. I can't help it if you're a..." His voice trailed off, and he cleared his throat. "Never mind."

I stood up and carried both of our dirty dishes to the sink, mostly so I could hide my grin. That little *Theo* said Subdued Porter was on his way out.

Good.

After setting the dishes down, I turned and leaned my hip against the counter, crossing my arms in front of my chest.

"Why are you censoring yourself with me?" I challenged. "I'm not your professor, you're not my student anymore, and we're stuck together for at least a few more hours. Clearly, you had a reason for coming here last night, so finish your thought. I'm a... what?"

His nostrils flared. "Fine, then. You're an asshole with an overblown sense of authority who gets off on making students beg."

Well. That was uncensored, at least. Also, categorically incorrect.

"My job is to teach my students. I want to see them succeed. Sometimes that means pushing them and holding them to a high standard. But I'm not on some power trip here—"

He shoved his chair back and stood up. "Then explain why I worked my ass off in your class and you still failed me."

"Because you didn't do the assignments properly," I shot back. "You fundamentally misunderstood what I wanted. I asked you time and again to come to my office hours, to let me explain things to you, but you clearly thought you knew better than I did."

"I'm a good writer," Porter said, voice vibrating with emotion. "Dozens of other teachers and professors have said so, and I didn't put nearly as much effort into their classes as I did yours—"

"I *know* you're a good writer! For fuck's sake, Porter. Everyone in the department sang your praises to me. *Porter Sunday is a unicorn student. Porter Sunday spins gold with his words. Porter Sunday wrote a classic Shakespearean sonnet on sexuality discrimination that made the entire department weep.* When Professor Chenault told me you wanted to take my class, I actually wondered, 'What can I teach this person? It'll be like trying to teach Marlon Brando how to act.'"

Porter made a scoffing noise.

"But I was here for it anyway," I informed him. "Hell, I couldn't wait to read your first assignment. And then you turned in this... this... beige fucking *cardboard*. Technically accurate, every comma in place, but just... bland as fuck. So, okay, I thought. No problem. Porter Sunday clearly has talent; he just needs to understand what creative non-fiction is. How cool that I get to show him. But I *couldn't* show you because you can't teach someone who refuses to be taught. I gave you feedback, Porter. So much feedback. But you refused to incorporate it into your work…"

"Bullshit!" His chin firmed, and his eyes sparked green fire. "You said to put my heart into it, my personality, my soul. For that last piece, about our family home, I wrote about Sunday Orchard—a place that's been in my family for generations. The place where my dad is buried. The place where my uncle and almost all my siblings and their partners still live to this day. There's no topic that has *more* of my heart—"

I sucked in a deep breath. "Then for fuck's sake, why didn't you let that come across? Porter, you wrote about apple varietals and growth timelines. About profit shares and hybridization. It was supposed to be a personal narrative, but it read like something out of an almanac, circa 1875. You took yourself out of the narrative almost entirely, which was the *opposite* of what I asked for. You're a brilliant writer, but it doesn't matter how accurate or technically perfect a piece is if you're not accomplishing what you've set out to do. And you wouldn't come and talk to me about it."

Some complex emotions worked across his face. Hurt, disappointment, anger, and then hurt again. "*Forgive me* if I wasn't willing to come listen to you tell me how awful my work was. *Forgive me* if I wasn't interested in one person's opinions on how to write creative non-fiction. And fucking *forgive me* for walking out on you right now before I say or do something we'll both regret."

He turned and stormed out of the kitchen area, shoving his feet into his shoes and yanking my jacket on before disappearing out the front door.

I closed my eyes and bit out a curse. *Well done, Dr. Hancock.*

I'd spoken the truth. I *had* tried my best to teach Porter. I also *had* been progressively more annoyed each time he turned in an assignment that was technically proficient and entirely missing the point. I *had* asked him repeatedly to come to my office hours… even if part of me had been secretly relieved that I hadn't had him in my space, where I'd be forced to deal with my inappropriate thoughts about the man for hours at a time.

But what had I just been saying to Porter about how it didn't matter how accurate your words were if you didn't accomplish what you set out to do? I definitely hadn't intended to make him storm out.

I scrubbed at the dishes a bit more savagely than necessary, hoping the manual labor would serve to calm me down and that a walk in the frigid morning air would do the same for Porter.

Once I finished the dishes, I threw several ingredients into the slow cooker for a stew I'd planned to make for dinner. Then I looked at my tablet, sitting right beside my comfortable, *empty* reading chair, and contemplated starting the new novel I'd downloaded.

For once, though, reading a new book didn't appeal to me. In fact, nothing about being alone in my cabin was appealing all of a sudden.

I decided I might as well clear a path to the wood pile before the next round of snow came, so I stepped into my boots. But just as I was lacing them up, I heard the deafening *brrrum* of a chainsaw out in the yard.

I grabbed my parka, pulled the front door open, and rushed outside to find Porter cutting branches off the giant downed tree in the driveway, handling the heavy saw as easily as he'd handled his fork at breakfast.

Meanwhile, I hadn't remembered that saw was in the shed, let alone the safety goggles and ear protectors Porter had found along with it.

"What are you doing?" I yelled. *Stupid question.* I gestured for him to give me the chainsaw. "Let me do that."

Porter looked me up and down as if judging whether or not I could be trusted with my own chainsaw… which was all the more embarrassing because his concern was valid. I'd gotten pretty competent with certain power tools while helping my grandfather, but that hadn't extended to chainsaws. "I don't think so," he decided.

I narrowed my eyes at him before reaching for the chainsaw. He yanked it away and held it up out of my reach. The edge of his mouth quirked up in a teasing grin.

"I don't want you to hurt yourself, Porter." The very idea of it made me shudder. "And I'm quite confident that I can do it at least as well as you can," I insisted.

"Really? Because this thing hadn't been oiled in years until I got to it, far as I could tell. And I grew up on an orchard. I've been using chainsaws since middle school." He gave me a look that could only be described as smugly innocent. "If you want, I could *teach you.*"

He was worse than a know-it-all. He was a know-it-all who actually *knew* it all. I was suddenly filled with the childish urge to throw him into a snowbank.

"No, thank you," I said primly. "You can hand it over right now. This is *my* chainsaw and *my* property, and I can figure it out just fine on my own."

Porter shook his head and sighed. "Can't teach a man who refuses to be taught," he mocked, throwing my own words back at me.

Infuriating.

But I refused to back down, and he finally gave up the chainsaw with an eye roll. "I'll get a handsaw from the shed, then."

I opened my mouth to argue, and he lifted an eyebrow in challenge. "Or did you want me to stay here in this cabin with you forever and ever, amen, *Theo*?"

I refused to speak the retort that came unbidden to my brain. *Only if I can gag you.*

And suddenly, I could imagine it. Porter trussed up in my bed, gagged and pliant. Telling me, as he had the night before, that he'd do anything I wanted, if I only told him what that was. Those teasing green eyes would still dance and challenge me even if his sassy mouth had to stay busy with other things, and…

"Christ," I muttered in disgust, turning away so I could trudge to the tool shed for a handsaw. "One of us won't make it through this day alive."

When I returned with the handsaw, he was standing with his feet braced and his arms crossed.

"Theo," he said slowly, like the word was still unfamiliar and he was testing it out.

"Yes?" I snapped, turned on despite myself.

"I have a wager for you. If, after an hour, I've removed more of this tree with the handsaw than you have with the chainsaw, will you admit that I know what I'm doing and let me use the chainsaw to finish getting the branches off?"

We both knew my chainsaw was never going to cut into the tree itself. The trunk circumference was way too large for the size chainsaw I had. Until we could get professional help up here, the tree wasn't moving. But if we could strip all the branches off and make it easier to access, the pros would be able to make a much quicker job of it.

"What do I get when I win?" I asked. Clearly, the man with the chainsaw would win. It was a no-brainer.

"I'll cook you dinner."

I shook my head. "Sorry, already put stew fixings in the Crock-Pot."

"I'll do the dishes."

"Already did that, too."

He exhaled a white cloud into the cold air. "Fine. What do you suggest? It hardly matters since I'm going to school you with this thing." He waved the handsaw in the air.

I thought about it for a long moment. What did I want from Porter Sunday? Lots of things, most of them highly inadvisable.

"If I win, I want you to let me critique the last essay you did for Professor Burton's class," I blurted, surprising myself as much as him.

Porter's lips thinned. "Um, *no*. I'm doing just fine in Burton's class, thanks, so I don't need your... help. And letting you point out all the ways I'm lacking isn't my idea of a good time."

"You're doing fine in Professor Burton's class because this is literally his last semester as a professor, and he's been half-checked-out since August," I retorted.

This was mostly an educated guess based on Jim Burton's behavior in other areas. I'd certainly never done anything as unprofessional as asking him to show me Porter's work. But judging by Porter's frown, my guess wasn't far off the mark... or else he'd been wondering the same thing.

"I would like to explain to you what I wanted to explain last semester. I want you to listen to me now the way you didn't listen then. Those are my terms. That's the prize I want."

"Fine," he gritted out. "It doesn't really matter because I'm not losing. We start now."

We spent the next hour busting our asses, trying to one-up each other as if I wasn't older and more sedentary and he wasn't drop-dead gorgeous with a muscular fit body and a really compelling facility with... ahem, *tools*.

About half an hour into our challenge, he'd worked up enough heat to strip off his borrowed jacket and push up the sleeves on the hoodie I'd lent him... which was short enough to remind me he was wearing sweatpants with no underwear. I would have called him out for trying to deliberately distract me, but I didn't think he was doing anything deliberately. The man was just sex on legs.

If I hadn't been so determined to win, I might have given up and just sat to watch him. But I wanted my do-over, damn it.

When my chainsaw finally sputtered and died, we were neck and neck—which felt like a win, even though Porter had been doing the job by hand while I had not. I spun toward the shed for more gas, and Porter began laughing.

"Good luck finding gas. The container in there is empty. How do you think I knew for sure I could win?"

I didn't bother responding, only hid my grin as I went past the shed to the thirty-gallon fuel tank tucked safely away from the buildings. After filling the chainsaw's tank up, I returned and winked at Porter.

"Never assume, Mr. Sunday. It makes an ass out of you and me."

CHAPTER FIVE

PORTER

We were both soaking wet and covered in a mix of snow and sweat from hours working on the world's largest downed tree. Stacks of brushy branches formed messy piles around the edges of the driveway, and the remaining trunk lay naked and forbidding, a long, heavy reminder that regardless of all our hard work, we weren't getting out of here anytime soon.

Because of the loud buzz of the chainsaw, we hadn't been able to carry on a conversation while we worked, which was probably for the best. Instead, we'd worked side by side in what became... well, not companionable silence, exactly, since it was more competitive than companionable and definitely not quiet. But the interlude had begun with me truly angry, in a way I rarely was, and had ended as more of a teasing challenge.

There was something about physical labor, especially outdoors, that was always soothing. It reminded me of all the times growing up on the orchard that my brothers and I had busted our asses trimming trees, harvesting apples, and generally hauling debris until our muscles ached and our stomachs cried out for a giant meal.

I couldn't even be too sad that I'd technically lost the challenge.

"Go on in," Theo said, nodding his head toward the small cabin. "You can grab a shower while I put this stuff away." His mouth quirked up in a smile. "Never let it be said that I'm not gracious in victory."

"Barely victory," I muttered.

I was still mildly peeved at him for cheating with the whole "spare source of gas" thing earlier, so I didn't argue. Instead, I jogged up to the cabin and helped myself to a long, hot shower without regard to saving him any hot water.

The scent of his fancy bodywash filled the steamy air around me as I scrubbed off the grime and tried to warm up. I wondered idly if the bodywash had been a gift from someone. It was a black pump bottle with "Salt & Stone" printed on it in gold lettering. The smokey, woodsy scent was perfect for this place and the man who inhabited it, but the fact someone else might have determined that—might have known him well enough to select the perfect scent and splurge on a gift of it for him—made my back teeth clench in annoyance.

I ran my hands over my body and tried not to think of him, but that was impossible. I'd watched him out of the corner of my eye while he worked to trim the largest branches off the tree with the chainsaw. His muscles had moved under his shirt and jeans, drawing my eyes away from my own work so much that I would have lost the damned contest with or without the spare can of gas.

Christ, he was sexy. This was not *new* news, obviously, about a man who'd been nicknamed Doctor Hot-Cock years ago. But being like this with him, when our student/teacher roles had been stripped away by circumstances *and* at Theo's insistence… even a monk would find themselves fantasizing about the man, and I was not a monk.

At least, not usually.

I hadn't hooked up with anyone since the summer, which was… shit, had it really been three months already? It had been way longer than that since I'd had a regular relationship worth speaking of. Between schoolwork, the gym, and the hours I'd spent both working and volunteering at the Hub, I barely had time for enough sleep, let alone satisfying sex… and I instinctively knew that sex with Theo would be all kinds of satisfying.

When I'd let myself fantasize about him before, I'd imagined us having… well, hate sex. A white-hot, clothes-ripping, I'm-gonna-regret-this-but-it-feels-too-good-to-care stolen moment in his office, maybe, if I ever deigned to come to his fucking office hours.

But after being here with him, sharing a bed with him, seeing him relaxed and vulnerable and teasing… I was starting to envision something much different but every bit as hot.

I still didn't understand the guy. I was still low-key angry after his explanation that morning. And I still privately thought he was a professor on a power trip who wanted to make students beg… but it didn't matter. There wasn't much I wouldn't let Theo Hancock do to me. There wasn't much I wouldn't beg for, sexually speaking, if he gave me half a chance.

I grabbed my cock under the pounding spray and began to imagine what that would look like. Me, kissing the smirk right off his face. Me, dropping to my knees and shutting him up by taking his cock in my mouth—

"Get your ass out of there before I haul it out," he shouted through the door. "You take any more of that hot water and I'm charging you for it."

I clamped my lips shut to keep the laugh inside and let go of my dick—now was not the time—but I refused to hurry. Instead, I finished rinsing off as slowly as I could, half in hopes he actually would come in here and try to haul my wet, naked ass out.

When I finally turned off the spray and reached for a towel, I called out, "I'm sorry, what did you say? I couldn't hear over the sound of that heavenly hot water pounding down on my sore muscles. You should try it. Feels amazing. Maybe give it twenty minutes to let the hot water heater catch up, though."

His grumble moved away from the door as I continued to laugh silently. The man was easy to tease.

After wrapping the towel around my waist, I realized I couldn't put back on the wet, frozen sweats he'd loaned me earlier. But I'd be damned if I was going to hide in here like a meek little maiden and ask for him to bring me something else. I gathered my courage and strode out into the cabin, ignoring the way the cold air hit my skin and caused my nipples to tighten.

Something crashed to the floor, causing me to glance up at Theo. His eyes were locked on me, even as he crouched to pick up the lamp he'd knocked over. Time slowed as I felt his eyes roaming over my chest and abdomen, down to the towel, where his gaze definitely lingered.

"You…" He swallowed. "Don't…"

"Have anything to wear? Yeah. Are my clothes from last night dry yet?"

"The, uh… the machine needs another dry cycle," he said, finally looking away to straighten the lampshade. "But I'll give you something that'll warm you up."

I quirked a brow, and wonder of wonders, Theo blushed.

Interesting.

"I meant *clothes*," he explained. "Warm *clothes*."

He moved to the dresser on the far side of the room, muttering something about *several layers of clothing* and *too many muscles.*

Even more interesting.

He pulled items out of the dresser, tossed them on the bed, and pointed to them without saying a word before skirting past me to get to the bathroom for his own shower. I leaned toward him—not threateningly but sort of experimentally—just to test a theory.

Theo's eyes flared with heat for just a second before he sucked in a breath and leaned away. "Excuse me," he said very primly, looking over my shoulder. He stuck his chin in the air. "Please stand aside."

Ugh. Nope, I so did not get this guy. This was where we were drawing the line, then? *You're not my student anymore, Porter.* And *don't censor yourself, Porter.* But also, *you're good enough to look at but not to kiss?*

I wasn't sure why this nettled me so much. Maybe because Professor "You May Call Me Theo" Hancock had been consistently throwing me off my stride since I'd woken up beside him that morning? Because I'd been hard for him for hours and had to forcibly stop myself from getting the release I needed in the shower? Either way, I hated that he could make me so frantic while remaining so perfectly in control himself. It made me want to provoke him.

"You're not scared of me, are you, Professor?" I murmured.

"Hardly." He narrowed his eyes. "And I thought we agreed I'm not your professor anymore."

"You're right. We did. And that's good because it seemed like you were looking at me some kind of way a minute ago. Almost like you might want to… kiss me." I let my voice go low and husky. "Which makes me wonder why you're trying so hard not to touch me now."

"Porter." Theo crossed his arms like a shield. "While you might not be my student anymore, you're still *a* student. And I would not kiss a student if he had lifesaving anti-venom on his lips and I'd been bitten by a snake."

Then he scrambled past me into the bathroom and slammed the door.

I stared at the back of the door in surprise. He'd just admitted both more and less than I'd hoped.

It was common knowledge that while professor/student relationships (or hookups) might not be smiled upon at Hannabury, they weren't forbidden. They simply needed to be disclosed to the administration to make sure that the student was never enrolled in the professor's class after that and that the professor didn't exert any undue influence over the student. It was similar to the way professors and other staff members weren't allowed to date their supervisors or direct reports—which, I remembered Nolan telling me, had caused a scandal once upon a time.

Neither of those situations applied to me and Theo.

Also, it must be noted, Theo had not denied looking at me or about what he'd been thinking.

So what was his problem?

I yanked on another set of Theo's clothes. This time, he'd loaned me a soft pair of flannel pajama bottoms and an old NYU tee that must have been from his undergraduate days. After pulling on the thick wool socks he'd set out for me, I padded over to the kitchen to see if I could help fix us a couple of sandwiches or something to tide us over until the stew was ready for dinner.

I had to admit that stew smelled amazing. The warm, hearty aroma filled the small cabin and made the entire place seem even cozier than it already was. Inside the fridge, I didn't find sandwich fixings, but I did find hummus, veggies, and fruit. I pulled a bunch of stuff out and made up a platter to share, hoping he wouldn't mind me making myself at home in his tiny kitchen.

Luck was not on my side because I was just coming in from fetching the hoodie I'd left outside when I remembered he hadn't taken any clothes into the bathroom for himself. By the time I stepped into the cabin, he was pulling on a sweater over the clean T-shirt, hiding all the delicious skin I might have gotten a peek of if I'd simply left the hoodie to die in the frigid driveway.

"I made us something to eat," I said, gesturing to the table where I'd set the platter. "Hope that's okay."

He slid his dark-framed glasses on his face and ran fingers through his wet hair to straighten it back from the mess the sweater had made. "Of course. Help yourself to anything while you're here."

His voice sounded strangely rough and unsure, as if our comfortable companionship from earlier had been zapped out of existence. I debated making a joke about helping myself to *anything*... but I figured that would only make things more awkward.

I busied myself fetching us a couple of glasses of cold water before joining him at the table. He popped back up to grab some pita chips from a cabinet to add to our stash, and then we dove in. My mouth was desperate to make all kinds of snarky comments to break the ice—things like the fact his students called that sweater his "touch me" sweater since the cashmere looked downright pettable, or the utter predictability of him not having something as pedestrian as deli turkey in his kitchen, or my realization that him cheating really invalidated our agreement to let him critique my last essay for Professor Burton—but I kept my mouth busy with food and waited for *him* to break the ice this time.

A few silent minutes later, he did.

"So you grew up in a small town like this, right?" he asked. "Little Pippin Hollow? Did you ever have dreams to move to the big city the way I dreamed of leaving it?"

I nodded. "Oh yeah. Still do. I was interviewing for a bunch of corporate jobs in New York and Boston last spring before... you know," I said, giving him a significant look. I hurried on, "It's not that I don't love small-town life. I'm gonna miss it, to be honest. But small towns really aren't practical if your goal is to make money."

"And that's your goal?" he asked, like the idea surprised him.

"Basically." I chomped a carrot stick. "See, my oldest brother, Knox, moved down to Boston and made a killing at his finance job for, like, ten years before moving back to Little Pippin Hollow. He helped put my brother and me through school, even though I was kind of a pain in the ass to him when we were kids—"

"You, Sunday?" Theo clutched a hand to his chest in faux shock. "Never say so."

I snickered. "It's all part of my charm. Anyway, it's not that our family was poor, really—not like some of the kids at the Hub who have to deal with food insecurity and not knowing if the electricity will stay on. But there were six of us Sunday kids, so there wasn't a lot of extra. Definitely no college funds and not a lot of money for daydreaming about the future, if you know what I mean. If my brother hadn't been super generous... well, it would have taken a lot more than two years of me commuting to Hannabury part-time for me to save up the money to become a full-time student, you know? And that really inspired me—"

He whistled low. "You worked two years to save money before you enrolled full-time?"

"Sure." I shrugged. "I worked nights and took a class or two every semester. I'm not scared of hard work, especially if it's for a purpose. And that's my point. I figure, once I've worked at a corporate job for a while and I've saved up a bunch, I'll be able to do good things like Knox did. Endow a scholarship for the kids at the Hub. Maybe more than one. And I'll give the Hub enough money to actually hire a full staff, too. Because those kids... they're *so* fucking bright. They need someone to make sure they're dreaming big, and they need to know someone's ready to invest in their futures when the time comes, the way Knox did for me. I swear, one of them is gonna cure cancer—probably Raquon, who's a little science geek with the sweetest heart. And one of them is gonna write the great American novel—I'm guessing Laci, who's thirteen and started a Bookstagram where she reviews YA stuff. And definitely one of 'em's gonna come up with a taco recipe that will revolutionize the taco industry because Edgar's only nine, but he has a really well-developed taco palate. It'll be a fucking crime if these kids don't get to pursue their passions."

Theo looked at me strangely. "And meanwhile, you're gonna be working a 'corporate job' somewhere. Not even a specific corporate job? Just… whatever they'll pay you the most for? What about *your* passion?"

"I don't really have one. Not yet, anyway. It's like we were talking about with you taking the Hannabury job." I nibbled a pita chip thoughtfully. "Serendipity, right? But it didn't just happen out of nowhere. It happened because you already had an impressive resume and track record at Brown before you took the step of applying for the job up here. It all kinda came together because you were in the right place at the right time with the right skills. I'm hoping the same will happen for me. I'll start making money to do the things I want to do, and then… you know, the passion will come."

He shook his head, looking a little like he had in class last semester. Like I was somehow missing the obvious. "Porter. You don't think you've found your passion yet?"

"Nope." I shrugged again. "Well, I mean, I love Sunday Orchard. I do. And if they needed me, I'd move back and help out in a heartbeat. But Knox is back in the Hollow now. He and his boyfriend are working alongside my second-oldest brother, Webb, and his husband, and… they all really enjoy it. Way more than I would. Which is handy because if I moved back there, I'd end up being 'Porter, the fourth Sunday sibling' again. As much as I love my family, I've gotta say, I like being known for who I am now, as an adult, rather than for the shit I pulled as a kid. I watch my brother Hawk struggle with the same thing. He loves the Hollow too much to leave, but it's been hard for him to break away from people's expectations. Like, I baked a cake for my Scout troop leader's birthday once, and everyone loved it, but that doesn't mean I want to be known as the Scout Cake Kid forever," I said with a chuckle. "You know?"

Theo shook his head, but he was smiling, too. "I grew up in Manhattan. We didn't do Scout cakes. But I know what you mean. People became known for what their parents did—for better or worse. Or for what neighborhood they lived in. Or for being the kid whose uncle was in that music video that one time. That kind of thing. It was very… superficial." He dragged a pita chip through the hummus. "Gotta say, I can't really see you in that life, Porter."

"Yeah?" The way he described it, I wasn't sure either, to be honest. "Well, if I find I hate it, I'll pivot. I'm not too worried. I'm really good with people."

"So why not stay in Hannabury and make a difference here?"

"Uh…" I blinked. "Did you not hear the part about the small town, no jobs thing? I'm working at the Hub right now, and they don't have enough money to pay me for all the hours I work, let alone to hire the program director they really need. If I stayed on after graduation, I wouldn't be able to pay my own rent without taking help from my family."

Theo nodded seriously and stared out the window at the snow that had started coming down again. "What if we could come up with a way for you to get the money?"

"Oh, sure." I snorted. "Prostitution, perhaps? Or, I know! I'll start a soliloquy-delivery service. Kinda like a singing telegram but *fancier*. For that hard-to-please professor in your life—"

"Creative non-fiction, Porter." Theo rolled his eyes. "You

know, the shit I tried to teach you? Well-crafted creative non-fiction can literally save lives. I can prove it to you." He leaned back in his chair.

I felt like I'd walked directly into his trap. "Back to this again?" I sighed. "I have no idea how you critiquing my writing will help, but I suppose you technically won the challenge earlier, so fine." I pushed back from the table and spread my arms wide. "I'm yours to command for the next two hours, Professor."

My words fell into the space between us like a molten-hot hand grenade with the pin already pulled. Sexual innuendo seemed to pour freely from my mouth, whether it was intended or not.

Theo inhaled a deep breath as if gearing up for the most impressive I-told-you-so lecture ever, full of "profound" advice about narrative and essay structure.

"What are some ways you could get money to fund a director position at the Hub?" he asked.

I frowned. His practical approach took the wind out of my sails and left me scrambling for a response. "Uh. Ask wealthy donors for contributions? Apply for grants? I don't know. Things like that?"

He nodded. "You got it in one. There are over a hundred thousand private foundations in this country alone. How do you get one to care about *your* program more than the others they get bombarded with? What makes the Hub special?"

"*Pfft*. I think that's pretty obvious. The Hub takes care of a really vulnerable, underserved population. It gives children a safe place to play after school, access to tutoring and mental health services." I tried to think of the other kinds of information charitable foundations might find critical. "You know, this year alone, the Hub will serve two hundred thirty-six children aged four to fourteen, from Hannabury and surrounding towns in Averill County, which has an average per capita income that's below the—"

Theo held up his hand. "Stop. You're telling me about the soil properties again, Porter. Dry facts."

I grit my teeth in annoyance. "Facts are important."

"Sometimes," he allowed. "But tell me the facts from *here*." He poked the center of my chest. "Like I'm sitting next to you having a snack, and you just found out I have fifty grand burning a hole in my pocket. Make it specific. Make it personal. Make me feel something. Tell me a story and convince me."

I struggled to come up with the kind of proposal concept he was looking for. "But... it's non-fiction," I said. "Facts aren't the same as a story."

He nodded excitedly. "Okay, see, now I think I understand what you don't understand."

I opened my mouth to say, *Good for you, I'm still lost*, when Theo cleared his throat and removed his glasses so he could buff the lenses on the softness of his shirt.

"There's a display of approximately one hundred seventeen old fishing lures that hangs at the Hannabury Courthouse. The lures were amateur construction, tied over a period of approximately thirty years. Some are quite intricately tied. Many appear to never have been used." He put his glasses back on. "You can go and check them out anytime the courthouse is open if you'd like to see them."

"What?" I wrinkled my nose in confusion. "I mean, I'm sure they're great if you're into fishing, but..."

"But you're not convinced? No. I'm not surprised. Okay, how about this." Theo cleared his throat and focused on nothing again. "When I was young, my grandfather made fishing lures out of dental floss and old bracelet beads from the thrift booth at the town's open-air market in summer. We would go into town every Saturday morning without fail and get two things: Hildie Upton's pumpkin spice muffins and any cheap broken beaded jewelry Morris Newton had in his stall that week. Then we would come back here and sit on the front porch, eating muffins and tying up flies, over and over again. Gramps made so many that after he died, I put together a display panel of intricate, hand-tied lures and donated them to the Hannabury Courthouse. They're currently hanging outside the judge's chamber because Judge Farino spent hours fishing with Gramps, and they remind him of good times on the river, but I like to think they're a part of the history of this town, too. Of how one person's castoffs became something more." Theo looked back at me. "Now, would you like to see them?"

I opened my mouth, then shut it again. *Yes. Yes, I really would.* But he already knew that.

Theo tapped his pointer finger on the table. "Every word of both stories was non-fiction, Porter. Every single thing I said was a fact. It's not about what you tell; it's about *how* you tell it."

I wanted to argue with him. "It can't be that simple," I insisted. "No one will give fifty grand to someone because I tell them a story."

"The movie adaptation of *Sully*, about the plane that landed in the Hudson River, grossed over $125 million dollars."

"That's…" We both knew I wanted to say it was different, but it wasn't.

"Tell me a story," Theo said in a gentle voice. "Just me. Right here. Don't think about it, just give me one story of how the Hub has helped someone, even if that someone is you."

The program *had* helped me, but it had helped many others way more than that. I opened my mouth and began telling Theo story after story of kids and parents I'd met through the program. One story became two, until I was telling him stories of people we'd changed for the better and far sadder stories of families we hadn't been able to help. Success stories and stories of heartbreaking failure where lack of resources had become a true impediment to getting kids onto a healthy path toward a thriving future.

We—or mostly *I*—talked for more than two hours, with Theo only interjecting here and there to point out how my stories could be adapted or crafted into clearer, more powerful expressions of the truth I wanted to convey—that a program like the Hub could do so much good if given enough funding for capable, consistent leadership.

He took off his glasses and made us a snack of coffee and cookies. I twisted in my chair, bringing one foot up on my seat and wrapping my arm around my knee. We were Theo and Porter. Equals. Almost, sort of, friends.

Those hours with him were eye-opening. Life-changing.

Years ago, Theo had been the one to show me that words were powerful—that was why I'd become an English major in the first place. Figured that now, he was the one to show me how and *why* they were powerful, by reminding me that the key was tying facts to emotions, even (or maybe especially) in creative non-fiction.

As the light began to fade outside, our discussion changed from grant proposals to true crime podcasts, biased journalism, and the fine lines involved in using non-fiction as entertainment.

After deciding to set my ego aside, I asked him a million questions about how he'd learned so much about creative non-fiction when his specialty was Renaissance poetry.

"Milton wrote a sonnet about the Duke of Savoy slaughtering the Waldensians in 1655." He gave me a wry smile. "I know... Poetry nerd much, Theo?"

I grinned. I'd been thinking more like *sexy* poetry nerd, but he wasn't wrong. "Go on."

"The poem is written like a prayer for vengeance, but it also serves as a historical record of the massacre. It's emotional, heart-wrenching. In it, he describes the Piedmontese throwing mothers with babies down the mountainside to their deaths, but it's done with this…" He searched for the right word. "This anger and impotent rage at the injustice. You can't help but feel very differently than if you'd simply heard a list of the historical facts in a bullet-point sidebar of a history book."

He met my eyes. "If I tell you there was a battle at Piedmont with two fatalities, you will shrug and move on. It happened so long ago, who really cares? But what if I tell you, *'Forget not: in thy book record their groans / Who were thy sheep and in their ancient fold / Slain by the bloody Piemontese that roll'd / Mother with infant down the rocks. Their moans / The vales redoubl'd to the hills, and they / To Heav'n. Their martyr'd blood and ashes sow / O'er all th' Italian fields where still doth sway / The triple tyrant; that from these may grow / A hundred-fold, who having learnt thy way /Early may fly the Babylonian woe.'*? And now what if I add that the triple tyrant refers to the pope?"

Hearing him recite poetry always fired me up, but this… when he was making such a strong point… reached into my gut and squeezed it tight.

"Yeah," I breathed. Better words failed me.

"William Hazlitt called it 'prophetic fury.' Prophetic fury in iambic pentameter. It's… seductive. And it has the power to reach deep into the heart and soul of humanity and change the course of events. Do you see what I mean?"

I did. And now I could see so clearly why he'd been frustrated with me last semester. I'd tried so hard to make my assignments "perfect" that I'd completely missed the point of making them *impactful*.

"Yeah," I said again. "I really do. That's… that's amazing. Thank you, Theo. I, uh… It's possible that I might have gone into last semester with a bit of a chip on my shoulder."

Theo nodded and stretched his arms up high so that his shirt rode up over his abs, and the sight made my mouth dry. "Yeah? Well. Happens to the best of us. But let that be a lesson."

"I kinda wish I could take the class with you again instead of Professor Burton." I grinned. "Not enough to stick around for another semester, mind you…"

"Eh." He shrugged and reached for his half-empty coffee mug. His long fingers wrapped firmly around the ceramic, and the muscles in his throat worked as he swallowed. "Now that you know, you'll do better. And Burton wouldn't fail you right now if you turned in ten pages of lorum ipsum, so it'll all work out fine."

"I'm not really happy with fine," I admitted. "I want to be the best."

"Is that so?" He leaned forward again, resting his chin on his hand. The entire force of his attention was centered on me, and it was heady as fuck. "Then pick a topic I might disagree with you on. Spin me a passionate tale using only facts. Win me over with the heat of your argument, Porter. Make it personal."

I frowned, trying to think of a topic we disagreed about… and just like that, his earlier disgust at the idea of kissing me came roaring back to life in my mind.

I couldn't help but grin as I looked at Theo across the table. What better way to prove my words had power than to convince Professor Hot-Cock to kiss me against his better judgment?

Game. On.

CHAPTER SIX

THEO

I HAD to admit to feeling just a little smug. After months of disappointment and frustration, I'd finally been able to prove my point to Porter by teaching him the power of a well-crafted piece of non-fiction. Now it was just a matter of providing constructive criticism to help him through his first attempt.

"I'm going to make some phone calls about tree removal while you get your thoughts together," I said before standing up and stretching again. I pulled out my laptop to look up the numbers I needed.

The second company I called said they'd be able to come out Monday morning if I was lucky, whereas the first company didn't even answer their phones due to the demand. I booked in for Monday and called one of my neighbors to ask about how the mountain roads were. According to him, our section of the mountain was blocked in on all sides by other downed trees. Thankfully, there was no evidence of car accidents or personal injuries in the area. After I hung up, I told Porter what I'd learned.

"Neighbor said we'd be lucky to get the road cleared tomorrow. Earliest they can do my driveway is Monday.

You're stuck here for at least three more nights." We were stuck *together* that long. And my bed hadn't gotten any bigger. In fact, I was pretty sure it shrank every time I glanced at it.

"Okay. I guess that's plenty of time for me to make a convincing argument, then, huh?" Porter said brightly.

"You think it's going to take you three days?" I deadpanned.

"I suppose it depends on how stubborn you are," he said.

The teasing light in his eyes as he gestured for me to take my seat at the table again should have been my first clue that I was in trouble. Then he began to speak.

"My first kiss was with a girl named Rochelle."

I blinked and opened my mouth to protest—what possible subject could he be arguing that began with an admission like that? I was afraid I knew—but then I shut it again.

He was twenty-six years old. An adult man who knew his mind. I was an adult, too, and capable of listening without being swayed. Wasn't I the one who'd told him to make his argument personal?

"Go on," I said roughly.

"I was sixteen at the time—we both were—but I'd been attracted to guys and *only* guys for several years by then. I hadn't officially come out, but I was pretty confident I was gay. My family low-key knew it. Rochelle knew it. Heck, the whole *town* knew it, and no one was very surprised since I already had two gay brothers and a gay uncle, and the Sundays were developing a bit of a reputation for being pretty gay. But Rochelle's father was the minister at a very fundamentalist church in Two Rivers, the next town over from Little Pippin Hollow. And Rochelle was a bit of a rebel. So she kissed me, out of the blue, right in the stands at the Averill Union Beavers football game one Friday night, just to prove a point. And it was..."

Curiosity drew me forward, almost against my will. "Yes?"

"It was *electric*," Porter whispered, his gaze holding mine. "Her fruity lip gloss, the baby powder scent of her, the way her mouth felt on mine… Christ, it did things to me. By halftime, I was having a full-blown sexuality crisis. Did this mean I liked girls? That I liked Rochelle? Was that possible? What would my family say if I came out as *straight*?" His lips turned up at the memory. "It took me a while—and a couple more kisses—to realize that it wasn't *her* I wanted. I'd been seduced by the forbidden. By the idea of doing something a little rebellious and a little wrong. Ultimately, I figured out it was way more fun to do that with guys." He glanced down at his fingers playing with the handle of his empty mug and laughed softly before meeting my eyes again. "Like *way* more fun."

I'll just bet it was. I swallowed hard and sat back in my chair, remembering my own first kiss. It hadn't been nearly that exciting… or maybe it was just the way Porter told the story.

Figured the man would be a natural now that he understood the assignment.

"After high school, when I started hooking up with guys more often, I chased that high," Porter went on. "Didn't take me long to learn that while it might be enticing to, say, kiss a straight guy who might not acknowledge me the next day or to hook up with someone in the stacks at the library on campus, the lure of the forbidden fizzled out really, really fast. There had to be more substance there for me to want more than a single kiss."

He paused for a moment, and I found myself fiddling with my glasses before taking them off and leaning in again. I wanted to hear more. Imagining him kissing other men—in the Hannabury library, for fuck's sake—gave me a strange, toxic combination of excitement and jealousy. A sick, elated feeling deep in my gut, like the sweet pain that came from touching a bruise.

Porter looked up and met my eyes. "A couple of years ago, I was walking past your classroom, and you were reading sonnets aloud to your class. It was the first time I heard your voice. And just like that—" He snapped his fingers. "I was attracted to you. Instant, holy-fuck, stop-me-in-my-tracks attraction. The kind of attraction that makes a person want to do foolish things, like declare an English major…"

"Porter…" I choked out. Every nerve in my body was standing at attention, dying to hear the rest of the story—*Oh, shit. He was attracted to me, even then? He'd declared an English major because of me?* But the few remaining shreds of sanity in my brain trembled like overused muscles under the onslaught of words and needed him to shut up immediately before they caved.

My attraction to him was already a stack of tinder soaked in high-octane fuel… and Porter held a fistful of matches.

He continued his story as if I hadn't spoken. "Of course, at the time, I didn't know who you were. No clue what you looked like. The only thing I knew about you was the sound of your voice reading poetry, and… it went straight to my balls. I just knew I could listen to you recite iambic pentameter for hours on end and never get tired of it." His cheeks flushed with the admission, but he didn't look away. "It wasn't until later that I figured out who you were. Dr. Theo Hancock—aka *Doctor Hot-Cock,* the most gorgeous professor on campus…" he said hoarsely. "And a total jackass."

I sucked in a shivery breath, and in my mind's eye, one match scratched down the striker in slow motion.

The world was tilting, sliding. I couldn't right it, and I wasn't sure if I should.

"Porter," I breathed again.

He shook his head at me, paying no more attention to me now than before. "I know what you're thinking. It's the lure of the forbidden, right? That's what made me so hot for you? Maybe so. All last semester, I fantasized about you. Couldn't stop. You'd be talking, and I'd wonder what it would be like if I shut you up with my mouth on yours. With my mouth on… well… *other* places of yours." He exhaled. "I was so full of these thoughts I avoided you like the plague. I didn't dare come to your office hours for fear I'd do or say something inappropriate. Hell, half my fantasies took place in your fucking office, and I figured if I ever spent any time there, I'd spontaneously combust."

I couldn't force myself out of the chair to walk away from the conversation, even though I knew it needed to be done. Instead, I sat there, silently begging for more.

"But I'd learned my lesson long before then, you know?" he went on softly. "I wasn't gonna act on this attraction because I knew better than to want something simply because it was forbidden."

"Oh," I said on an exhale. "Good. Right."

His green eyes met mine. *Held.* "Then class ended. And I still couldn't stop thinking about it. God, I was so angry at you, Theo. At times, I thought I hated you. But even so, I still craved your kiss. So now, I can't help wondering… what does that mean? Is it really the forbidden that makes me want you as much as I do? Or is there something more there, a true attraction that could lead to something incendiary? I need to know…"

Time sat heavily between us while the match caught fire with a dangerous flare of heat.

Porter ran his tongue over his bottom lip, then finished in a whisper, "…and I figure there's one surefire way to find out."

I wanted to punish him for stirring me up this way. To prove him wrong. To show him once and for all he was only after it for the thrill of the thing. He couldn't possibly want me for any other reason than that. He'd already established how much he disliked me.

What else was there to know?

I lunged across the table and crashed my mouth into his.

His hands came out to clutch at my sweater to keep from tipping backward in the chair. He tasted like sweet, creamy coffee with a hint of the oatmeal cookies we'd eaten after lunch. The scratch of his stubble abraded my palms as I held his face to mine and devoured that sultry mouth.

The mouth that had teased me all day, that had tortured me last spring, that had cycled through my dreams more times than I could count...

The reality of it blew those dreams away. I couldn't stop. He was like Sisyphus, who'd slyly asked Thanatos to demonstrate the chains, and I was Thanatos, bound up in them for all eternity.

Porter's throat and mouth made noises that went straight to my dick. My brain begged me to stop kissing him, to get us back onto safer footing, but my body simply refused. It was too good, and rational thinking could go to hell.

Thankfully, I wasn't the only one overwhelmed with desire. Porter grabbed my shoulders and pulled me closer until I fumbled around the table between us and ended up straddling his lap. His hands moved down my back and up under my sweater. As soon as the dry skin of his palms skimmed up my bare back, my entire body erupted in goose bumps.

I wanted this kid, this *man*, more than I'd wanted anything for as long as I could remember. With my one remaining functional brain cell, I finally ripped my mouth from his and leaned back. "Wait. *Wait*. Fuck. Wait."

Porter's pupils were blown, inky black eating up the vivid green. His cheeks were flushed, and his lips were shiny from the kiss.

My kiss.

"This is—" I began, but he clamped a hand over my mouth.

"Don't say it," he growled. "If you fucking dare tell me it's wrong or some other high-minded bullshit, so help me, I'll—"

I yanked his hand away and kissed him again, grabbing the back of his head to keep him pressed tightly against me. He groaned into the kiss and tightened his arms around me. For several hungry beats, we explored each other again until I could barely breathe. I pulled away again.

"Okay, wait. I just… give me a minute. Okay?"

Our audible panting filled the room with leftover heat and desperation.

"It's not the forbidden thing, Theo," Porter said firmly. "It's more than that."

Yes. It was definitely more than that, for both of us. But that didn't make it *right*.

I moved off his lap and made it back to my own chair, leaning forward with my elbows on my knees so I could wiggle my hips to adjust my strangled dick.

"We can't do this," I said, holding up my hand. "And before you argue with me, please understand I am not saying I don't want to. Clearly, I want to very, very much. But I am months away from becoming head of the very department you're graduating from. I know that I'm not your professor anymore, but I—"

"No one needs to find out."

A small puff of air escaped me. Christ, he really was temptation incarnate.

"Right now, we're going to take a few deep breaths and slow down," I said, speaking to myself more than to him. "I'm not saying no, Porter. I'm saying… wait."

Porter inhaled a deep breath through his nose and held it before letting it out. "Okay. You're right. I don't want to do anything you'll regret."

Once again, I was surprised by his maturity and under-standing, even though I shouldn't have been. Porter Sunday wasn't the typical undergrad. He was a twenty-six-year-old man who'd worked hard to get himself into college. A man who was so devoted to his work helping underprivileged children at the Hub, it seemed like he spent more of his hours there each week as an unpaid volunteer than as a paid employee. It took a special person to do that. To care as much as he did.

"Dinner," I said, pushing myself to stand and stretch and trying very hard to block out the memory of Porter's mouth on mine, his hands on me, and the sound of his whimpers and groans in my ears. I put my glasses back on, like they were some kind of armor. "Maybe you can grab us a couple of beers."

We moved efficiently into awkward mode, moving around the tiny kitchen space without touching each other. I didn't want things to be uncomfortable between us. Despite our antagonistic semester earlier in the year, and wholly aside from this conflagration of desire between us, I found I *liked* Porter Sunday. More than I'd expected.

Once I'd served the stew and placed the wide bowls at each of our places on the table, I sat back down and held my beer bottle out for a toast. "To unexpected snowstorm company."

He smiled back. "To impromptu angry sonnet perfor-mances, and the gracious unwilling hosts of those performances."

I chuckled.

We clinked our bottles and took a sip before diving into the meal. Thankfully, the outdoor work had burned off enough calories that I was hungry for dinner despite the snack platter we'd shared a few hours earlier.

"You should know, you have a lot of friends in the English department," I told him. "Jean Chenault thinks you're the second coming of Alan Ginsburg, and Sally Diaz basically forced me to read that sonnet of yours that was published in the student magazine. It was… incredible, honestly."

His cheeks flushed. "That's nice to hear. But creative *fiction* hasn't really been my problem." He winked at me, which made my stomach tighten. "I have a very good imagination."

I couldn't help but chuckle. "Seems like creative non-fiction isn't really a problem for you anymore either," I admitted wryly. "You were, ah… extremely convincing a minute ago."

"Really?" His eyes sparkled, and it made my pulse speed. "No notes, Professor? No in-depth critique of my performance?"

I licked my lips, chasing the lingering taste of Porter. "Nope." I forced myself to eat another bite of stew before getting us back on a comfortable track. "So… does your family know you like to write?"

"They know I write. I wouldn't say I *like* to write necessarily. I love to read, and I share that passion with my brother Hawk—he's an even bigger reader than I am—but for some reason, I find it hard to sit still long enough to spend much time writing. I prefer being outside or being active. *Doing* life, instead of writing about it. You know?"

"Oh yeah. I'm the same. It's one of the reasons I moved here. Living in the city made me feel… unmoored, a bit. Removed from the outdoors. Walking in a park or along the river is so structured. It's not the same as hiking in the woods. And I like being able to work on projects with plenty of room to spread out. I have plans to replace the tool shed with a big workshop so I can work on some DIY projects easily in winter. Eventually, I want to add on to the cabin and build it out a bit."

"You definitely need a dedicated bedroom," Porter decided. "And what if…"

His eyes got dreamy as he started brainstorming renovations, and we even pulled out a notebook to sketch various layouts. Porter had insightful ideas and explained several of the building projects he'd helped with on his family's orchard over the years.

"I do miss that kind of work," he said, pushing his bowl away and leaning back in his chair. It was the first time I'd missed having a comfortable sofa or seating area for us to move to for the evening. He'd been right earlier when he'd commented about my place not being ideal for having company over. Hopefully, the expansion I planned would allow me to turn this central room into a living room instead of my bedroom.

"You're welcome to come up here and help out anytime," I said without thinking. "There's always plenty of work to do. Clearing scrub, chopping and hauling wood, fixing things that seem to break every time I turn around."

"I'd like that. But I, uh… I don't know where I'll be after the semester is done."

"Oh, right." I stood to bring our bowls to the sink. "Have you started looking for a job?"

"Sort of? I got to the second round of interviews at a couple places last spring, but then I didn't graduate. I'm planning to follow up with some of them, but I don't know if that'll work. I had to tell Parabola Media down in New York that I failed a class and they needed to remove my name from contention…"

I turned and crossed my arms. "You're welcome."

Porter's mouth dropped open in surprise. "Excuse you? They were going to pay me eighty-five grand a year!"

"Parabola Media are a bunch of vampires who'd work you into the ground and steal away every shred of joy you possess," I corrected. "I've known people who worked there, and it never ended well. Seriously, Porter, name one person you know who went to work for a big-city media or marketing company who's happy right now. Go on, I'll wait."

His nostrils flared, and his mouth opened, but then he shut it again. "I don't happen to know any personally, but…"

"Uh-huh. And how much was your rent going to be?" I added. "For a lifeless box you'd only see in the dark of night."

"We already talked about this, Theo. I want to make money so I can do good with it. The best place to make money is the city. And the passion will come, if I…"

"Damn it, Porter, for a guy who's so incredibly smart, you're being so incredibly dumb. You've already *found* your passion. You want to work with the kids at the Hub."

"And you want me to write grants for that? Great. And assuming I write the most compelling proposals ever and donors start flinging money at me left and right, how long will it take for me to see that money? And what will I live off in the meantime? No trust fund, remember? And nobody left me an *inheritance-cabin* either." He threw his arms out to encompass my little house. "My plan is the best one I can think of."

It was on the tip of my tongue to offer for him to stay. To live with me. But I bit it back. This place was barely big enough for one person, let alone two. And I wouldn't be able to have him in my space like this if we were simply going to be… friends.

"I'm sorry, Porter," I said. He glanced at me in surprise. "Not for failing you, because I stand by that decision. But I'm sorry for interfering in your future plans. I just…"

He raised both eyebrows. "Just…?"

"I just want you to be happy," I admitted. "I want you to live your dream."

A teasing twinkle appeared in those green eyes I knew I'd be fantasizing about for a long, long time. "Really? Then sleep with me, Professor Hot-Cock. That's one dream you can make come true easily. And I promise you, it will for damned sure make me happy."

His words made my heart take off running in my chest

like a scared rabbit being chased by a pack of rabid wolves. It was terrifying and exciting in equal measure.

"I told you," I said, trying one last time to do the right thing. "It would be incredibly risky for both of us if anyone found out—"

"Theo. We're stuck in your house in a freaking blizzard, because a tree fell down after I came out here to rage-recite poetry at you, because you failed me last semester, because I was too fucking attracted to you to actually have a conversation and figure out what I was supposed to be doing for my assignments. It's already the most ridiculous of circumstances, so why not add one last wild and crazy thing to the mix? When the road is clear and I leave here, we'll forget this ever happened."

I snorted. "Impossible." Forgetting had seemed unlikely before I'd actually gotten to know Porter. Before I'd kissed him. Before I'd…

Porter stood up and moved into my personal space. Our chests brushed, and I felt one of his knees push my legs apart. He deliberately removed my glasses, folded them neatly, and set them on the table. "Give me this," he breathed, leaning in but not quite touching his nose to my cheek. "Please."

He was a taunting child, daring me to fling myself off a tall cliff into deep water.

And it was crystal clear I was going to jump happily and enjoy the entire blessed ride down.

CHAPTER SEVEN

IF YOU ASKED anyone in Little Pippin Hollow, they'd tell you Porter Sunday was the persuasive one. The one who shook down his older brothers for candy money and made sure every kid on the playground got an equal number of turns, even if I had to throw a royal fit to make it happen.

So maybe it shouldn't have been a surprise that I was being obstinate and pushy with Theo. Not when he was trying to deny us both something we clearly wanted.

Theo Hancock was fire, and I craved heat enough to enjoy the burn.

"Please," I whispered again, brushing my nose along his cheek until my lips reached his earlobe. His skin was warm and sweet with a hint of salt. My teeth clamped lightly down on the plump lobe as I sucked it.

His arms came around me in a sudden clamp, holding me tightly as he turned his head to press his open mouth to my neck. "One time. That's it."

"Not enough," I gasped as one of his hands moved down to grab my ass.

"This is not up for negotiation. Once is all I can give," he growled between nips of my skin. "Take it or leave it."

"T-take," I said, unable to believe this was real. This was happening. "Take me. Take whatever you want."

Never had I sounded so desperate, so willing to do any and everything he might want of me. But I was.

Theo strong-armed me over to the bed before putting his hands on my shoulders and pushing me down until I sat on the edge of the bed. He loomed over me, the intensity of his gaze burning my gut and hardening my dick.

"What do you want, Porter?"

My mouth hung open in paralyzed disbelief. How did I admit to him I was putty for him to mold and manipulate according to his own whims?

The edge of his lips curled up. "I like you like this. *Speechless*. It's refreshing. Unexpected." He leaned in and ran the tip of his tongue along the edge of my ear. The deep rumble of his voice vibrated through my chest. "Sexy."

An embarrassing noise of submission escaped my throat. "I'm never like this," I breathed. "Usually, I'm..."

His hands distracted me as they reached for the hem of my shirt and pulled it over my head. "You're?"

My breaths came shallow and fast. "I'm..."

"Hm, let me guess." He ran his hands across my chest and shoulders, down to my biceps, where he squeezed them in appreciation. "Bossy."

I huffed out a laugh. "Assertive. Strategic. Persuasive."

"Mm." He leaned over and dropped an open-mouthed kiss to one shoulder before dragging his tongue down my arm and nipping the tender skin inside my elbow. "You're awfully pliable for someone so assertive."

Amusement lit his eyes, but they still held enough heat to make my cock leak. I shifted my hips. "Only for you."

Theo knelt down between my feet and looked up at me. The sight of him there between my knees made me dizzy. My eyelids closed, and I concentrated on not passing the fuck out.

"Gonna come like this," I murmured under my breath. "In borrowed pants. With you fully dressed."

He reached out a hand and cupped my erection, squeezing all the blood I currently owned and making black spots edge my vision. I sucked in a breath and thought of spiders.

"Look at me."

I blinked my eyes open in time to see him pulling the touch-me sweater over his head. I thought of all the students who would pay money to watch this man disrobe. He could make millions, a dollar at a time, doing a naughty-professor striptease.

When he was finally shirtless, the defined muscles of his chest and shoulders revealed just how much time he must spend in his outdoor pursuits. He wasn't big like I was, but he definitely could wipe the floor in a wood-chopping competition with the average college professor.

"Fuck," I said, squeezing my eyes closed again. The low rumble of his laugh made my stomach erupt in nervous bubbles. I liked this, liked *him*. The experience of this simple, flirty hookup was more exciting than every interlude I'd ever had with another man.

How was that possible?

Theo's hands moved up to yank at the cord holding the elastic waistband in place at my hips. "Stand." Once I stood up, he pulled them down to my ankles and helped me step out of them until my hard dick bobbed in front of his face.

"Feed me your cock, Mr. Sunday," he teased, meeting my eyes again with a knowing look. He was very aware of what he was doing to me.

"I will come on your face before that happens," I bit out between clenched teeth. "You even open those lips, and I —*ohfuck!*"

The wet heat of his mouth engulfed me as his fingers bit into my bare hips and ass to hold me in place. I grabbed for

Theo's hair and held him in place. His tongue bathed my cock with toe-curling pressure until the black spots in my vision turned into exploding stars.

"Fuck, fuck," I barked into the small space around us. Thankfully, he had no neighbors to hear me. "Oh god. Oh."

When my orgasm ended and his affectionate sucks and teasing licks slowed down, I fell onto my ass on the bed again and buried my face in my hands.

There was no need to say, "I told you so." Surely the warm salt of my release on his tongue was proof enough I hadn't been exaggerating.

Theo stood up and scrambled to get his pants down before taking himself in hand and jerking off with his dick in one hand and a firm grip on my shoulder in the other. The muffled grunts and gasps coming from his throat were mesmerizing, and I lifted my head to watch.

Professor Hot-Cock was stroking himself off inches from me. Just as I leaned in to return the favor of his delicious mouth on me, he erupted. His hot spunk hit my chest and chin, but before he even finished coming, he'd grabbed the back of my head to crush his lips to mine.

We both scrambled back on the bed, coming together in a sticky tangle of naked arms and legs while we kissed frantically before finally slowing back down to soft touches and sweet kisses. It wasn't enough.

"You'd better not say that was my one time," I warned. "Because that didn't count. At all."

He lifted an eyebrow. "Are you saying the performance didn't reach your lofty standards?"

I rolled him onto his back and climbed on top of him, lazily cleaning us up with a balled-up tee before kissing his stubble-burned lips and cheeks. "That's right. You didn't understand the assignment, Theo. I give it an *F* for effort."

"How about an *F* for fuck?" he said with a laugh, squeezing my ass in his hands and pulling my cheeks apart.

"God, yes."

He continued to laugh as I teased him with kisses on his most ticklish spots. He was sexy as hell. The fantasy of getting naked with him didn't hold a candle to the reality.

When I lowered myself down his body to his dick, he tried to warn me he needed more time. "I'm not twenty-six," he said without a trace of embarrassment. I appreciated his confidence. It was something I'd been attracted to all along.

"I'm not in a hurry." I continued to explore his body, running soft fingertips down the inside of his thighs and around the back of his knees before feeling the toned muscles of his calves. "You're sexy as fuck. One night isn't going to be enough to enjoy all of you."

Theo sat up and ran his fingers through my hair. "If you weren't a student…"

I crawled forward and straddled him, grasping his jaw in my palms. "If I wasn't a student… what? What would you do?"

He leaned in and kissed me slowly. Deliberately.

Thoroughly.

"I'd chain you to this bed and spend way more than a weekend with you," he murmured against my lips.

My heart hammered against my ribs. "Would you? Or are you cum-drunk? Those words sound awfully oxytocin and dopamine-laced…"

He pulled back and met my eyes. His mouth no longer curved up, and his eyes no longer held the teasing sparkle from earlier. "Porter… this isn't the sex talking. I was drawn to you when you were my student. Even before I knew I *liked* you, I couldn't resist you. So confident. So friendly. So passionate. So talented. Even when you kept fucking up in my class and I wanted to write you off, I couldn't. You drove me crazy, but there was something about you that…" Theo shook his head like he, the master of words, was suddenly unable to articulate what he wanted to say. "It was like the first time I read T.S. Eliot— I knew I only under-stood a fraction of it, but I couldn't put it down. The cadence and the rhythm spoke to me, and I needed to uncover all its layers, even if I had to read it a hundred times."

The things he said, the serious way he said them, thrilled me to the core. It was hard to believe this person I'd wanted for so long could possibly want me just as much. I knew Theo wouldn't lie about it—that wasn't him… but there had to be a catch.

"But I'm too young, right?" I prompted. "For you to want anything serious with me."

"Are those your words, or do you think they're mine?" The familiar tones of his professor voice came through, calm and deliberate.

I chewed at my lip while I considered. "I worry you wouldn't give me a real chance even if I wasn't a student in your department."

Theo reached out to pull my lip from my teeth. "And why would *you* want to be with someone who's a *grumpy, life-destroying jerk*?"

I snorted. It should have felt awkward having this impor-tant conversation while sticky and itchy with his dried release on my skin. But it didn't. Being with him was easier than I'd ever imagined it would be.

"Aren't you the one who said people can be more than one thing?" I teased. "It's called being a *mature and fully artic-ulate human being.*"

"So you *did* hear that part," he grumbled. "Figures."

"You are grumpy," I went on. "Sometimes. Though, I'll note, that didn't stop me from having a *major* crush on you. But now…" I ran a hand through his messy hair. "This is a very different side of you. And I like it. I already knew you were gorgeous and smart as hell, but you *care*. You care about your students. You care about teaching. You care about improving lives. And you're not afraid to work hard to get shit done, even if it means breaking a sweat."

His eyes reclaimed some of their teasing sparkle, and his thumbs caressed my jaw. "You trying to get me to break a sweat right now?"

"Definitely. But that's not all." I tried to put my thoughts and feelings into words. My stomach swirled with nerves, but if he was being serious… I didn't want to lose a chance with him because I couldn't make my case. *Make it personal*, right? Speak from the heart? Okay, I could do that.

"The thing is, Theo, everything I've learned about you just makes me want to learn more. You're funny and kind. Generous and protective. Sexy as fuck. But also… I think you're looking for something, just like I am. You might have more figured out than I do," I admitted. "You know *where* you want to be, and you've figured out how to make a living doing what you're passionate about. But I think you know there's more out there, too. More than just a cabin with a single reading chair. There's connection. And community. And all kinds of things that will broaden your horizons. I don't think you've found that yet… and I want to be with you when you do."

Truthfully, *I* wanted to be the something he was looking for, but I wasn't about to say anything quite that cheesy when he'd already promised this was only a one-night stand.

Theo's eyes widened almost imperceptibly. I could tell he was teetering between breaking the tension with a joke and responding with complete candor.

Instead, he bit out a curse and kissed me hard on the mouth again, holding my face to his with renewed vigor. I was so hot for him in that moment, it was enough. I would take what I could get from him and be grateful, even if it left me wanting more in the future.

After a while of rolling around on the bed again, he yanked me up and nudged me into a hot shower, where we shared a long, soapy grind until he finally took us both in hand to finish us off. We kissed until the water ran cold and quickly dried off before slipping under the covers in bed and curling up together for warmth.

"Tell me what you'd do with the Hub if you had all the money in the world," he said in a soft, midnight voice.

I knew time was ticking away on my Theo clock despite my willing it to slow the hell down. I stayed awake as long as I could, unfurling my dreams to him one kid, one concept, one financial need at a time, until both of our voices slurred with sleep.

Hours later, in the darkest part of the night, Theo's beard stubble scratched me awake as he nuzzled my balls and stroked my cock into full hardness. "Want you again," he admitted in a sleepy grumble.

"Have me," I whispered back.

His mouth moved behind my sac until his hot tongue landed on my hole. I grabbed for his head and held him there gently. I might have thought it was a dream, but no dream of mine could have compared to this.

After thoroughly debauching me, he urged me to roll onto my stomach, proving that Doctor Hot-Cock was actually thrillingly, delightfully vers. He fumbled in the bedside table until finding what he needed and moving slick fingers to my hole to begin stretching me open. Theo's hot body leaned over me and whispered words into my ear. I couldn't even make them out over the pounding of blood in my head and my own desperate sounds filling the room.

When he finally ripped open a condom, lubed himself up, kneed my legs further apart, and began pushing inside of me, I reached back to grip his hip to keep him from pulling away.

His thrusts started off slow and deliberate until my body welcomed him. I let out a deep, drawn-out groan of pleasure, which he took as permission to move faster.

Having Theo inside of me was so fucking perfect, so right,

I wanted to beg him to stay with me forever. I was selfishly grateful he was fucking me from behind and in the dark so there was no chance he'd see the way I had to clench my jaw to keep from blurting out something awkwardly sentimental —*be with me, let me have this forever, never stop*—that would linger in the air long after our magical interlude was over. My feelings were too much too soon—or maybe just too much, *period*. I was still a student; he was still a professor. And when I graduated... I'd be leaving town for good unless some grant-writing miracle occurred between now and then. This night might be all we ever got, and I didn't want to taint the memory of it by speaking aloud all of the things I wanted but couldn't have.

"Porter," Theo groaned into my hair as he slowed his movements down to a languid roll. "Baby, you feel..." He ducked his head down to press his lips to the nape of my neck while he reached around to take me in hand. The left-over slick on his fingers was enough to feel amazing as he jacked me off.

He increased the pace of his thrusts and strokes until both of us came with a combination of grunts and shouts, locked together tightly.

Theo withdrew from me, and I collapsed onto the bed, not caring one bit about the mess that made. Theo didn't seem to care either. He took care of the condom and collapsed directly on top of me with a breathless, disbelieving little laugh, like he might be thinking the same thing I was:

This wasn't one-night-stand sex. This was life-changing. This was incomparable. This was the kind of sex that demanded a future between us.

Eventually, Theo got up and got us cleaned off before climbing back into bed and taking me in his arms. As our bodies cooled, he stroked his hands down my back and my shoulders, pressed tiny kisses to my temple, sifted his fingers through my hair like he was memorizing the shape and feel of me.

But I was too busy thinking to give in to the sadness that threatened to swamp me. Regardless of what Dr. Theodore Hancock said about this being one night only, I fell asleep swearing silently I would make sure this wasn't our only night together.

Yes, I'd give him the rest of the semester. I'd treat him like he was the distant, stodgy professor nemesis he'd always been to me. I'd temporarily "forget" this one night the way I'd promised.

But when I was no longer a Hannabury student, I would do my best to make him remember in a way he'd never, ever forget again...

I had a bone to pick with fate... and I was going to win.

CHAPTER EIGHT

THEO

I was a liar.

After telling Porter I would only sleep with him once, I continued to use his body for my pleasure over and over for the next forty-eight hours. When the tree workers finally cleared my driveway Monday morning, it was time to take Porter home.

It felt like I was dropping off a part of me and watching it walk away forever.

Worse. Watching it walk away so it could linger at the periphery of my consciousness for the next few months, tormenting me with what I wouldn't let myself have.

Never had I played it so cool. If my students thought I was stoic in class, that was nothing compared to the overly casual way I said goodbye to Porter Sunday.

"So. Good luck with everything," I said as he opened the passenger door, letting in a blast of arctic air.

He stared at me. "That's it? That's all you're going to say?"

I couldn't get enough air in my lungs, and my stomach felt like it was full of restless vipers. I clamped my back teeth against the impulse to tell him to stay, to close the door and come home with me where he belonged.

"I mean it. I wish you all the happiness in the world." I hesitated. "You deserve it."

He let out a long exhale before meeting my eyes. "Let me make one thing clear, *Professor*. I care about you. There is a spark here, a fucking fantastic one, and we both know it. This could be something incredible. Hell, it already has been. Don't… don't screw it up because of your jacked-up ethics nonsense."

"My job security isn't nonsense," I said, losing the warm glow I'd had a split second before. "Neither is your degree."

Porter reached out to take my hand, but when a group of students walked across the street ahead of us, he changed his mind and pulled his hand back. "I know. And I respect that. But there are only seven weeks left until I'm no longer a student."

I opened my mouth to tell him I couldn't make him any promises until then, but he stopped me with a quick kiss to my cheek after making sure the students had passed. "See you in seven weeks and one day, Professor," he whispered. "And that's a promise."

He was out of the vehicle, hands in his hoodie pocket, sneakers squeaking across the snow, before I could say another word. I watched him as he walked up the path, as he jogged up the stairs, as he disappeared into the house.

Fuck, I was so screwed.

We'd talked about his temporary living situation. Finding a place to live for only one semester hadn't been easy for him, and he was due to move out by New Year's. He'd told me if he didn't have a job lined up already, he'd need to move back in with his family in Little Pippin Hollow.

I didn't want that to happen. Hell, I didn't want Porter leaving Hannabury—leaving *me*—at all. But neither did I want to hold him here with promises made when circumstances had thrown us together in a single bed. I didn't believe for a minute that a corporate job in the big city was right for him, but it wasn't my choice to make.

I backed the car out of the drive and made my way to campus to prepare for the following day's classes. Thankfully, Monday classes had been canceled also, due to the residual power outages and downed trees around town, so I had time to recover my equilibrium.

Assuming such a thing was possible.

Once in my office, I threw myself into work to force my brain to get over its little fairy-tale weekend. This was the real world—my career, my never-ending list of papers to grade, the textbook I was co-writing with the head of the gender studies department on gender roles in Renaissance literature, the final exam that needed to be finished up.

Surely if I threw myself into the ocean of busywork, it would drown out the fire Porter Sunday had lit in my blood.

FIVE DAYS LATER, I could say for sure that the flame of Porter Sunday was still blazing merrily inside me. The man seemed to be everywhere on campus. When I grabbed a salad between classes at the campus deli, he was at a table in the corner typing on his laptop, and I wanted so badly to know what he was working on. When I knocked on Jim Burton's door to ask him about a scheduling issue, Porter Sunday was in there for his office hours, and I had to bite back a sarcastic tease about how he'd managed to locate the English faculty offices at long last. And when I drove by the Hub one afternoon, planning to drop off some soccer balls I'd found on deep discount, Porter was outside with the kids, hanging handmade snowflake ornaments in the tree in front of the rec building.

Every time I saw him, he was ten times more beautiful than the last... which was saying something, considering how fucking beautiful I'd already known he was. After being with him intimately, I was more aware of his body, his movement, the way his lips curled up in amusement. Every inch of him made me squirm with a restlessness I couldn't shake.

When I returned to my office after my lunch break, Jim Burton popped his head into my office. "Got a minute?"

"Sure," I said, trying to get a handle on my dark mood. "What's up?"

I followed him into his office, where he turned his laptop to face me. "Press release assignment in my Creative Non-Fiction class. Take a look."

I peered at the words on the screen and knew immediately who'd written it. The press release introduced the new full-time director to the Hannabury Youth Hub, and it was obvious the director was Porter himself. The quotes he'd used in the assignment were hilarious, considering I knew he would have had to get actual quotes from classmates for it. And his resume details, which I knew had to be accurate for this assignment, were even more impressive than I'd imagined, showing that he'd had a long and varied experience at various youth organizations and that he'd minored in Nonprofit Management and Social Innovation. This was news to me.

"This is… excellent," I admitted with a smile. "Quite an improvement over the one he did for me last semester on the off-season appearance of the apple ermine moth."

Jim nodded in satisfaction. "Something's gotten into him the past week or so. He's been even more engaged than ever." He puffed out his chest. "I like to think I'm having an influence on the man."

I fought back a laugh. "Certainly seems like it. That's why we're gonna miss you around here, sir," I said, anxious to leave Jim's office before my partiality for his student became obvious.

"There was another reason I wanted to share this with

you, Theo," he said, indicating the chair in front of his desk for me to take. "Have a seat."

As the head of the English department, Jim had been a well-respected mentor to many of us, and generally, I took every opportunity to learn from him I could. Reluctantly, I settled into the chair and watched Jim take his.

"I was so inspired by young Sunday's assignment that I wanted to see if I could help bring more awareness to the Hannabury Fund, which oversees financing for the Hub, and perhaps make a private donation. The work Sunday's doing is important, and I'd like to see the events he outlined in this assignment—" He tapped his laptop screen. "—become a reality. I figured it'd be a shame to lose him if he moves out of the area after graduation. So I contacted Marsia Grossberg at the Hannabury Fund to ask where their funding came from…"

I was pretty sure I knew where this conversation was going. "Oh? She's a lovely person. Does good work over there," I murmured.

He lifted an eyebrow at me. "She does indeed. Thanks, in part, to a generous endowment by a certain Sutton Family Foundation." He tilted his head. "The same Sutton Family Foundation that built the new physics wing of the science complex. The same Sutton family who gave us Professor Emeritus *Darren* Sutton from the physics department."

"I'm not sure I understand what you're getting at, sir."

He snorted. "Cagey doesn't suit you, Theo. I recall you once mentioning that you'd inherited your home from your grandfather, a noted physics professor here at Hannabury. At the time, I didn't put two and two together. But now that I think of it, you do share a resemblance. Darren wasn't any good at being cagey either."

I laughed and shook my head.

Jim tapped his chin with a stubby pointer finger. "It strikes me that a family with the kind of financial power to endow a physics wing might also be able to, say, *enhance* the program budget at the Hub." He shrugged. "Just a thought, Dr. Hancock. Just a thought."

"The Sutton endowment is earmarked for education," I said instinctively, but he was right... and my gears were already turning.

When I'd told Porter that my grandfather liked to tinker with gadgets in his tool shed, I might have been slightly underselling the situation. In truth, my grandfather had been an amazing inventor—one who'd held patents for creating various types of diodes and voltage regulators, whatever those were. I also hadn't mentioned that my grandmother had come from a family of wealthy investors. Though they'd lived simply in faculty housing and on their acreage in the woods, it was by choice and not necessity. They'd preferred to spend their money endowing the Sutton Family Foundation to fund various education initiatives.

The foundation wasn't something I spoke about often. In fact, I rarely even thought about it since thinking of my grandparents often conjured up a homesick feeling that had nothing to do with my physical home itself. But *technically*, I was the director of the foundation, though I rarely changed the way my grandfather had allocated the funds. And *technically*, the only stipulations my grandparents had put on the money were that it be used in Hannabury and that it be used for education.

I couldn't believe I hadn't thought of this before.

"Do you not consider the Hannabury Youth Hub to be a center of education?" Jim went on, unaware that I was already more than convinced. "A place where children can learn dignity and confidence, independence and fun? How to be good citizens of this community and how to give back when they go on to bigger and brighter futures?"

Of course I did. And Jim was right: I could easily set up an endowment for the Hub that would cover the cost of a director and make sure the program was funded for years to come. It was exactly the sort of thing my grandparents would have wanted the money spent on.

They would have liked Porter Sunday. They would have liked him a *lot*.

"Would it be an unethical decision," I began slowly, "for my family foundation to make a donation that financially benefits a student in our department?" *Especially one I have feelings for?*

He shrugged. "I don't see endowing a youth program as financially benefitting a certain student. Who's to say the powers that be will select Mr. Sunday as the director? You don't know that for sure, do you?"

"I suppose not," I agreed.

Technically, the Hannabury Youth Program was administered by the Hannabury Fund. And there was no way Marsia would deny Porter the director position if he wanted it. From what I'd heard, and what I'd observed myself at things like the Fun Run, Porter *was* the Hub. If they could keep him, they would.

I felt the world lifting from my shoulders. I could do this. My family's foundation could make even more of a difference to the at-risk youth here in town, and by doing so, Porter might get a chance to implement the programs he dreamed of.

"Thank you for your advice, Dr. Burton. I appreciate it, as always."

I stood and nodded to him before turning to leave. When I got to the door, Burton stopped me. "Oh, Theo? Did you ever meet Zahid Hasan? He worked with your grandfather in the physics department. Young guy. Came from MIT."

"Maybe? Was he tall with glasses and a prominent Adam's apple?"

Burton grinned. "That's it. The type to wear pocket protectors like a walking stereotype. Anyway, he fell in love with one of his graduate teaching assistants." He met my eyes. "Love at first sight. They waited until she was no longer a student before acting on it, of course. But he and Anne are married now, and they both teach at a university down in Pennsylvania. They're research partners and a powerhouse in the department."

"Oh?" My palms began to sweat. "That's, uh… nice for them. Not sure why you think I'd be interested."

"Remember that you're human, Theo." He winked. "We all are. You're not going to handle running this department very well if you don't remember there's more to life than what you can find in a four-hundred-year-old book."

"*'The web of our life is of a mingled yarn, good and ill together,'*" I teased, quoting *All's Well That Ends Well*.

Burton's eyes danced. "I'll do you one better from the same play, young Padawan. *'Get thee a good husband, and use him as he uses thee.'*"

I blinked at him, feeling my face go red, but managed to hold back my laughter until I was out in the hall.

Jim Burton had a point. And I would take it to heart.

But first, I had several weeks of work to do and plans to set in motion.

CHAPTER NINE

PORTER

Seven weeks. It had been seven weeks since I'd touched Theo. Seven weeks since I'd allowed myself to do more than fantasize about a future together. After a single chance meeting at Professor Burton's office, I'd mostly avoided going to the English building except for classes—it was just too painful to see Theo when we couldn't be together, especially when I wasn't even sure how he felt about me.

Did he regret our time together? Was he secretly glad that he had an excuse not to take things further?

I was not an overthinker by nature—I left that to several of my brothers—but suddenly, I found myself spiraling and second-guessing. Theo was important to me. Our time together at the cabin had made me rethink the whole direction of my life, just as surely as walking past his classroom on that fateful day sophomore year had. I wanted to know that Theo felt even a little bit of the same passion for me.

In the meantime, I'd kept busy by focusing on my assignments in my one and only class—where I was *killing it*—and by doing exactly what Theo had suggested—writing grant proposals to get more money for the Hub. It turned out there were a lot of places that were willing to support a program like ours, if we had someone with the time and talent to write the proposals. I couldn't help feeling grateful for the way things had gone down in Theo's class last semester because I had an abundance of time… and thanks to our frantic-mad weekend at the cabin, now I had the talent, too.

There were no guarantees that I'd get the grants I'd applied for, obviously, or that the Hub would choose to keep me on full-time even if I did, but it felt good to know that this was one last thing I could do for the kids.

I was at the library, uploading my final assignment as an undergraduate, when Marsia, the head of the Hannabury Fund and my de facto boss at the Hub, texted to ask me to stop by her office before taking my usual shift at the Hub later that day. She said she had "good news."

Intriguing.

I was almost positive it couldn't have been about any of the grants. Charitable foundations like the ones I'd applied to were all about the delayed gratification, and I knew we'd have to wait weeks (or maybe even longer) to see if any of them came through.

So I was shocked when I walked into Marsia's office to see a bunch of my coworkers assembled with beaming smiles and to have her greet me with, "Surprise, Porter! We'd love to offer you a *paid*, full-time position as Director of the Hannabury Youth Hub."

"No way," I breathed. "Are you kidding? Did one of the grants come through? Was it the New England After School Alliance? Or, no, was it the Caldimont Foundation? They were offering fifty thousand a year, under certain circumstances, but I didn't think we'd hear until February—"

"Er. No. Neither." Marsia's smile didn't fade. "It was actually a local program. The Sutton Family Foundation, which was created by one of Hannabury's most beloved science professors. They endowed the Sutton Wing of the science complex, and they've been longtime supporters of our work.

Their representative reached out last month to make us this offer—"

"Marsia! And you didn't say anything? I've been dying for weeks, wondering if I should have accepted those interviews in Boston," I complained jokingly—I was too thrilled to ever complain about anything for at least a full year. "This is… this is amazing. And you're sure you want *me* to…"

"Porter," she snorted. "Of course we want you! Everyone at the Hannabury Fund believes you're the best person to run the Hub full-time. No one is more dedicated. Just look at all the extra effort you've put in, writing those grant proposals for us! The excellent marks in your Nonprofit Management courses, plus the personal endorsements from your advisors in the English department, were the icing on the cake. We just wanted to wait until you were finished with your semester to offer you the job so you wouldn't be distracted… and to give you the opportunity to apply for other jobs in case that was what you truly wanted."

"There's nothing I want more than this," I whispered. This was partly a lie; a future with Theo wasn't something I could control, but now that I had this job, it was firmly in the realm of possibility… assuming he wanted it, too.

"Good." She grinned. "We look forward to seeing what you do with the program, starting in January."

My dream job, right here in Hannabury.

"Thank you," I said in a shaky voice.

"Thank you, Porter, for making this a program we're all very proud of. And another surprise. Henriette, here, has volunteered to take over your shift today since we figured you were up all night finishing your final assignment. No one wants our new director to get overtired before he officially takes the job." She winked, and my coworker Henriette laughed out loud. "Do me a favor and swing by HR to fill out some paperwork, then go celebrate your accomplishment! Congratulations!"

After thanking her again and practically floating to the HR office to complete the necessary paperwork, I headed back across campus to where I'd parked my car. My phone rang with a call from my brother Webb. "Hey," I said, smiling before even hearing his voice.

"Hey, troublemaker. Drew wanted me to ask when you were coming home. I said I thought you were waiting to do your graduation walk until the spring, so—"

"I got a job!" I blurted, voice shaking to match the shaking hands and knees I still had from the meeting. "A real job. *The* job. To run the Hub."

"What? You're kidding?" Webb said. "Shit, Porter, that's fantastic! One of your grant applications came through?"

"No," I said with a laugh. "I mean, maybe? I don't know yet. But this was a large endowment through the university fund given by a local family foundation or something. I'm not sure exactly. My head started spinning after she told me about the job, and it *kept* spinning when I saw the salary on the HR forms I filled out. The only stipulation was that the program has to implement some activities to educate and inspire kids in the sciences with specific emphasis on physics. The wording is broad, though, so I can get creative. We could make balloon cars or measure the volume and weight of snowballs. Remember when Gage helped Aiden build that automated dog treat dispenser for the science fair? Or when Aiden's Scout group built Popsicle stick trebuchets? That kind of thing."

"That was a blast," he said. "Until my son decided to build a bigger one with scrap lumber and use rotten apples as ammo."

I laughed, feeling light and free. I told him the specifics of the offer and confessed I might not be able to stay in Little Pippin Hollow very long over the holidays. "I'll need to move by the end of December since my sublet is up, and I'll probably want to get some work done so I can jump into the new job with both feet."

"Understandable. We can come help you move after the holidays. I'm not sure if we have any spare furniture lying around, but Luke's mom has an uncanny ability to find deals on stuff. I can ask her to keep her eye out."

"That would be great. Thanks." The thought of moving for the second time in six months was depressing. I tried not to think about it too much, but I would need to get creative to find housing in a college town in the middle of the school year.

"But you're definitely not taking part in the graduation ceremony until next May, so you can be with your friends, right? You want us to come out to Hannabury later this week and, I dunno, take you out for a beer or something? Seems kind of anticlimactic to end your final, final semester without celebrating."

"Oh, I'll be celebrating. My friends were already going to take me out tonight, and they don't even know about the job yet. But I do want to spend a couple of days looking at places to live, and I'll come home after that. Maybe we can celebrate my degree over the holidays," I said. "Tell Drew and Marco I'm expecting a feast of my favorites."

"Will do. We're proud of you, Porter." We talked for a while longer before ending the call. It was nice to hear his familiar voice, and I realized I was looking forward to seeing everyone over the holidays.

Within moments of ending the call, the family text chain blew up with congratulations emojis and graduation GIFs.

As I looked up from my phone, I saw someone exit the front door of the English building.

Theo.

I stared at him, drinking in his long-legged confidence and the way his dark-framed glasses set off his hair. He turned his head when someone behind me called out to a friend. Our eyes met and locked on each other. Words hung unspoken in the crisp winter air between us.

I was no longer a student in his department. But technically, he was still responsible for the final granting of my degree on behalf of the department. I wondered how long that process took.

I'd told him I would approach him the day after finishing the semester, but that didn't mean he was free. For all I knew, he was inundated with papers to grade and exams to review.

For all I knew, he was dreading our meeting.

My heart tripped over itself in the vain hope he would say something, call out to me with an admission of longing, of sleepless nights and desperate hope—the same things I'd been experiencing without him.

But another shouted laugh came from behind me, breaking the moment and causing Theo to frown before nodding slightly in my direction and then walking away.

I trudged the rest of the way to my car, wondering if I should cease my stupid hopes and acknowledge he might not have the same feelings for me I had for him. Just because I wanted more and sensed there was a magnetic connection between us didn't mean he felt the same way. Was I being naive to think I could convince him to give us a try?

Maybe when I went home for the holidays, I could ask my family for help. If I explained everything, they'd help me come up with a plan or tell me I was being ridiculous.

My phone continued to blow up with congratulations messages, but I was too melancholy to respond. Instead, I turned my phone off.

I dropped my vehicle at home, did some half-hearted packing, and walked to the bar to meet my friends a few hours later. Suddenly, I felt like getting wasted. When I entered the bar and found a table already taken by my class-mates and covered in appetizers, I exhaled a sigh of relief.

"You guys are a sight for sore eyes," I admitted.

Nolan shoved a tequila shot in my hands. "To the college graduate! May you live long and prosper!"

I threw the drink back and felt the familiar burn. Even though I hadn't had a drink since the night I ended up at Theo's house, I still credited them with putting my life on a different path than it might have taken if they hadn't convinced me to go rant poetry at my former professor.

"Finally," I agreed, reaching for a clean glass and helping myself to the pitcher of beer in the center of the table. "It only took six and a half fucking years."

They all cheered and laughed, clinking glasses with me and giving me hell for being a "graduating grandpa." We shared the relief of finishing the semester and talked about everyone's plans for the holidays.

It took about three hours and who-knew-how-many more drinks before I couldn't stand it anymore.

"I'm in love with Doctor Hot-Cock," I blurted out in the middle of Sean's summary of a recent basketball game.

"No, man, I said shot clock," he explained with a divot of confusion on his forehead. "Shot. Clock."

Beck slapped a hand over his mouth. "Sean! Shut it, we're getting ready for some major tea. Spill it, Sunday. You can tell mama."

"That night, you know? It was that night," I admitted. "You know that night."

They all looked at each other. "What is he talking about?" Toru asked in a stage whisper.

"Oh! Fuck. You went to his house, didn't you?" Nolan asked.

"*We* went to the professor's house," Toru reminded him. "All of us. I remember that much, even if you don't. And Porter got out so he could do his performance piece and…" They frowned. "Shit, I don't remember."

Sean pulled Beck's hand down. "I do! I remember you texted us the next day to say you were fine but that you and tequila were breaking up for at least the rest of the semester. I figured you were as hungover as the rest of us, so it made sense that you haven't been coming out with us on Thursdays… But Jesus Christ, Sunday, I feel like you left out a few pertinent details if you somehow fell in love with the man! Tell us *everything*." He leaned forward on his elbows and propped his chin in his hands. Beck did the same. "You may begin now."

I explained the basic events of the weekend—leaving out anything salacious—and then concluded, "He wouldn't be with me because of the whole… student/teacher thing." I waved my hand in the air. "*Pfft*. Ethics, shmethics. You know? If he wanted it badly enough, he'd have done it."

"Mmm, I dunno. Couldn't he be like… fired or some shit?" Beck asked.

"And could it have threatened you getting your degree?" Toru wondered in concern.

I groaned. "Don't join his side. You're on my side, remember? The side of no thoughts, just vibes."

"Yes. Obviously." Toru waved their hand in the air, just like I had. "Well, whatever could or couldn't have happened doesn't matter anymore, darling. Semester's over. You're an alumnus now. Ain't nothin' but a thing. Methinks we need to hire a car and driver for another visit up the mountain. Who's with me?"

Everyone's hands shot up… except mine.

"Oh, no," I said firmly. "Hell no. No way. I'm not making a drunken fool of myself like that again."

"He's right," Nolan said, nodding enthusiastically. "That was how he ended up in this trouble in the first place."

"I don't want him to think I'm a kid," I whined… exactly like a kid.

Beck leaned toward me. "Did you fuck him?"

I refused to answer it with words, but my face turning fire-engine red did all the talking anyway.

"Oh my God," she said with a laugh. "High-five, bro."

I squeezed my eyes closed as she lifted my arm and high-fived my limp hand. "It's more than that, Beck. I have real, capital-*F* Feelings for this man. I need help."

Nolan nodded again. I was surprised he didn't have cervical spine injuries from all the drunken nodding I'd seen him do this semester. "We're here for you. For sure. *For sure.*"

Toru took a delicate sip of wine they'd gotten while I hadn't been looking. "What if you took a home-cooked meal up to his place tomorrow night and surprised him with a romantic interlude?"

Nolan bobbed his head. "Candles and shit. I like it."

Beck pursed her lips in thought. "Or… or what about writing him a sonnet. Super-meta, right?"

"Didn't we do that last time? That poem was killer. It slayed." Sean spoke around a mouthful of jalapeño popper. "I mean, I assume it did. I don't remember a word of it. Did we actually write one?"

I shook my head. "Not that I recall. I ended up reciting Shakespeare's, pretty sure."

Toru sniffed. "Angry sonnets have their place, of course, but they are not the way to a man's heart."

"Muffins," Nolan said, shooting me with a finger gun. "Muffins are the way."

"Nonsense." Toru rolled their eyes. "*Love sonnets,*" they insisted. "Love sonnets are the way."

"A love sonnet?" I snorted. "No, that's…" I paused for a long moment. "Wait. A *love sonnet.*"

Toru nodded smugly. "It's what us English scholars like to call a *mirror moment,* baby." They buffed their fingers on their sweater. "And my parents said it was a useless major. Pfft."

My heart kicked up speed, only partly fueled by tequila. "I'm going to sonnet the fuck out of him."

Everyone cheered and reached forward to clink various glasses, or cheesy appetizers in Sean's case, in celebration of my decision. "To Porter and Doctor Hot-Cock! May you weasel your way into his withered Grinch heart and make it grow to ten times its size."

The conversation returned to a discussion about everyone's plans for the holidays and the remaining shopping and wrapping everyone had to do. Nolan sniffed and glanced over from the corner of his eye. "I still think a candle wouldn't go amiss," he muttered.

No. It wouldn't. I'd candle *and* sonnet the fuck out of Theo Hancock.

And this time, I would force him to take me seriously.

THE FOLLOWING day at work was nonstop. The kids were jacked up on holiday sugar treats, and they were all talking a mile a minute about how grateful they were it had been the last day of school before the holiday break.

I spent the first half of the day discussing new programming for preschoolers that would begin in January, brainstorming some marketing ideas, and decorating my new, tiny, closet-sized office, which came complete with a brand-new laptop, a dedicated phone line, and the world's oldest, creakiest desk chair.

After working for the Hub the past several years, I already had notebooks full of ideas on how I'd like to grow and expand the program if I had the wherewithal, including coordinating with the local schools to identify families who would benefit from the Hub's programs and integrating the Hub with other local early intervention efforts for at-risk kids. I'd been holding myself back from believing this could happen for so long I felt like a cannonball that had finally been launched. I knew I needed to pace myself eventually, but for now, I was just enjoying the newfound freedom to turn my ideas into reality.

Once the kids showed up in the afternoon, I didn't have another minute to even think, much less worry about what I had planned for later that evening.

Which was probably for the best. Last time, I'd had no script, and things had worked out pretty damn well in the end… *mostly.*

"Hey, Porter," Raquon called as he entered the main room and shucked his coat. "Happy graduation. You're done with school forever. Wish I was. I can't wait until I can work on science experiments all day."

"Uh-huh. Wait, how'd you know I was done with college?" I asked as I finished setting up a holiday craft station for the younger kids.

Raquon froze in place. "Oh! Uh… I mean… doesn't everyone know? You've been in college for like ten years, right? 'Bout time you kicked it."

His sister Kyrie elbowed him hard in the ribs and rolled her eyes. "Nice job, dummy."

"Hey," I warned. "No name-calling. And for your information, Raquon, it's been six and a half years. Not ten." I set out some markers. "Even though it felt like ten," I added under my breath.

As soon as the majority of the kids arrived, I announced the various activities we had planned for the afternoon. "To recap: greeting card making over here by Tim. Star suncatcher making by the window, but please be careful not to get glue on the glass this time. For those of you who are scheduled for music lessons, Miss Jones is waiting for you in the music room. And those of you who absolutely can't stand to be locked inside on this freezing afternoon may shoot hoops on the court as long as Jada is out there keeping an eye on everyone. Be sure to come back when you're done because the Hannabury faculty brought goodie bags for each family to take home."

Everyone moved off in different directions. I turned on a

holiday music station before moving between the two craft activities to help out. Time passed quickly, the way it always did on Fridays, and I made sure to check in quietly with a few of the kids who might struggle at home with the upcoming school vacation.

I appreciated the distraction because otherwise, I would have been thinking of nothing but Theo. What was he doing? Was he remembering what I'd said about coming for him when the semester was over?

When it was finally time for us to clean up and get ready for the parents to pick the kids up, I felt a strange vibe in the room, like the kids were expecting something. While the faculty had provided bags of food and small gifts for each family, they weren't the kind of gifts that would make these kids feel very pampered. I hoped the anticipation wasn't about that. Had I built it up too much by mentioning it?

"Porter! Someone's here asking for you," Laci said with a singsong tone in her voice.

I turned around from where I'd been cleaning up the last of the shredded tissue paper leftover from the star suncatcher project and saw a very nervous-looking Dr. Theodore Hancock standing in the doorway, holding a giant bouquet of colorful flowers.

My heart leapt into my throat, and all I could think was *He remembered. He definitely remembered.* "Theo—uh… Dr. Hancock?"

"It's Theo, Porter," he said, clearing his throat. "For you… just Theo."

Everyone stood still and watched with knowing smirks on their faces. None of them looked confused about who he was or what he was doing there. "What… What's going on?"

He walked into the room and held the flowers out to me. "I wanted to ask you to dinner. Last night, I mean. But you weren't here at the Hub, and when I called, you didn't answer your phone."

My face heated. "It was turned off. I was… out with friends. Celebrating." *Making plans.*

He scraped his lip with his teeth, a nervous gesture I'd never seen him do before. It was endearing as hell. "I thought that might be it. So I… made alternate arrangements."

Laci bounced on her toes and made a muffled squeal sound. Kyrie let out a giggle. Raquon elbowed her.

"Okay…" I said, looking around. "Yeah. I'd like that. Dinner, I mean."

Edgar rolled his eyes. "This is excruciating. Get to the good part, Doc."

The edge of Theo's lips twitched up. "I brought dinner to you. Well, to everyone. There's a taco truck outside. And since it would be a little excessive to bring it here just for the two of us, I—"

Laci blurted, "He invited all our families! Isn't he the sweetest!"

"*Unlimited tacos*," Edgar clarified with an awed voice. "For *all* of us. They're already parked out there next to the basketball court. And just sayin', Doc, if Porter won't date you, I've got a single uncle and two older cousins you could check out. Because seriously, nothing says love like unlimited tacos."

Laci and Raquon grabbed my hands and pulled me down the hall and out the door to the parking lot. Sure enough, Hannabury's most popular food truck was happily twinkling like a beacon with its strings of fairy lights while the mouthwatering smells of fresh tacos wafted in the crisp winter air.

I looked back at Theo in shock as his gesture sank in. "You did this? For me? Why?"

He handed me the flowers and leaned in to kiss me on the cheek. "Because I figured if I wanted to get your attention, the best way would be by taking care of the kids you love."

"You were right," I agreed softly.

The kids raced past us to get in line at the truck's serving window. Parents got out of their cars to join them. Music poured from the speakers on the truck and filled the area with a festive atmosphere.

I turned to Theo, flowers in one hand, and looped a finger into his belt buckle. "Hi." I breathed him in. "*Hi.*"

"Hey. Congratulations on no longer being a Hannabury student," he said with a teasing grin.

"Thank fuck," I whispered against his cheek.

"Porter… I have a lot of things to say to you, but first and foremost…" He glanced around at the kids and the impromptu party atmosphere he'd created. "Will you come home with me tonight?"

I laughed, so relieved I couldn't stand it. "I was planning on it. I, uh… might have already picked out a sonnet to scream at your house if I had to."

He pulled back and smiled at me. "You were planning on coming to me?"

"Seven weeks and one day, remember?"

Theo's smile lit up the parking lot even more than the food truck's twinkle lights and the giant floodlights over the nearby basketball court. "Seven weeks ago, I wanted to ask you to wait for me, but I couldn't. I needed to make sure you didn't feel obligated or pressured."

"I understand," I admitted. And I did, when I wasn't under tequila's dubious influence. "You were in a difficult position. And we didn't know where I'd be after the semester was over either."

"And now?" he asked eagerly.

"Now… I'm going to be program director here at the Hub," I said with excitement I couldn't conceal. "I wrote a whole bunch of grant proposals exactly as you said I should, but it turned out I didn't need to because the Hannabury Fund got an endowment from a local foundation. Turns out this former Hannabury physics professor was an inventor, and…"

I blinked as several pieces of information slid into place in my brain.

"Theo," I began calmly. "What did you say your grandfather's name was?"

He ran a hand through his hair. Took his glasses off to buff them against the hem of his shirt, then set them back on his face. "I, uh… I'm not sure I mentioned it."

"Sutton," I supplied. "As in the Sutton Family Foundation?"

Theo looked uncharacteristically sheepish. "Maybe?"

"You… you did this?" My eyes widened, and my face went hot. "You… you *endowed me*?"

"It wasn't for you," he said quickly. "I mean, it *was*. I hoped it was. But the endowment was for the Hub. I didn't want to say anything because I didn't want to pressure you. If you changed your mind about anything, like wanting that big-city job or… or being attached to me, I wanted you to be able to make that choice free and clear. But, if you wanted to stay… I wanted you to have that option."

"Oh. My. God. You… you gave me my dream job, Theo. You… you made it possible." I swallowed hard as tears threatened.

"The job is yours, Porter, because you earned it. I have no say in who the Hannabury Fund chooses to run their program, and I swear your name was never mentioned during the entire process of the endowment. Whatever happens with you and me, whether you want to be with me or not…"

"Stop talking," I whispered.

Theo frowned. "But…"

I shook my head and pressed a finger to his lips. "I thought words were power. You taught me that. But actions speak a thousand times louder, don't they? You haven't just given *me* a gift. You've given a gift to all of the kids in this community. If I wasn't already half in love with you, Theodore Hancock, I would be now."

"Love?" His gaze flicked between my eyes. "Are you sure?"

"Frantic-madly," I promised in a whisper, twining my arms around his neck, flowers and all. "I can't believe you did all this, and I didn't even have to yell Sonnet 147 at you to get your attention this time."

Theo's hands grasped my waist like he never wanted to let me go. "You've had my attention all along, Porter Sunday. Do you remember the first line of that sonnet?"

I felt light-headed and managed to nod jerkily.

My love is as a fever, longing still.

"Good," he said, his voice deep and full of want. "Because that is how I feel about you. And I'm going to prove it to you day by day." He leaned down until his lips rested against mine.

"Starting tonight?" I asked with a grin.

"Starting *now*," he said, and then my terrible, brilliant, generous, amazing jerk of a professor, my Doctor Hot-Cock, the love of my life, kissed me right there in the middle of the impromptu taco party…

And for the two of us, there could be no happily ever after more randomly, wonderfully poetic than that.

EPILOGUE
THEO

The Following May

WATCHING Porter walk across the stage in his cap and gown was surprisingly emotional for me. My colleagues had insisted I be the one to hand him his diploma and shake his hand. It had been several months since the dean of the college had learned of our relationship, and she assured me that she saw nothing untoward about my involvement in Porter's commencement exercises.

I'd kept the information secret, however, so seeing the look on his face when he stepped up onstage to accept his diploma was a gift.

"Congratulations, baby," I murmured as he stepped forward to take the folder from me and shake my hand. "I'm so incredibly proud of you."

His cheeks turned pink, but his huge grin was enough to make me mirror it like a besotted fool. And I *was* a besotted fool. Since getting together at the end of the last semester, Porter and I had been inseparable. His new apartment had only been used on the nights we'd decided to stay close to campus for bad weather. Most nights, we'd slept together at the cabin. As soon as the weather warmed up enough to start our cabin addition project, we'd spent even more time there working to get the new bedroom finished as quickly as possible.

It was finally done, and the two of us would be hosting his family for a graduation cookout this afternoon after the ceremony. What Porter didn't know was that his brothers had already moved his stuff out of his apartment earlier this morning and deposited it at my place before turning in the keys to his landlord.

We were officially living together as of today, and something about the official-ness of it made a weight lift off me I hadn't known I was carrying.

I love you, he mouthed before winking and heading toward the other end of the stage to let the next student approach.

It wasn't the first time he'd *officially* said the words, with no disclaimers. It was more likely the thousandth. He'd first told them to me on a moonlit night full of stars when we'd gone outside to search the trees near the cabin for a hooting owl. The hush of the winter air and thick snow all around us had made the setting feel otherworldly. He'd turned to me and stepped into my personal space until our cloudy exhales mixed together.

"I'm madly in love with you," he'd breathed.

I'd closed my eyes to memorize the feeling of being love-drunk with him. "I love you, too. So very much. Stay with me, please. I don't ever want to let you go."

We'd kissed for hours that night, until our hands and toes felt numb with cold and our noses were bright red. It was a memory I carried close like a secret, even though my love for Porter Sunday was anything but.

I was open and free with my feelings toward him. The department knew it, his friends and the parents and kids at the Hub knew it, and he'd even met my family on a weekend jaunt to New York in February. Meanwhile, the Sunday family had welcomed me with open arms—literally—the first time we'd met, each of them enveloping me in a bear hug before demanding to know my feelings on romance novels, heirloom apple varietals, processed foods, and… cows.

Now I had a forest full of Sunday brothers set up in giant tents and an oversized RV parked beside my house to celebrate not only the graduation but also the acquisition of a new building just off campus to house the Hub program. Thanks to an incredible marketing campaign Porter had begun in Hannabury and the two nearest towns, he'd managed to get several local companies to pledge recurring donations to support the upkeep of a building donated by a government grant he'd won for the program.

His family had shown up to spend several days working on the building to finish minor repairs and much-needed painting before the program could officially move into its new digs. The plan was to have it done in time for the Hub's summer programs next month.

Even though Porter hadn't been upset to discover my family foundation was the one behind the Hub's original endowment, he still refused to accept any additional money for the program from us. Instead, he'd thrown himself head-first into applying for grants—he even let me help write the proposals—and had been thrilled when some began coming through.

Thankfully, several of the program volunteers had offered to help his fundraising efforts, which had included intro-ducing him to some of the wealthy families in town.

Once the commencement ceremony was finished, we all met outside for pictures in the gorgeous Vermont sunshine. I congratulated several of my other students before making my way to the large group surrounding Porter.

"It's about time you finished your degree," I said in my sternest professor voice.

Porter turned to me with a grin. "No thanks to you."

I shrugged. "You're welcome?"

He launched himself at me, nearly bowling me over into the grass as I grabbed him around the waist to keep from falling. He kissed me hard on the mouth before moving his lips to my ear. "I wouldn't have it any other way, Theo. I hope you know that."

"I do. And I can't say I disagree. Thank you for not giving up when I discouraged you last year."

He pulled back and cupped my face. "Never stop teaching me how to use my words to make a difference. Thanks to your advice, I was able to convince my boyfriend to take a chance on me."

"Please." I rolled my eyes. "I'm just a sucker for an angry sonnet, Sunday."

I kissed him again before letting him pull away so he could return the well-wishes from a nearby classmate. I turned to his uncle and shook his hand. "Congratulations, Drew. You raised a fine man."

The older man's eyes sparkled with humor. "Didn't do much, actually. He's always been his own sort. But thanks all the same. I'll take your gratitude out in that brisket you've been smoking since yesterday."

Porter's sister, Emma, leaned in. "And you can thank me for my role by making sure nobody bothers me when I take a long, hot shower in that fancy outdoor setup you have."

My cheeks heated at the mention of the outdoor shower. Once I learned we wouldn't be able to do the bulk of the addition work ourselves due to our schedules and building codes, I decided to do a very different project to add to our enjoyment of the house.

I'd built a large outdoor shower set away from the house to better see the night sky without light pollution. Porter and I used it embarrassingly regularly. It had seen quite a few white-hot moments in the few months we'd had it. I didn't dare picture his sister in the damned thing.

"Me too," Porter's brother Knox said. "I find the idea of that shower very… inspiring."

His boyfriend, Gage, nodded enthusiastically. "I'll join you. You need a back-scrubbing assistant, baby, and I volunteer as tribute. It's a public service, really."

"You're a giver, Goodman," Knox agreed in a voice that made Gage shiver.

Drew's partner, Marco, weighed in. "Fill out the sign-up sheet on the clipboard at the cabin. I believe there's an opening tomorrow morning at six."

I buried my face in my hands as Porter poked me in the ribs. "Pervert," he said happily. "I told you it wouldn't stay our little secret."

"It's not even in sight of the house!" I said. "How do they know about it?"

Porter gave me a teasing grin. "I mean… you *did* pass around tequila shots last night. And you know what tequila does to me."

I laughed. Of course I did. That was why I'd passed around the shots.

Everyone continued to give us hell the entire way up the mountain to the cabin, where three long picnic tables had been placed near a large gas grill. Camp chairs sat out around a fire ring further away from the house, still set up from the tequila-soaked night before when my friends and Porter's friends had welcomed the other Sundays to town. It turned out that my colleague John and his boyfriend, Teagan, were already friendly with Knox and Gage, which was a crazy coincidence… the kind I'd gotten used to since having Porter Sunday in my life.

For the first time ever, I felt like part of a large, loving family. I glanced around the clearing and realized how happy

Gramps would be to see so much joy and laughter, love and energy filling the land he'd claimed for our very own.

Porter had been right, all those months ago, when he said there was something I'd still been searching for, despite having my dream job and living in my dream place. Now I also had a man I loved—and a comfortable sofa where the two of us cuddled nightly—and I finally felt truly content.

"Thank God the rest of the Sundays are all sleeping outside," Porter said when the two of us moved inside to our brand new bedroom to change into casual clothes. "Even with twice as much space now, I'm thrilled we only have one bed."

I grabbed his wrist and yanked him into my arms to kiss his cherry-red lips. "Just think. If I hadn't had just the one bed, you might have been safe from me all those months ago."

He kissed me long and hard before pulling away. "Nah. Even if there'd been twenty beds, I still would have ended up in yours."

We changed quickly, but before Porter could open the bedroom door, I caught him around the waist and pressed my lips to his ear. "Same code word tonight?"

"Twenty-seven." He laughed and pressed back into me. "I'm starting to refer to it as the 'old man sonnet' in my head, you've used it so often lately. And it's not even about sex."

"Forget Shakespeare, then. I'll pull out some Edna St. Vincent Millay. *'And lust is there, and nights not spent alone.'* How's that for old man?"

I felt Porter's entire body shudder against mine. "You give good poem," he admitted in a low voice.

"There's more where that came from if you just say the word…" I teased the side of his neck with my mouth and tongue.

"Sonnet twenty-seven," he breathed. "Please."

"Mm. Methinks not, fair squire. We have a million Sunday lumberjacks outside who demand fresh meat."

Porter groaned and pulled away. "You can't hand me a softball like that and expect me not to tee it up, Theo."

I followed him outside, where music was blaring from speakers and a couple of the guys were setting up a cornhole game that Gage and Knox had brought along. The boards had been painted with caricatures of truly manic-looking cows because Knox claimed they helped Gage aim. I was curious to know what that was all about, but I was confident that I'd hear about it in short order.

"Hey, Porter!" his friend Nolan called from a group of fellow classmates taking up one of the picnic tables covered in shared dishes. "Did you ever remember your angry sonnet so you could recite it for Doctor Hot... I mean, uh... Dr. Hancock?"

Beck let out a whoop. "Oh shit. What about the love sonnet? Surely you told him that one."

I stared at my life partner, the man I held no secrets with. Or so I'd thought.

"You *wrote* me sonnets?" I asked. "Original ones? Of your own pure brain? Oh my God. I need to hear these."

His eyes widened, and he clapped a hand over my mouth. "No. Nope. I'm not sharing, even if you torture me. Trust me when I tell you it was mostly tequila doing the writing—"

"Mmm. I seem to remember we argued about you trying to rhyme 'sex me' with 'wrecks me,'" Toru mused. "Though, I can't remember whether that was the angry sonnet or the romantic one."

"See, I remember gems like 'cockblock' and 'Hancock,' and I personally feel like we achieved some greatness there," Nolan said with an enthusiastic nod.

"Everyone's a critic," Porter complained. He gave his friends a narrow-eyed look. "Zip it, or I'm calling you a ride home. I've got Steve on speed dial."

They howled with laughter and began answering Porter's

brothers' interrogations. I listened to every detail and saved my own interrogation for later.

Porter might claim he wouldn't give up his sonnets under torture, but I knew better. I'd have him reciting them for me—and maybe coming up with a few more—before the night was over since the torture I had planned for Porter Sunday was long and drawn out, detailed and excruciating. And just like every moment with Porter Sunday, I planned to enjoy it to the fullest.

Somehow, despite my best efforts to circumvent it, the universe had brought me exactly where I needed to be and given me the perfect man to share it with. These days, I was more than merely content; I was blissfully happy...

And I didn't have a bone to pick with fate about any of that.

HAWK AND THE PHROZEN PHALLUS

A CHERRY PICKED BONUS SCENE

CHAPTER ONE

HAWK

SAFETY NOTE: Allow frozen toys to thaw a little before putting against your delicate naughty bits. Frostbitten nether regions are no fun.

"This hike has been awesome," I said, stretching out my hamstrings and looking around at the springtime scenery at the top of Balderdash Peak. "Fresh air and sunshine always clear out the cobwebs."

"Mmmhmm. And don't forget sharing your thoughts on *Dangerous When Wet: A Pride and Prejudice Variation*. That was my personal favorite part," Jack said, setting his backpack on the ground and kneeling to take out our cooler bag. "Very inspiring."

I grinned. "I'm so glad you agreed to my campout idea, even though we have to rush back to get to Hannabury for Porter's graduation tomorr—*uh*. Jack? What the hell kind of sausage is that?" I asked, eyes bugging at the size of the cylindrical package Jack pulled out of the bag. "I thought we were grilling burgers."

"Oh, we are. *Later.* First, though," he added with a maniacal grin on his gorgeous face as he straightened back up. "I'm a little concerned about you, Bird."

"Me?" I frowned. "*You're* the one who's been working so hard hiring seasonal staff at the diner, you haven't had a free minute in days."

"True," he said mock-sadly. "We've both been so busy that we've hardly spent any quality time together. You've probably been feeling… neglected, baby."

I raised an eyebrow. "I have?"

One thing I had not felt since the day that Jack Wyatt walked into my life eight years ago was *neglected*. And no matter how busy the diner was, or how much Jack and I had on our plates dealing with our families and friends and new roles regarding the resort, we always, *always* made time for each other. We'd learned the hard way that we were strongest when we were a team.

"Mmm," Jack went on. "And you look… warm."

I swiped a hand over my forehead. The spring day *was* warm, and our hike to the top of Balderdash Peak had been our longest hike since autumn. I was a trifle sweaty, it was true. But the mischievous glint in his eye set my heart pounding in a way that had nothing to do with unseasonable temperatures.

"I'm feeling fine," I said cautiously.

Jack shook his head solemnly. "Are you, though? Heatstroke, Bird. It sneaks up on a person."

The sound of my laughter, clear and free, rang through the empty clearing. "You know, I do believe I heard that somewhere once."

"Fortunately for you," Jack said, slapping the package against his hand, "I'll always be here to take care of you." He bit his lip. "Ideally before this bad boy melts."

Melts?

"You're scaring me," I lied. "What did you bring and why do I feel like keeping my ass as far from you as possible?"

"You remember that story you told me the first night we made love? A little something about a popsicle…"

My eyes widened and my heart picked up a crazy rhythm. "You… *no.*"

"Oh, yes," Jack countered, grinning wickedly. "Definitely, definitely yes."

Look, being engaged to Jack Wyatt was like living in my longest-running fantasy on a daily basis.

Waking up in his arms, falling asleep to the sound of his breath in my ear, feeling his hand on the small of my back when we stood in line at Winter Fest, seeing his smile across the breakfast table, hearing the deep satisfaction in his voice when he called my name across the crowded diner, spending time hiding with him in our ravishing room acting out every hot-as-fuck scene from my latest read… every second of it was high-octane jet fuel for my brain.

Needless to say, in the months that we'd been together, there hadn't been a single time when I'd thought, "You know what would spice things up?" because I was existing on the high end of the Scoville scale twenty-four-seven… which was why I hadn't given the freezable dildo a single thought since Jack had given it to me last summer.

My fiancé, on the other hand, had not forgotten.

In fact, it seemed he had been *plotting.*

"Strip," he commanded, unwrapping the prized item from its plastic baggie. "I have big plans for you tonight and the clock's ticking. Take your clothes off, Bird."

We were far away from any trails or camping sites, but even then, the idea of letting him play with me in that way in public sent shivers down my spine. "Now? In broad daylight?"

"Mmm. While you're still sweaty and hot from the hike and I just spent two hours on the trail staring at your ass? Yup."

Oh. Well. When he put it that way. The idea of anything

frozen against my hot skin was... tempting. The idea of playing with Jack that way was more tempting yet.

It took me less than a second to yank my sweaty shirt over my head and shimmy out of my boots and shorts. "You, too, Mr. Wyatt," I said in a voice gone husky. "If we're getting caught in flagrante, I'm not going down alone."

The tent wasn't even set up yet, so I grabbed one of the sleeping bags, unzipped it, and tossed it down in a patch of new grass. I knew from experience if we didn't stay in the sun, the spring air in the shade would make it too cool to enjoy anything frozen.

I lay back on the sleeping bag but stayed propped up on my elbows so I could watch him take off his clothes. As soon as Jack saw me watching, he turned it into a delicious striptease.

"Fuck, yes. That's it baby," I called with a wolf-whistle. "Work it for me."

Jack's grin was magnetic as always. This week's spring busy-ness aside, he'd been noticeably less stressed about work over the last few months, and when I'd asked him about it, he'd confided that making me an equal partner in running the diner had taken a lot of the pressure off him. That melted my heart in a lot of ways—I loved being his partner in all things, but it filled something inside me to know I made his life easier and better the same way he did for me.

Not to mention that now that we were running the diner as a team, we both had free time for other things. Me, for my environmental committee and Nature Scout activities; Jack to become a farm-to-table consultant for lots of restaurants in the area, including the restaurant at the new resort; and both of us to make plenty of new memories on the mountains we loved.

I bent my knees and spread my legs, giving Jack a show of my own. I enjoyed the cool breeze on my hot skin almost as much as the intensity of my fiancé's gaze on my naked body.

"Tease," he grunted before speeding up the clothes removal.

When he finally crawled on top of me, I took a moment to enjoy the feel of his strong muscles, the scent of his clean sweat, the sound of his low groan as our cocks pressed together, and the salty taste of his lips as I pulled him closer for a deep kiss. When his tongue entered my mouth, I tasted the familiar lemon-lime flavor he added to his water bottle.

Being with Jack Wyatt put me into a delicious sensory overload that surpassed all of the dreams I'd ever had of him. Even this many months after getting together, the excitement hadn't waned at all. If anything, it had grown in a way I hadn't expected before beginning our relationship.

Who would have known that getting to know him even better would turn me on exponentially? That every time I made love to him, I'd only want him *more*? Like reading my favorite Pride and Prejudice retellings, every kiss with Jack was perfectly familiar and just the tiniest bit different and exciting at the same time. It was the best of all possible worlds, and I didn't think I'd ever get used to the fact that I'd get to have this *forever*.

The ice-cold temperature of the dildo against my inner thigh shocked me into a gasp. "Fuck! What are you... *oh god...*" I arched back as he moved the toy around my hip to the heat of my lower back and down into the top of my crack.

It felt so strange, so wrong, and so fucking good.

Jack's lips moved to my ear where his teeth grazed my lobe. "You're so hot like this. Outside, under the trees where anyone could see you laid out for me, waiting for me to fuck you with this toy."

I let out an embarrassingly impatient noise. My need for Jack was always on a simmer in my blood, but this... today... knowing he'd planned this interlude with me and *for* me? I was on a hair trigger. Click, *boom*.

"You going to beg me to fuck you, Bird?" His low voice

slid into my ear like hot honey. "Penetrate you with this frozen dick until you beg for my hot cock to warm you back up?"

My groans turned into a whimper as the dildo moved lower across my hole. It felt amazing. The sun beat down on us and the heat of Jack's body over mine added to it. The relief of the cold toy was too much. The contrast of it made my dick stand up and my balls draw in.

"Too cold to fuck me with," I said, secretly wanting him to try anyway.

"Mm. Maybe. But maybe it's just right," he cooed. "Maybe you need to be a little uncomfortable so I can see your hole tighten around this thing and hear you beg me to take it out."

I shuddered out a breath. He knew I would do anything to turn him on, including taking an ice-cold dildo up my ass.

"Jack," I whispered.

His low chuckle vibrated between us. "I can't tell if that's a warning or a sweet little beg. I'm going to assume it's the latter." His lips moved to my temple and down to my mouth. As soon as his hot tongue entered my mouth, the tip of the ice-cold phallus pressed against my hole.

Somehow, he'd magicked lube on it while I'd been distracted with his growly whispers. The cold, slick surface moved into my hot hole, churning up a delicious mix of antic- ipation and nerves in my belly. I wanted him so damn much.

"Oh, yeah. *Shh.* That's it. Such a good boy," he murmured. "Take it for me. You can do it."

"F-fucking f-freezing," I said, sucking in a breath and puckering around the intrusion. It was ice cold and hot as fire. It felt delicious and so damn weird. I both wanted it out... and didn't want the teasing to end.

The slick toy moved in and out in shallow thrusts as my ass clenched around it. I threw my head back and gritted my teeth. "Fuck!"

I couldn't decide if I liked it or hated it, but I knew for sure I liked the glassy look in Jack's eyes as he stared, transfixed, at my hole. "Fuck," I said again, shifting from a curse into a groan as I realized he was moving down my body to get a better look.

Instead of moving my legs wider apart to look, he took my cock into his hot mouth and began sucking me off. I screamed again, shocking a nearby bird out of the trees. The intensity of the sensations in my groin made my brain begin to short-circuit.

"Fuck me," I begged. "You. With *you*. Please."

He knew what I meant. Within seconds, it was Jack's hot, slick cock replacing the frozen toy in my hole and his strong body thrusting wildly inside of me. I wrapped my arms and legs around him and held on as he pounded into me.

"So hot," he grunted. "So good for me. Jesus, Hawkins, I love you so fucking much. More than I thought possible. Every day, it's more than the day before, and I think… this is it now. It can't be more than it is this second. But then… but then…"

I moved my hand into his hair and held him as close as I could, clinging to him and comforting him, trying to hold out when all my body wanted was to jump off the cliff and enjoy the fireworks on the way down.

"Love you," I said into his warm skin. "Love you. *Love you*." My words ended in a gasp as his hand reached for my cock and pulled the orgasm out of me.

My release came quick as his thrusts lost their rhythm and Jack came deep inside of me with a curse.

Afterward, we lay in a sweaty, panting pile of limbs, spent and happy.

Jack pushed the damp hair off my forehead. "That. Was. Epic."

"You have excellent ideas," I sighed.

"You brave enough to rinse off in the river with me?" he asked with a smile in his voice. "Before we set up our tent?"

It was only spring which meant the river was mostly snowmelt. I lifted an eyebrow at him. "I'm the one who had Frosty's dick in my ass a minute ago, Jack Wyatt, and you're asking if I'm brave enough for a cold dip? Surely you jest."

He pulled back to look at me with the affectionate gaze that still made my stomach contract. "Fair. Clearly I'm the one afraid of freezing my balls off. In fact, instead of taking a swim, we should just rinse off with a washcloth or something. Hypothermia is at least as dangerous as heatstroke. Probably."

I moved to stand up before reaching a hand out to pull him up.

"We're about to find out. If you were scared of the cold, you should have thought about this before thinking you were going to be cute by bringing that thing in the cooler bag."

"No, but... that was for *you*." His laugh was a gift I held close and treasured.

I shrugged and turned toward the river. "You can wait out here if you want to. But I wonder what my nipples will do in that cold water. Could be dangerous," I said archly.

I didn't turn back to look at his reaction because I knew him well enough to know he loved my nipples. And there was no kind of danger, real or imagined, that Jack would let me wander into on my own.

"And I can only imagine my poor nuts turning into raisins. Yeah. You stay here, Jack. You probably don't want to see any of th—*oof!*"

Jack's arms wrapped around me from behind. "Fine. I'm coming," he said against the back of my ear. "If you wanted to act out *Dangerous When Wet*, all you had to do was say so. You don't have to play dirty."

"My hero," I whispered in his ear as I led him into deeper water.

My nipples and nuts did, in fact, turn into raisins. But after some diligent attention from Jack's hot mouth, they sorted themselves out in no time.

PERFECTLY, INCANDESCENTLY HAPPY

A CHERRY PICKED BONUS SCENE

CHAPTER ONE

JACK

Life with Hawk Sunday was never boring.

"Psspss. Tch, tch, tch. Pssspsspsspsspssst."

It was shortly past sunrise and I was still a little bleary as I followed the strange sounds down the wide, oak staircase and around the corner to our large farmhouse kitchen. The floor was chilly under my feet and though the radiators were dutifully clanking and hissing, there was a distinct draft blowing through the house—enough to make me wish I'd thrown on more than a pair of flannel pajama pants when I'd noticed the empty spot in the bed beside me and gone in search of my missing fiancé.

Most mornings, Hawk was the late riser of the two of us. Not only did he work every bit as hard as I did, especially now that he was taking on a more active role in some environmental initiatives around the Hollow, but my man also had a late-night reading habit to keep up... and he didn't shirk his duty. Sometimes I'd come home from the diner and find him passed out in our hidden library with a paperback on his chest. More often, a stifled gasp or muffled groan would rouse me from sleep in the wee hours of the morning, and I'd roll over to find him curled beside me in the darkness, reading some brand new Pride and Prejudice variation—Hawk's drug of choice—on his Kindle with the brightness turned low.

Hawk claimed it was the most satisfying feeling in the world when he could wake in the night, glance out the window at the stars flickering over the dark treetops on our land, cuddle against my warmth, and listen to me snoring softly as he cracked open a story.

Personally, I thought it was much a more satisfying feeling to reach over, haul his lean, naked body against mine, watch him toss his Kindle on the bedside table, and get him to gasp and groan for entirely different reasons.

Also, I did *not* snore, no matter what Hawk claimed.

But all of that nocturnal reading (and, *ahem*, not-reading) meant that it was unusual for Hawk to wake before me, and even more unusual for him to drag himself out of our bed before I did, especially on a rare Saturday when neither of us were scheduled to work.

"Baby?" I reached the kitchen and glanced around the cheery space with a frown. The scent of freshly brewed coffee filled the air, but the room was cold and Hawk-less.

One of the French doors moved in the breeze and I walked around the island to glance out at the back porch... which was where I found the love of my life sitting cross-legged on the deck, shivering slightly in only a t-shirt and pajama pants, and making strange hissing noises in the direction of the forest.

Well. Okay, then.

I grabbed a striped throw blanket from the little nook where we ate most of our meals, grinning a little as I did so. I'd gone my whole life without seeing the point of shit like throw blankets—if a house was warm enough and a person had adequate clothing, why clutter up a space with useless textiles?

Hawk, on the other hand, claimed they gave the space character. That they'd made our house a home.

Frankly, I thought *Hawk* was the one who did that, and since the blankets made him happy, I didn't utter a single word of protest—not even when the silly things began taking over each room of the house, since it seemed every member of the Little Pippin Hookers needed to crochet, knit, or weave something for their precious Hawklet.

And damned if the blankets weren't occasionally useful. Like when snuggling in front of the television on a Sunday afternoon. Or when your future uncle-in-law dropped by unexpectedly mere moments after you and your very naked partner had finished fucking on the kitchen floor. Or, like now, when the man you loved had awoken in the morning and decided to begin speaking in tongues while courting hypothermia.

I slid out the open door, closing it behind me to keep the warmth inside, and knelt to drape the blanket over Hawk's shoulders. "Morning."

"Morning." Hawk glanced up at me, brown eyes shining in welcome. "There's coffee in the—"

"Mmhmm. I saw." I sat behind him, spreading my legs on either side of his body, and pulled him back to wrap my arms around his chest. Still half-asleep, I buried my face in his neck and inhaled deeply, feeling my cock stir. Hawk smelled like clean laundry and the bodywash—*my* bodywash—I'd used on him in the shower last night. As I nuzzled his ear, I strongly considered beginning our day with porch sex...

At least until a distinctly cold breeze gusted through the trees, skittering leaves and pine needles across the porch, and I dismissed the idea.

"Hawk. Baby. What the hell are we doing out here?" I mumbled into his skin.

Hawk snorted and leaned forward just enough to remove the blanket separating us. With a bit of finagling, he draped the blanket over my shoulders instead, then nestled back into the shelter of my arms with a happy sigh. The feeling of him squirming against me was distracting enough that I almost missed his explanation. "We're waiting for Potato."

"For…"

"Potato," Hawk repeated. He pointed to a small ceramic bowl a couple of feet away, which seemed to have been freshly filled with cat treats. "I got him his favorite Greenies. He always comes when I have Greenies. And I've been *psp-psp-psp*-ing at him for five minutes."

"Ohhh. Right." I'd always known Hawk was an animal lover, but I hadn't realized just how deep the love affair went until we lived together. He didn't just enjoy his family's pets or livestock, he loved *all* kinds of animals--even the beady-eyed, acorn collecting, trash-picking, garden destroying kind. But he really, *really* loved the stray cats that roamed the area, and had even tried to lure them inside when the weather started getting chilly, probably to make sure each one had an adequate supply of throw blankets.

Unfortunately, the closest he'd come after several weeks of effort was getting one cat—a tiny fluff-monster with bi-colored eyes and russet-brown fur that Hawk had named Potato—to eat treats from a bowl on the porch and consent to be petted. Ordinarily I wouldn't care much about this, not being much of a pet-person, but I knew Hawk cared a lot.

"Maybe Potato's sleeping in," I offered. "It's Saturday, after all."

Hawk shook his head, worry in his voice. "He hasn't come in days, maybe even a week, and last time he was here, he seemed… off."

"He's a stray cat, babe. Who the heck knows what kind of health problems he, ah…" I broke off with a wince. The last thing I wanted was for Hawk to torture himself thinking of what might have befallen his feral friend. "I mean… he was probably adopted," I declared. "By the family that bought the house over on Chicory." I hooked a thumb down the mountain in the direction of town. "You know, I bet that's exactly what happened. I bet he's playing with their kids right now."

Hawk turned his head to give me a withering look that said he knew exactly what I was doing. His lips twitched with amusement. "Golly gee, Jack, do you think so? Or maybe he and the Muellers' dog have stowed away on a train and are headed out west for a big adventure!" He rolled his eyes. "Maybe with little hobo sticks on their shoulders?"

"Shush," I grumbled, poking his ribs lightly to make him squirm. "I'd rather think of him that way than have either of us assume the worst." I paused for a moment. "Though personally I'm voting no hobo sticks, given that Potato lacks opposable thumbs."

He let out a burst of startled laughter, but a moment later, the laughter ended in a sigh. He pulled my arms more tightly around him. "I know you're right. You are. But I can't help worrying. And there's a part of me that just wants to *know*, you know? It's really rough feeling like the one who's always..." He swallowed. "Left behind."

"Ah." I propped my chin on his shoulder. "We're not actually talking about Potato, are we?"

"We are!" he protested. Another sigh. "Partly."

"No word from Reed, I'm guessing?"

Hawk shook his head. "Gage texted. I left him a message. Luke DM'd him on Instagram. Drew sent him an email. Even Porter called to ask him some advice about a literature professor at school he's got a problem with. And I *know* it's not super unusual for Reed to go radio silent, sometimes for a lot longer than two weeks. I *know* he travels constantly and his work keeps him hopping doing..." He turned his head and wrinkled his nose. "What do think-tanks do exactly?"

I shrugged.

"Anyway, I'm sure he's fine. But it was nice having him

home for a while there, and I… I miss him." Hawk's shoulders slumped. "A lot."

"Uh huh. And?" I prompted.

"And…" Hawk sighed. "I miss Crys. She was a good friend. And I knew she didn't plan to stay in the Hollow forever, but she left really abruptly." He glanced up at me, eyes narrowed in annoyance. "She didn't even give you two weeks' notice at the diner."

I stroked a hand down his forearm beneath our shared blanket. "I appreciate your loyalty, baby, but I'm not upset. Shit happens, and we made things work. Van and Ernie at the Bugle, though, they were way worse off. Crys *and* that other kid quit right around the same time—"

"Other-Chris," he supplied.

"Right. Him. And Van and Ernie were down two barbacks at once."

"Yeah." Hawk was silent for a moment. "And did you hear Mrs. Nordwick from the Hookers is moving in with her sister in Portsmouth? And Alan Tracey got a job down in Worcester, so he's leaving too, which means he won't be able to play Santa in the kids' play in December and they might have to cancel it? I dunno." He thumped his fist lightly into my knee. "Change sucks, that's all."

Christ. Even after months with Hawk in my life and in my bed, after weeks with my ring on his finger, there were moments when my feelings for this sweet man simply swamped me. He was the kindest, purest soul I'd ever met; a person who cared about not only every square centimeter of Little Pippin Hollow, but every being—whether crotchety human or feral cat—who lived here.

"Sometimes change does suck," I agreed gently. "Sometimes when relationships change, it means you're pulled away from the people and places you love, and that's hard. But I'd argue that sometimes it's necessary. Things have to change so you can find the life, the *love*, that's meant for you. Sometimes change is a good thing, baby."

I bit his shoulder lightly and felt his body come alive, primal need and deep affection arcing like electric currents between us as they always had… or, at least, as they had since I'd pulled my head out of my ass last summer and recognized the beauty in front of me for what it was.

"Welllll, when you put it that way..." Hawk arched his neck, giving me better access to lick over the place I'd bitten. "I suppose there are *certain* changes I approve of," he conceded. He twisted in my arms and wrapped his arms around my neck. "For example, last year, I wouldn't have been able to do this." He pressed a soft kiss to my jaw.

"Mmm. So true. And last year *I* wouldn't have been able to do *this*." I nipped at his lower lip, and when he opened his mouth on a gasp, I cupped his jaw in my hand and tilted his head back to kiss him deeply, savoring the sweet-tart flavor of his moan on my tongue.

When Hawk pulled back, his eyes were glazed and his hands were tangled in my hair. "You make…" He sucked in a shuddery breath. "A compelling argument."

I laughed. "Very open-minded of you," I said solemnly, "to admit that you were wrong."

"Hey! I didn't say *wrong*." He shifted further so he was straddling me. "Just that I'm willing to be convinced that change is good." His hard cock rubbed against my stomach and he groaned. "Preferably someplace warmer. Preferably *now*."

I didn't need to be told twice.

HAWK

"And then she fell from the horse, hit her head, and woke up with amnesia—"

"Hold up," Jack said from behind me. "Elizabeth Bennet

fell from her horse—the spirited thoroughbred she'd insisted on buying because she's a talented equestrian, with the money that she inherited because she's secretly a nobleman's daughter—and got *amnesia?* Baby, how long is this book?"

I stifled a laugh as I clomped down the narrow trail in the forest behind our house, with Jack on my heels. The sun was warm enough that I'd stripped off my windbreaker on the way *up* the trail an hour ago, and although the weather forecasters claimed we were in for a cold and snowy November, there was no sign of it on this October day. The air was autumn-crisp, the trees had donned their most colorful leaf-peeping 'fits, I was feeling pleasantly sore after spending the morning doing dirty things with my fiancé on the hardwood floor and the afternoon hiking—two of my favorite activities ever—and since Jack and I both had the day off, I was looking forward to an extended round two when we got home… in approximately five more minutes.

In short, life was perfect. Perfectly perfect. The kind of perfect that I would never, ever want to change because, no matter what Jack said, change *almost* always equaled awful.

I gave Jack a teasing glance over my shoulder. "I haven't even told you about the pirates yet."

He shook his head, disgusted. "Poor Lizzie. And where was Darcy when all of this bullshit was happening? Don't tell me—off somewhere brooding about something, and practicing his inscrutable look for when he comes in at the eleventh hour to save the day."

I stopped short and turned around, arms folded over my chest. "You will not," I said in my most threatening voice—which, unfortunately, was not very threatening, especially when I was talking to the man I'd been in love with for the better part of a decade, "talk about Fitzwilliam Darcy in that dismissive tone, Jack Davidson Wyatt."

Jack let out a long, low whistle. "Wow. Middle-naming *and* last-naming me. Serious stuff."

"It is." I lifted my chin. "I have come to feel fond acceptance for your football-watching obsession, Jack. I have even learned to love your snoring—"

"I do *not*—"

"But this is a bridge too far," I said. I was mostly—only *mostly*—teasing, and the look in Jack's eyes said he knew it… and found it all kinds of adorable… which was the best feeling in the world. "Since it's a lovely day and I'm feeling magnanimous, however, I'll accept your apology." I rolled my hand in a *get on with it* gesture.

"Magnanimous," Jack repeated slowly, testing the weight of the word on his tongue. He stepped closer, so his chest bumped against my folded arms, and he grasped my hips. "That's quite the vocabulary word. And here I thought I sucked your brains out through your dick mere hours ago, *Henry Hawkins Sunday*—"

My face went hot as flashfire memories of this morning seared my brain, which made it a little hard to come up with a witty retort… But it didn't seem to matter anyway, since Jack's eyes were busy scanning the area and his face wore a faraway, distracted expression.

"What?" I demanded, unfolding my arms so I could look around also, but I saw nothing except forest.

Jack shook his head, his gaze focused on me again. "Nothing," he said, though the tiny frown between his eyebrows belied his words. "What was I saying?"

"You were apologizing for your thoughtless words about our lord and savior Fitzwilliam Darcy," I reminded him. "At least, you'd gotten to the part where you said *Henry Hawkins Sunday*, and I'm almost positive the abject apology part was forthcoming."

He laughed. "Henry. Hawkins. Sunday," he repeated, like each word filled him with delight. He slid his hands down my arms and laced our fingers together, then lifted my left so he could run his thumb over the shiny gold engagement band there. He tilted his head. "Have you considered what you want to do when we get married?"

"Do?" I blinked. "What do you mean, do? If you're trying to distract me, Jack—"

"I meant with our names. Like, you could go with Henry Hawkins Sunday-Wyatt. Or Wyatt-Sunday. Or just Sunday. Or just Wyatt." Startlingly blue eyes met mine. "I don't care what you choose, but I'd like to share a name with you, I think."

I tried to suck in oxygen, but my lungs had forgotten how breathing worked and I ended up making a series of short gasping sounds. If Jack was trying to get out of apologizing… he was absolutely succeeding.

Total, unmitigated success.

"I mean, only if you're into it." He shrugged offhandedly, like it didn't matter to him one way or another, though I was pretty sure this was a lie.

"You'd… become a Sunday?" I managed to whisper. "Really?"

"Of course." His eyebrows rose. "Is that what you want?"

"I… yeah. Yes." I couldn't have stopped my smile if I tried. "I mean, let's think about it for a minute and make sure, but… I want to share a name with you, too. I want to share everything."

He grinned. "Good." He wrapped our joined hands behind my back, pulled me against his chest, and lowered his mouth to mine…

Then stopped.

"Do you hear that?" he whispered against my lips. The frown was back on his face.

I paused and listened, then shook my head. "Nope."

"I'd swear it was coming from over—" He lifted his head. "There. Hear it?"

If I strained my ears, I could just barely hear a faint, high-pitched noise. A bird call maybe. Or an animal.

"Do you think something got hurt?" I wondered, suddenly worried. "Come on, let's look."

I tugged Jack along the path toward home, stopping every so often to listen for the noise. Eventually, when we were so close to our house that I could see the chimney through the gaps in the trees, the sound became a bit louder. Closer.

Jack and I exchanged a look, then he moved left into the underbrush, his heavy boots clearing a path through the ferns and his strong arms helping me over a fallen log, until finally we saw what we'd been looking for. Under the low branches of a pine tree sat an ancient wooden crate tipped on its side, and inside the crate was…

"Potato!" I cried softly. "Oh! Oh, wow. Look, Jack, he—"

"She," Jack corrected, staring at the cat… and the four tiny, brown-and-white kittens crawling around her. "Definitely a she."

"I don't want to get too close and spook her right now, but we need to bring things for them," I decided. "Food. And water. And something to keep them warm—"

Jack darted a look at me. "I know where we can find a blanket or two."

"—and if Potato will let us, we should try to take her and the babies home with us, at least for the winter. I think we should call them Jane, Lizzy, Mary, and Lydia," I said seriously. "Not Kitty because that would be too on the nose."

"Are you being—?" He gaped at me. "Five cats, Hawk. One, two, three, four, *five*. You want us to take in *five* cats." He shook his head. "Baby, I'm not sure if I've ever explained to you that the reason I never had a pet of my own is because I'm not much of a pet guy—"

"Or maybe you didn't *used* to be a pet guy?" I suggested, biting my lip.

He narrowed his eyes. "This is going to be like the throw blanket situation, isn't it? You say, 'Jack, you don't mind if I get one or two little cats for the back of the sofa, do you?' And

I say, 'Hawk, this is your home. You don't need permission.' And suddenly, there are multiple cats in every room, draped on every chair and bed—"

I rocked up on the balls of my feet. "But you admitted that the blankets came in handy, remember? That time you wanted to try countertop sex, and Uncle Drew stopped by to surprise us with a pumpkin flax loaf, you pulled the plaid one around me like a kilt and I think Drew really believed I was wearing it on purpose—"

Jack snorted. "No, sweetheart. He really didn't."

"Would you consider it, at least?" I pleaded. "I won't insist, if you're really against it, obviously. And we don't know if Potato will even be happy with us, if she's not socialized, and we'd need to get a vet involved, but I've always wanted a cat. Or… five cats."

He pursed his lips thoughtfully. "I don't know, Hawk. That would be quite a… *change*."

"It would," I agreed with a sigh. "I know. But—"

"And my fiancé tells me change sucks, so…"

I looked up and caught the teasing glint in his eyes. "Oh my god. You're still trying to get me to admit I was wrong, huh?"

Jack shrugged, unrepentant, and grinned broadly. "Hawk, you wound me--"

I cupped his gorgeous face in both of my palms, running my thumbs over the stubble there. Nothing in the entire world had ever made me as happy as I was every single minute I was with this man, and I knew nothing ever would. So I lifted up on my toes and kissed him gently… and then not-so-gently because my fiancé was seriously fucking hot and I couldn't help myself.

"Fine. *Fine*," I admitted breathlessly, several minutes later. "Sometimes change doesn't suck. Sometimes it's totally and completely necessary. Sometimes it brings you all the things you wanted and didn't think you could ever have."

Like a new home. A new name. A new purpose. And love. Always love.

"So now will you think about becoming a pet guy?" I demanded.

Jack grinned and traced one blunt fingertip over my cheek. "Pretty sure I don't have to be a pet guy, 'cause I'm already a full-on Hawk guy." He rolled his eyes. "We can keep the damn cats."

I threw my arms around him exuberantly. "You're gonna love them," I promised. "Eventually."

His big arms wrapped around me, pulling me tight. "I'm gonna love *you*, Hawk Sunday," he whispered in my ear, his voice strong, his promise unwavering. "And that's something that's never going to change."

If you haven't read Jack & Hawk's story yet, grab Cherry Picked
HERE → *https://readerlinks.com/l/2395435*

*And if you haven't met the rest of the Sunday Brothers yet, binge
the series HERE* → *https://readerlinks.com/l/3027689*

Ready to meet the final Sunday brother? Grab The Pretenders of
Copper County *HERE* → *https://readerlinks.com/l/4135215*

ABOUT MAY ARCHER

May is an M/M author who lives in Boston. She spends her days planning vacations, mainlining diet soda, avoiding the gym, reading M/M romance, and when all other forms of procrastination fail, writing it.

Visit her website at mayarcher.com to sign up for her newsletter to hear about sales and upcoming releases, freebies and behind the scenes info and more! Or join her Facebook group, Club May!

facebook.com/may.archer.author

instagram.com/mayarcherauthor

amazon.com/May-Archer/e/B075JQVGLX

patreon.com/MayArcherRomance

bookbub.com/authors/may-archer

www.ingramcontent.com/pod-product-compliance
Lightning Source LLC
Chambersburg PA
CBHW032246310726
48973CB00008B/2316